JEKEL LOVES HYDE

by Beth Fantaskey

GRAPHIA

Houghton Mifflin Harcourt
Boston   New York

For my husband, David,
and Paige and Julia

All rights reserved. Published in the United States by Graphia,
an imprint of Houghton Mifflin Harcourt Publishing Company.
Originally published in hardcover in the United States by Harcourt Children's Books,
an imprint of Houghton Mifflin Harcourt Publishing Company, 2010.

Graphia and the Graphia logo are trademarks of
Houghton Mifflin Harcourt Publishing Company.

For information about permission to reproduce selections from this book,
write to Permissions, Houghton Mifflin Harcourt Publishing Company,
215 Park Avenue South, New York, New York 10003.

www.hmhbooks.com

The text of this book is set in Minion.

The Library of Congress has cataloged the hardcover edition as follows:
Fantaskey, Beth
Jekel loves Hyde/Beth Fantaskey.
p. cm.
Summary: As seventeen-year-old Jill Jekel and classmate Tristen Hyde work together on a
chemistry project, hoping to win a scholarship for her and a cure for his curse, they also un-
cover family secrets and a chemistry of their own.
[1. Experiments—Fiction. 2. Supernatural—Fiction. 3. Stevenson, Robert Louis, 1850–1894.
Strange case of Dr. Jekyll and Mr. Hyde—Fiction. 4. High schools—Fiction. 5. Schools—
Fiction. 6. Murder—Fiction. 7. Pennsylvania—Fiction.] I. Title.
PZ7.F222285Jek 2010
[Fic]— dc22
2009019390

ISBN 978-0-15-206390-0 hc
ISBN 978-0-547-55027-5 pb

Manufactured in the United States of America
DOM 10 9 8 7 6 5 4 3 2 1

4500285192

"I had long since prepared my tincture . . . and, late one accursed night, I compounded the elements, watched them boil and smoke together in the glass, and when the ebullition had subsided, with a strong glow of courage, drank off the potion.

The most racking pangs succeeded: a grinding in the bones, deadly nausea, and a horror of the spirit . . . I knew myself, at the first breath of this new life, to be more wicked, tenfold more wicked . . . and the thought, in that moment, braced and delighted me like wine."

—Robert Louis Stevenson,
The Strange Case of Dr. Jekyll and Mr. Hyde

Prologue

Jill

I BURIED MY FATHER the day after my seventeenth birthday.

Even the sun was cruel that morning, an obscenely bright but cold January day. The snow that smothered the cemetery glared harshly white, blinding those mourners who couldn't squeeze under the tent that covered Dad's open grave. And the tent itself gleamed crisply, relentlessly white, so it hurt a little to look at that, too.

Hurt a lot, actually.

Against this inappropriately immaculate backdrop, splashes of black stood in stark relief, like spatters of ink on fresh paper: the polished hearse that glittered at the head of the procession, the minister's perfectly ironed shirt, and the sober coats worn by my father's many friends and colleagues, who came up one by one after the service to offer Mom and me their condolences.

Maybe I saw it all in terms of color because I'm an artist. Or maybe I was just too overwhelmed to deal with anything but extremes. Maybe my grief was so raw that the whole world seemed severe and discordant and clashing.

I don't remember a word the minister said, but he seemed to talk forever. And as the gathering began to break up, I, yesterday's birthday girl, stood there under that tent fidgeting in my own uncomfortable, new black dress and heavy wool coat, on stage like some perverse debutante at the world's worst coming-out party.

I looked to my mother for support, for help, but her eyes seemed to yawn as vacant as Dad's waiting grave. I swear, meeting Mom's gaze was almost as painful as looking at the snow, or the casket, or watching the endless news reports about my father's murder. Mom was disappearing, too . . .

Feeling something close to panic, I searched the crowd.

Who would help me now?

I wasn't ready to be an adult . . .

Was I really . . . alone?

Even my only friend, Becca Wright, had begged off from the funeral, protesting that she had a big civics test, which she'd already rescheduled twice because of travel for cheerleading. And, more to the point, she just "couldn't handle" seeing my poor, murdered father actually shoved in the ground.

I looked around for my chemistry teacher, Mr. Messerschmidt, whom I'd seen earlier lingering on the fringes of the mourners, looking nervous and out of place, but I couldn't find him, and I assumed that he'd returned to school, without a word to me.

Alone.

I was alone.

Or maybe I was worse than alone, because just when I thought things couldn't get more awful, my classmate Darcy Gray emerged from the crowd, strode up, and thrust her chilly hand into mine, air-kissing my cheek. And even this gesture, which I knew Darcy offered more out of obligation than compassion, came across like the victor's condescending acknowledgment of the vanquished. When Darcy said, "So sorry for your loss, Jill," I swore it was almost like she was congratulating herself for *still having* parents. Like she'd bested me once more, as she had time and again since kindergarten.

"Thanks," I said stupidly, like I genuinely appreciated being worthy of pity.

"Call me if you need anything," Darcy offered. Yet I noticed that she didn't jot down her cell number. Didn't even reach into her purse and feign looking for a pen.

"Thanks," I said again.

Why was I always acting grateful for nothing?

"Sure," Darcy said, already looking around for an escape route.

As she walked away, I watched her blond hair gleaming like a golden trophy in that too-brilliant sun, and the loneliness and despair that had been building in me rose to a crescendo that was so powerful I wasn't quite sure how I managed to keep my knees from buckling. Not one real friend there for me . . .

That's when I noticed Tristen Hyde standing at the edge of the tent. He wore a very adult, tailored overcoat, unbuttoned, and I could see that he had donned a tie, too, for this occasion. He had his hands buried in his pockets, a gesture that I first took as signaling discomfort, unease. I mean, what teenage guy wouldn't be uncomfortable at a funeral? And I hardly knew Tristen. It wasn't like we were friends. He'd certainly never met my father.

Yet there he was, when almost nobody else had shown up for me. Why? Why had he come?

When Tristen saw that I'd noticed him, he pulled his hands from his pockets, and I realized that he wasn't uneasy at all. In fact, as he walked toward me, I got the impression that he'd just been waiting, patiently, for his turn. For the right time to approach me.

And what a time he picked. It couldn't have been more dead on.

"It's going to be okay," he promised as he came up to me, reaching out to take my arm, like he realized that I was folding up inside, on the verge of breaking down.

I looked up at him, mutely shaking my head in the negative.

No, it was not going to be okay.

He could not promise that.

Nobody could. Certainly not some kid from my high school, even a tall one dressed convincingly like a full-fledged man.

I shook my head more vehemently, tears welling in my eyes.

"Trust me," he said softly, his British accent soothing. He squeezed my arm harder. "I know what I'm talking about."

I didn't know at the time that Tristen had vast experience with this "grief" thing. All I knew was that I let him, a boy I barely knew, wrap his arms around me and pull me to his chest. And suddenly, as he smoothed my hair, I really started weeping. Letting out all the tears that I'd bottled up, from the moment that the police officer had knocked on the door of our house to say that my father had been found butchered in a parking lot outside the lab where he worked, and all through planning the funeral, as my mother fell to pieces, forcing me to do absurd, impossible things like select a coffin and write insanely large checks to the undertaker. Suddenly I was burying myself under Tristen's overcoat, nearly knocking off my eyeglasses as I pressed against him, and sobbing so hard that I must have soaked his shirt and tie.

When I was done, drained of tears, I pulled away from him, adjusting my glasses and wiping my eyes, sort of embarrassed. But Tristen didn't seem bothered by my show of emotion.

4

"It does get better, hurt less," he assured me, repeating, "Trust me, Jill."

Such an innocuous little comment at the time, but one that would become central to my very existence in the months to come. *Trust me, Jill . . .*

"I'll see you at school," Tristen added, pressing my arm again. Then he bent down, and in a gesture I found incredibly mature, kissed my cheek. Only I shifted a little, caught off-guard, not used to being that near to a guy, and the corners of our lips brushed.

"Sorry," I murmured, even more embarrassed—and kind of appalled with myself. I'd never even come close to kissing a guy on the lips under any circumstances, let alone on such a terrible day. Not that I'd really *felt* anything, of course, and yet . . . It just seemed wrong to even *consider* anything but death at that moment. How could I even think about how some guy felt, how he smelled, how it had been just to give up and be held by somebody stronger than me? My father was DEAD. "Sorry," I muttered again, and I think I was kind of apologizing to Dad, too.

"It's okay," Tristen reassured me, smiling a little. He was the first person who'd dared to smile at me since the murder. I didn't know what to make of that, either. When should people smile again? "See you, okay?" he said, releasing my arm.

I hugged myself, and it seemed a poor substitute for the embrace I'd just been offered. "Sure. See you. Thanks for coming."

I followed his progress as Tristen wandered off through the graves, bending over now and then to brush some snow off the tombstones, read an inscription, or maybe check a date, not hurrying, like graveyards were his natural habitat. Familiar territory.

Tristen Hyde had come for . . . me.

Why?

But there was no more time to reflect on whatever motives had driven this one particular classmate to attend a stranger's burial, because suddenly the funeral director was tapping my shoulder, telling me that it was time to say any final goodbyes before the procession of black cars pulled away from the too-white tent and the discreetly positioned backhoe hurried in to do its job because there was more snow in the forecast.

"Okay," I said, retrieving my mother and guiding her by the hand, forcing us both to bow our heads one last time.

We sealed my father's grave on a day of stark contrasts, of black against white, and it was the last time I'd ever find myself in a place of such extremes. Because in the months after the dirt fell on the coffin, my life began to shift to shades of gray, almost like the universe had taken a big stick and stirred up the whole scene at that cemetery, mixing up everything and repainting my world.

As it turned out, my father wasn't quite the man we'd all thought he was.

Correction.

Nothing and no one, as I would come to learn, would turn out to be quite what they'd seemed back on that day.

Not even me.

And Tristen . . . He would prove to be the trickiest, the most complicated, the most compelling of all the mysteries that were about to unravel.

Chapter 1

Jill

THE FIRST PERIOD of the first day of my senior year kicked off with an academic ritual that I'd dreaded since my earliest days in school.

The choosing of partners.

"Come up and get your get new lab manuals, a copy of the text, and then pair up at the lab stations," our advanced chemistry teacher, Mr. Messerschmidt, said, directing our attention to the front of the room, where his long desk held neat stacks of books and papers waiting for us. He did a quick head count, lips moving as he pointed at us, one by one. "We're *supposed* to have an odd number," he added, frowning, like the tally hadn't turned out as planned. "So somebody'll have to work alone this year, if everyone shows."

No . . . not an odd number . . .

I felt my heart race, the way it always did when there was a chance that I might end up alone. One year in gym class, I'd been the odd girl out for square dancing two weeks in a row, standing in solitary shame against the wall until the teacher forced somebody else to switch out so I could have a turn. And even though chemistry was my best subject, that was no guarantee that Jill Jekel would find a partner here, either.

As I moved to get my manual and book, I tried not to look desperate, even as I made vague attempts at eye contact.

Becca was in the class, but she was so popular . . . I looked in her direction, but Seth Lanier was telling her some joke, making her laugh. She'd probably team with Seth . . .

Tucking my stick-straight, brown hair that was forever escaping from my ponytail behind my ear, I reached for the lab manual, trying to look relaxed and nonchalant. I could always act like I *wanted* to work alone, if worst came to worst.

"Hey, Jill."

I glanced over to see Darcy Gray edging in next to me, snapping up a manual, and I felt a surge of hope, albeit one tempered with skepticism.

Darcy seemed to be winding up to tell me something. Or *ask* me something. Was there a chance that *Darcy Gray* was going to ask me to partner? Because we were the two best students in the room . . . It made sense . . .

"What's up?" I greeted her, hoisting the heavy book Mr. Messerschmidt had picked for us. Sterne and Anwar's *Foundations of the Chemical World, 17th Edition.* A classic, trustworthy text. My father had kept an earlier edition in his office at home. It was, of course, still there, if we ever unlocked the door to that sacred, forbidden space.

"I just wanted to tell you that station three sucks," Darcy said, taking her own copy from the pile. She scowled at the cover, like she disapproved, not even looking at me as she spoke. "I had three last year, and the Bunsen burners don't work right. It totally screwed me over, and Messerschmidt wouldn't let me change."

"Oh." So that was it. Darcy was tipping me off about a faulty lab station. Which was nice, I guessed. But not what I'd hoped for. I felt my cheeks warming, wondering if Darcy had any clue that I'd sort of expected her to ask me to be her partner. "Thanks."

"No problem," she said, still not looking at me as she headed for station one—and her boyfriend, Todd Flick. Gorgeous Todd, not a brain in his head, but he'd take Darcy's directions without complaint or question. He was probably the perfect partner for somebody as domineering as Darcy.

But why had she bothered to warn me about the lab? We were competing for valedictorian, and she could have just let it go. Could have let fate take its course, maybe to my detriment. Was Darcy that confident that she'd take first place?

Probably.

Hugging my books, I took a deep breath and turned around to face the whole class. As I'd expected, most of my classmates already seemed to be pairing up as surely as the animals on Noah's ark. It was like watching that square dance all over again as students moved around the room, coalescing into teams, gravitating toward desks. A few stragglers were still coming up for books, but in general, it appeared that the world was, as usual, operating two by two, with me as the odd girl out.

The odd, odd girl.

Just try to have some dignity, I told myself, squaring my shoulders and starting my solitary march toward the back of the room, eyes fixed on the farthest station, in the corner. I figured I might as well take the last table if I was going to work alone. At least I wouldn't have people staring at the back of my head, thinking about the empty chair at my side.

But just as I was about to put my books down, Becca grabbed my arm, laughing her easy laugh. "Jill, where are you going? Get over here!"

I blinked at her with surprise. "What?"

"Our station," Becca said, pointing to lab three. "I grabbed one for us."

"Us?"

Becca looked at me like I'd lost my mind. "Duh, Jill. We're partnering, right? I mean, you have to save my butt! You're the one who understands this stuff!"

"I . . . I . . ." I stammered for a second, still uncertain. Becca Wright had picked me not necessarily because we were friends— she had too many friends to count—but because I was *serviceable* for her. Which, I supposed, in her eyes was a pretty darn good reason for us to link up. Not insulting at all to a person who would never imagine worrying about having a partner.

So why was I little hurt to be seen mainly as a human study aid?

And Becca had set us up at station three, which Darcy claimed didn't work right. "We should switch to lab ten," I suggested, pointing to the back of the room. "I heard lab three . . ."

"No way," Becca interrupted, still smiling. "I want to be near Seth, and he's on five, right behind us."

I hesitated for one more second, knowing that if Becca had her heart set on being near Seth, she wouldn't budge, even if the malfunctioning burner threatened to set us both on fire.

I gave one last glance to the empty table at the far end of the class.

Then I went with Becca to lab three, awkwardly climbing on to the high stool. Hearing somebody behind her, Darcy turned around to see who was getting stuck with the misfiring burners and gave me a surprised, incredulous look like, "Didn't I just warn you about that lab?"

I smiled weakly and shrugged, and Darcy rolled her blue eyes before twisting back around to face front.

"Okay, everyone," Mr. Messerschmidt announced, clapping his hands to summon our attention. "Are we all set? All partnered?" He counted heads a second time, then consulted a sheet of paper in his hand, frowning again. "We still seem to be missing someone . . ."

Just then the door opened and in walked Tristen Hyde. Late. And not seeming to care that the whole class was already assembled. He strolled right in front of Mr. Messerschmidt and picked up the textbook, checking the cover and nodding like I'd done. Like he recognized the book as a good one, too.

Mr. Messerschmidt watched this performance in silence, mouth set in a firm line. "You're late, Mr. Hyde," he finally said when Tristen took his sweet time collecting the lab manual.

"Sorry," Tristen said absently, more focused on trying to jam the manual into his battered messenger bag, like he had no intention of looking at the rules and regulations.

I noticed that he'd gotten a light tan over the summer, and the sun had highlighted his thick, dirty-blond hair, and I wondered for a second where he'd been, what he'd done over the last few months. Tristen was a cross-country runner, a track star. Maybe he'd just been . . . running? Or had he traveled back to England? I'd heard that his dad was a psychiatrist, here for some kind of visiting professorship. Maybe they'd gone home for the summer break?

I definitely couldn't recall seeing Tristen around town. Then again, I hadn't really seen anybody around town. I'd worked in the basement of Carson Pharmaceuticals cleaning equipment and inventorying stock. A pity job that my dad's old boss had wrangled for me. Although I'd hated the work, it had been really nice of Mr. Layne to look out for me, given what my dad had been accused of doing at Carson in the months before his murder on their property.

We were fortunate, too, that Mercy Hospital was desperate for nurses, so Mom hadn't lost her job when she'd had her breakdown right after Dad's funeral.

Yes, things could have been worse. So why didn't I feel luckier?

Still standing at the front of the room, Tristen took some time to survey the lab stations, looking for a spot. He didn't seem panicked or desperate, even though it must have been obvious that everybody was already paired up.

"Do you have a pass or an excuse?" Mr. Messerschmidt asked, holding out his hand.

"No," Tristen said, still coolly appraising the class.

"Oh." Mr. Messerschmidt didn't seem to know what to make of Tristen's total lack of justification or concern. My teacher's hand flopped to his side. "Well . . . take a seat, please."

"Sure," Tristen agreed, starting to make his way down the center aisle.

"We have an odd number this year," Mr. Messerschmidt began to point out.

"That's fine," Tristen said, heading toward the empty table at the back of the room. Lab station ten, where I'd nearly ended up.

"I *suppose* we could have one team of three," Mr. Messerschmidt suggested as we all followed Tristen's solitary progress. "You could join—"

"No, I'm good," Tristen interrupted, thudding his messenger

bag on the table, claiming the space. He slid onto the stool and began to leaf through the textbook, sort of shutting Mr. Messerschmidt—and all of us—out.

There was a weird moment of silence, during which we all stayed swiveled toward the back of the class, looking in Tristen's direction. He continued reading.

"Well, then," Mr. Messerschmidt finally said, clapping his hands again, ending the interruption and regaining control of the situation, which Tristen had somehow hijacked with nothing more than a casual disregard for . . . everything.

Over the course of the next half hour, our teacher proceeded to guide us, page by laborious page, through the contents of the lab manual, advising us of all the ways we could inconvenience the local emergency crews, the school district, and the Commonwealth of Pennsylvania by variously scalding, searing, asphyxiating, and blowing each other up if things were mishandled.

I'd had Mr. Messerschmidt for basic chem the year before, and I knew all the proper procedures, but I turned the pages anyway, as directed.

But now and then, for some reason, my mind would wander back to the far end of the classroom. To Tristen.

Did he even remember that day in the graveyard? Should I tell him, someday, that he'd been right—and wrong—back then? That some things had gotten better . . . but some had gotten much, much worse as the police had delved into my dad's activities, exposing a double life? Late nights at Carson labs. Murky images on security cameras. Unexplained thefts of chemicals that seemed innocuous enough, but which Dad had stolen, nonetheless.

And then there was Mom, who still seemed to be hanging on by her fingernails.

My grief had softened a little as Tristen had promised on that day he'd held me. But I wouldn't say life was "better."

Would I tell Tristen all that someday?

Of course, I knew I wouldn't. We hadn't even talked again, except to say hi in the halls now and then. I wouldn't go bare my soul to him just because we'd shared one close moment in a cemetery.

Yet I found myself glancing over my shoulder at him. And when I did, I saw that Tristen wasn't following along with his lab manual. It wasn't even on his desk. He was still reading the textbook, which was spread open before him, and his mouth was drawn down in concentration, like he was engrossed in some concept or theory that challenged him.

I watched his face, his mouth, thinking, *Those lips have brushed against mine.*

How weird that touch seemed in retrospect. Tristen was like a million miles away from me although we were in the same room. How was it that he'd ever held me, stroked my hair?

Like the rest of that whole period of my life, it all seemed part of some crazy dream. A crazy *nightmare.*

I must have stared at Tristen so long that he sensed me watching, because he glanced up from his book, caught me observing him, arched his eyebrows . . . and smiled. A smile that was at once surprised, questioning, and maybe a little teasing. A grin that managed to say, "Me? Really? I'm flattered, I guess!"

NO!

I whipped back around, face flaming. Why had I been studying him?

Becca had noticed the whole thing, too. She elbowed me and whispered, "What was *that* about?"

"Nothing," I told her, meaning it. "Nothing!"

Then the bell rang, rescuing me, and I gathered up my books, refusing to look in Tristen's direction again. Fortunately Becca was immediately shanghaied by Seth—or maybe it was vice versa—so I was spared more questions.

But I wasn't quite in the clear. As I made my way toward the door, Mr. Messerschmidt called out above the din of chattering students. "Jill! Darcy! Hyde! Come here! I have something for you three."

Turning to see what our teacher wanted, I noticed that he held a few folded sheets of lime green paper. "I'm coming," I said as Mr. Messerschmidt began waving the papers, using them to summon us.

Under the room's fluorescent lights those colorful flyers *looked* like a cheerful enough invitation. But in truth, the bright leaflet with my name on it would turn out to be the ticket to a lot of dark places.

Dark places in my school.

Dark places in my home.

Dark places in *myself.*

Standing shoulder-to-shoulder with Tristen and Darcy, who would take the wild ride with me, I opened the flyer and read.

Chapter 2

Jill

"I UNDERSTAND THAT this is the first time three students from a school as small as Supplee Mill have been invited to participate in the competition," Mr. Messerschmidt noted as Darcy,

Tristen, and I crowded around his desk, silently reading the information he'd handed to us. "The Foreman Foundation is very selective."

I only half heard my teacher. I was trying to concentrate on the words on the green paper and not get distracted by the fact that Tristen was practically bumping against me as he looked over his own flyer. I was still so embarrassed to have been caught looking at him, and by Tristen's obvious misinterpretation of my *nonexistent* interest, that I just wanted to get to my next class. Still, I pushed my slipping glasses up to the bridge of my nose and tried to focus, because Mr. Messerschmidt seemed so excited about this contest he'd apparently nominated us for.

And, at first glance, it did look like a pretty good opportunity. *The Foreman Foundation for the Promotion of Scientific Inquiry . . . national scholarship contest . . . original experiment in the categories of chemistry, physical sciences, biology . . . Presentation at the University of the Sciences . . .*

College was looming next year, and I needed scholarships to supplement the money saved for my education. I wasn't exactly sure how much Dad had earned as a senior chemist, but things definitely seemed tight without his salary. Lately Mom had even been trying to work extra shifts at the hospital when she could get up the energy.

"How much is this worth?" Tristen cut to the chase, flipping the paper over, looking for a sum. "It looks like a lot of work."

"It's a thirty-thousand-dollar scholarship," Mr. Messerschmidt said just as I found the number myself.

Thirty. Thousand. Dollars. Once I saw it in print, the figure was pretty much all I noticed.

Darcy seemed kind of impressed, too. "That's a decent chunk

of change," she admitted. "It won't cover all my tuition at Harvard, but it's nice money."

"And a nice bit of *work*," Tristen reminded us. "Hours in the lab conducting original research—and more time to develop a presentation. That's a lot of effort." He glanced at me. "Don't you think, Jill?"

I was surprised to be singled out, and pushed my hair behind my ear, irrationally nervous as I met his brown eyes. "I—I don't know . . . I mean—"

"It's not just the money." Mr. Messerschmidt cut me off before I could stammer out more nonsense.

I looked away from Tristen and trained my eyes on the paper, not wanting to see him laugh at me. Because I was pretty sure he'd been starting to smile at my failure to articulate a simple thought.

"Imagine how a win would look on college applications," our teacher continued. "Universities would sit up and take notice."

"Meaning more scholarship money," Darcy said shrewdly.

I glanced at my rival, with her bobbed blond hair, her clear blue eyes, and her confident pose, manicured hand on hip, and thought with jealousy that Darcy probably really would get into Harvard, as she already seemed to assume.

Mr. Messerschmidt also smiled with approval at Darcy's ability to connect the dots. "Precisely." He plucked my flyer from my fingers, pointing to the copy. "And see—you can work alone or in pairs."

Pairs again.

"And split the cash, then?" Tristen asked, squinting at the small print.

"Yes, half the money—but double the chance of winning," Mr. Messerschmidt noted. "You guys are good, but a lot of talented students will compete for this. Two heads would definitely be better than one. And you'd still get all the prestige. That can't be halved."

Mr. Messerschmidt had a point. It was probably better to play it safe and have at least a decent shot at $15,000, which was nothing to sneeze at. It was like a year of education if I went to a nearby state university, like Kutztown or Millersville, and lived at home. And even at Smith, my dream school . . . my long shot . . . the money would go a long way.

But Darcy was already looking from me to Tristen and back again with an exaggerated frown. "Sorry, kids," she said. "But Darcy Gray works solo."

Had either of us begged for her help?

I looked to Tristen, mouth starting to open, about to suggest that maybe, just maybe, we might want to consider a partnership. Just to improve our chances.

But before I could speak, he said, with a laugh, "And Tristen Hyde doesn't work at all!" Then he crammed the flyer into his messenger bag, where presumably his lab manual was also crumpled and already forgotten. "Or at least not *that* hard."

Then both Darcy Gray and Tristen Hyde turned on their heels and headed for their next classes, leaving me. The odd girl out.

"That's a shame," Mr. Messerschmidt mused, shaking his balding head at their abrupt departure. "For both of you."

"Um . . . how's that?" I asked, taking time to refold my flyer, tuck it into my chemistry folder, and zip that into my backpack. What did my teacher consider unfortunate for me and . . . who did he even mean? Darcy or Tristen?

"I really thought the whole idea of a Jekel-Hyde team of chemists might be just interesting enough in itself to get you an advantage," Mr. Messerschmidt said. "Too bad Tristen's not interested."

My hand stopped in mid-zip, and my head jerked up.

Jekel and Hyde.

Of course, it wasn't the first time I'd thought of our names in that way. When Tristen had arrived at Supplee Mill at the start of our junior year, people had made the connection and joked about us being soul mates. Not only was the teasing embarrassing, but it was obvious that nobody really remembered the old Robert Louis Stevenson novel *The Strange Case of Dr. Jekyll and Mr. Hyde*, which we'd all read in freshman lit. In the book, mild-mannered Dr. Henry Jekyll had created a formula that changed him into his evil alter-ego, "Mr. Hyde"—a ruthless killer. It was far from a love story. Thankfully, since Tristen and I hardly ever crossed paths, the jokes had quickly gotten old and pointless, and before long, like everybody else, I'd pretty much forgotten our names were even linked.

Certainly, when Mr. Messerschmidt brought up the connection again in the context of a chemistry competition, that was the first time in months I'd thought about the coincidence of Jekel meeting Hyde again—and connected us both to the old locked box in Dad's sealed home office.

I resumed zipping my backpack, but my thoughts were a million miles away.

Or would that be over one hundred years away?

Me, Tristen, and that box . . . The one I'd been warned never, ever to touch.

And certainly never to *open.*

Forget it, Jill, I told myself, shouldering my backpack and abandoning the idea almost as quickly as it had crossed my mind. I'd been told to leave the box alone, and I would follow my parents' rules.

At least that's what I thought I'd do until two nights later, when my mom called me to a family meeting—convening what little was left of our family—and confided a nasty little secret that she'd been hiding specifically from me.

Chapter 3

Tristen

"HEY, TRISTEN."

I looked first to my arm—surprised and more than a little unhappy to discover a hand resting there—and then shifted my eyes to learn that it was Darcy Gray who dared to touch me, uninvited, as I shoved books into my open locker.

"About that chemistry scholarship," Darcy said without removing her hand. "I've been rethinking working alone."

My mouth began to twitch with amusement, and I arched my eyebrows. "Really, Darcy? Have you?"

Unfortunately I didn't have the opportunity to advise Darcy that *I* had not rethought *anything* related to the contest—including the partnership that she was about to suggest—because we were both interrupted by yet *another* hand very unwisely clamping down on my shoulder.

I turned slowly to see Todd Flick's narrow, suspicious, simian eyes glaring up at me as he demanded, "Why the hell are you touching my girlfriend, Hyde?"

Forgetting Darcy entirely, I turned my head to stare pointedly at Flick's knuckles. "Take your hand away," I advised. "Now."

Although I'd heard much of quarterbacks being the smartest players on American football teams, Flick wasn't bright enough to do as I said. Instead he issued an ultimatum, snarling, "You have two seconds to explain, Hyde—or I'm gonna *kick your ass.*"

After that, just as my grandfather had predicted, I forgot pretty much everything. Again.

Chapter 4

Tristen

IN HIS REMARKABLE Symphony No. 5 Ludwig van Beethoven required only four notes—three rapid Gs and a long E-flat—to evoke in generations of listeners a sense of impending doom.

Sitting in a Pennsylvania diner, my father, the preeminent psychoanalyst Dr. Frederick Hyde, managed—of course—to best even the great German composer, with a grim, one-note, growling sigh that caused the blood to run cold in my veins.

"Rrrrrrrr . . ." Dad shook his head as he sliced neatly into a thick slab of rare prime rib. "I hardly know what to say, Tristen."

"Sorry, sir," I apologized yet again, picking up a french fry and dredging it through a puddle of ketchup. "I know you're disappointed."

"'Disappointed' is hardly the word," Dad said, glancing up at me. "You *pummeled* a classmate, Tristen. Sent him to the hospital with a *broken arm* that will end his football season. I am far, far beyond 'disappointed.'"

"Yes, sir." I slouched lower in the booth. "Sorry."

"Sit up, please, Tristen," my father directed, using his knife to point at the french fry in my fingers. "And use utensils. This may not be The Ivy, but it's still a step above a *kennel*. There's no excuse for eating like an *animal*."

"Sorry," I said again, straightening my spine and abandoning my food entirely.

My father dabbed a napkin against his impeccably trimmed, tribute-to-Freud beard, then resumed eating his dinner in a profound silence that managed to speak volumes about me while I stared out the window, watching the people of Supplee Mill as they went about their business on Market Street. A few blocks away Todd Flick was probably just leaving Mercy Hospital with a freshly set bone. I reached up and pressed my fingers against my own bruised face, wincing.

Dammit.

Yet things could have turned out much worse. At least Flick was going to be okay.

Still, the story that had emerged had been unnerving. Apparently it had taken two of Flick's teammates to subdue me. How could I not remember *that*?

My fingers again traced the purple, swollen skin just below my eye.

"Hurt, Tristen?" Dad asked.

I looked across the table to see that he'd finished eating and crossed his knife and fork atop the plate. "Yes," I admitted, dropping my hand. "A little."

"Good. Maybe the pain will deter you from fighting in the future."

"We can only hope," I agreed.

Dad gave me a long level stare that made me regret even the hint of sarcasm.

Then, when he was sure his point had been delivered, he leaned back in the booth, adjusted his eyeglasses, and began drumming his fingers against the table, head cocked, observing me as if I were one of his patients. A particularly difficult case who showed no signs of progress, in spite of years of intensive treatment.

"Well, Tristen," he finally began, "now that we've both had a chance to calm down, why don't you explain—again—what happened at school today."

I averted my eyes and fidgeted with my water glass, erasing the condensation. "I tried to tell you in the car. I don't remember."

Daring to check his reaction, I saw a muscle in Dad's jaw twitch. A warning sign. "Tristen, please don't start with that again."

"It's true." I leaned forward. "Can't you at least give me the benefit of the doubt?"

"No, Tristen," Dad said, mouth set in a firm line. "Because if I validate this 'blackout,' then I am validating a component of the *stories* your grandfather filled your head with—"

I could feel the muscle in *my* jaw starting to jump. "Grandfather swore they weren't stories. If you'd just listen—"

"Tristen, no." Dad cut me off sharply, leaning in, too, so we were eye-to-eye. "For the last time—the *very* last time—there is no 'Hyde curse.' I will not speak seriously of nonsense!"

"But—"

"Your grandfather suffered from dementia in his final days." Dad overrode me again, actually reaching across the table and clasping my arm. I suppose the gesture was meant to be reassuring, but he held too tightly, and it came off as confining, almost threatening. "Those 'crimes' he confessed to—they never happened. There was no 'evil alter ego.' No late-night forays that ended in violence. No 'blackouts,' for god's sake."

"But—"

Dad squeezed harder, his fingers surprisingly powerful, given that the only exercise they ever got was turning the pages of his academic texts. "The *Case of Jekyll and Hyde* was a *novel,* Tristen," he said, boring into my eyes. "A work of fiction. A good book, with some admittedly interesting insights into man's dual nature. But a *tall tale.* There was no 'real' Dr. Jekyll, no 'formula,' and no 'real' Mr. Hyde. And we are, quite obviously, *not* descended from a fictional character. It's ludicrous!"

I stared at my father's eyes, which were a peculiar metallic gray. Eyes the color of two padlocks and nearly as impenetrable. I had inherited my mother's brown eyes. Sometimes when I looked in the mirror, I could almost see her in my reflection. I loved and despised those moments.

Where was Mom?

I watched my father's opaque eyes, searching again.

When my mother had first disappeared, vanishing in the middle of the night three years before, the police had nosed around Dad, sniffing for signs of foul play. But they'd found nothing. Of course they'd found nothing, I reassured myself.

My father was imperious and overbearing, but my parents had loved each other, in their own curious way. Mom had understood how to tease out of Dad a gruff, grudging, but genuine affection that I never got to experience now that she was gone.

No, even if there was a Hyde curse—even if the Hyde men were descended from *the* evil "Mr. Hyde" and genetically doomed to commit unspeakable acts of violence—surely Dad wouldn't have harmed *Mom.*

Then again, I didn't believe Dad's assertion that my mother had abandoned us of her own free will as part of some midlife crisis that she'd snap out of eventually. That was "ludicrous," to use his own word.

Someone had harmed her. *Killed* her. But who?

I blinked at Dad, utterly confused, and pulled my arm free.

What did I believe?

My father seemed to sense that I was struggling inside and seized upon my uncertainty. "Tristen, I am one of the world's best psychotherapists," he said with his characteristic, shameless hubris. "I have spent my professional life exploring the workings of the mind. And I am telling you right now, there is nothing wrong with you—aside from the fact that you've let your grandfather's ridiculous stories cloud your thinking."

"But my nightmares," I noted. "My dreams. Even Freud said dreams were important. That they are the subconscious expressing its true desires."

And the dreams that I suffered—if they represented my true desires, I wasn't just sick, or deviant, even. I was a *psychopath*. The nightmares had started out chaotic, little more than random images of gore. More recently, however, they had begun to coalesce into a narrative dominated by a river, a knife—and a girl's pale, vulnerable throat.

"Oh, Tristen." Dad smiled at his teenage son's effort to educate the great Dr. Hyde about *Freud*, of all topics. "You talk as if you've never read Jung." His smile faded. "The images that appear in our dreams are influenced by—*complicated* by—the dreamer's history, his circumstances. And the images in your nightmares were placed there by my father. Your subconscious isn't playing out its hopes. It is expressing your very *conscious* fears. You don't secretly want to kill anyone."

He did have a point. I *didn't* want to kill. If anything, I desperately wanted Grandfather to be wrong. I just wanted to be normal.

My father sat back, looking out the window and shaking his head. "If I'd had any idea my father would have such a terrible impact on you, I would never have allowed you to visit him so often. I would have forbade it."

"No, don't say that!" I objected. "Without Grandfather I wouldn't have studied music. I wouldn't compose!"

Dad returned his attention to me. "Nor would you be *infected* with this foolish notion that you are predisposed to become an *insane killing machine.*"

I knew we'd reached the end of the discussion. Or perhaps not quite the end, because he reached out again, taking my wrist more gently this time. "Tristen," he said, his tone softer, too, "if there was a 'Hyde curse,' I would also suffer, wouldn't I? According to your grandfather's fables, *all* the Hyde men go mad, correct?"

"Yes," I agreed, looking away, unable to meet his eyes, because, even discounting Mom's disappearance, there had been times after Grandfather had started talking so freely, so desperately, that I'd looked back on my father's behavior and wondered if *something* wasn't quite right.

"Tristen, look at me," Dad ordered, removing his glasses, as if to eradicate any small barrier that might impede my understanding. I forced myself to meet those gray eyes. "Yes?"

"There is no curse," he said softly and convincingly. "Let the idea go before you really *do* harm your psyche."

"Fine," I agreed, primarily so I could end the discussion and unlock my eyes from his. "Whatever you say."

However, I wasn't convinced. Not convinced at all. If only I could have really confided in him, told Dad about that evening I'd been with that girl by the river. And that night in London—the *rest* of the story about Grandfather and what I suspected . . .

Of course I couldn't, though. That last secret—it would have to go with me to my grave.

Slipping his glasses back onto his narrow nose, my father shifted in the booth, reaching for his wallet. "I need to return to campus," he said. "Will you be all right?"

"You're going to back to work *now?*" I asked. "It's nearly eight o'clock."

"This fellowship is important," Dad reminded me. "I didn't suspend my practice in London—and your education at one of England's best academies—in order to sit in a rental house in the Pennsylvania countryside. I need to prepare lectures and conduct research that will impress my American colleagues."

The suspicion that I kept fighting off crept back yet again. I could understand that the fellowship at the prestigious Severin College of Medicine was a good chance to introduce Dr. Frederick Hyde to an even wider, international audience, but lately his hours had been getting longer and longer. How much research could he do?

Dad summoned our server with an imperious wave, signaling for the check. As they settled the bill, I again watched out the window. And who should walk into my line of sight but Jill Jekel and Becca Wright, the two unlikeliest of friends.

One wore a short denim skirt and tight T-shirt, the other a lacy blouse. Not sexy lacy. Virginal, wedding-veil, Victorian lacy.

One gestured actively with fuchsia-tipped fingers. The other struggled to keep her small pale hands wrapped around a huge artist's portfolio.

One sometimes showed up in my nightmares, falling into my arms, feeling the prick of a blade against her skin . . . One was . . .

"Interested, Tristen?" Dad asked, jerking me back from my reverie.

I realized that he was watching me as I followed Jill and Becca's progress down the street. "No." I shook my head. "Not at all."

As the words came out of my mouth, I was certain that I told the truth. Yet I felt, for some reason, like a liar, because both of those girls, they did intrigue me, in very different—sometimes disturbing—ways.

Chapter 5

Jill

BECCA WRIGHT was stretched out on my bed kicking her tanned, pedicured feet in the air as she flipped through *Foundations of the Chemical World* like it was *Star* magazine and she was looking at photos of beautiful people, not molecular models.

I stood in the corner at my easel, adding a bright sun to my canvas but keeping one eye on Becca's halfhearted attempt at studying, wondering how long she'd keep up the charade.

After about two more minutes the book slammed shut and Becca sat up, twisting her long legs into a pretzel, the same way we used to sit together on a rug in our kindergarten classroom.

Why had we stayed friends for so many years, long after Becca had gone on to be popular? Was it just because we still lived on the same block and ended up walking to school together every day? Or did she really just need me even more than like me? That was probably the truth . . .

Outside, lightning flashed as a late-summer storm blew closer, and no matter how Becca felt about me, I was glad she was there while Mom worked an evening shift.

"Jilly?" Becca ventured when the thunder faded away. "I was just thinking."

"Yes?" I dabbed more chromium yellow on my canvas. "About what?"

"The stupid way Messerschmidt grades us," Becca said. "You know, how he only gives two real tests the whole year, so if you flunk one, you're doomed."

"I'll help you study," I promised. *Like always* . . .

"Yeah, and you'll end up trying to teach me everything at the last minute," she said matter-of-factly, like neither one of us had any choice in the matter. "It'll take hours."

I shrugged. "I don't mind."

"Well . . . what if you just helped me during the test?" Becca asked.

The suggestion startled me so much that my hand jerked, messing up my painting. But I gave her a wobbly, uncertain smile in case she was joking. "Becca, you don't really want to . . . *cheat?*"

She untwisted her legs and hopped to the edge of the bed. "Just think about it, Jill," she said in a way that told me she *wasn't* kidding. "You practically give me all the answers anyway. What does it matter if I memorize them right before the test or if you text me under the table *during* the exam?"

I shook my head, not believing that Becca was honestly suggesting that we should cheat. "We could get caught," I reminded her. "It would go on our records! And we'd probably get in-school suspension!"

Not to mention the embarrassment . . . Not to mention that cheating was WRONG.

"No," I said more firmly. "I couldn't do it."

Outside, rain began to fall, and I dabbed a new brush into azure, convinced that the talk of cheating was *done*.

"Hey, Jill?"

I glanced up to see my friend staring at my feet, and I looked down, thinking I must have dropped paint on my ballet flats. "What?"

"Don't those goody two-shoes ever feel a little tight?"

My cheeks flamed. "Becca . . . I'm just afraid . . ."

"Oh, just forget it," she muttered, standing up and walking to the window. "I'll just fail."

I dragged my brush against the canvas, trying to fix my mistake and wondering if Becca had any idea how unfair that comment was. She was smart enough to do the work on her own . . . but pretty enough that she'd never really had to do anything for herself.

"I should get going," she said, "but this storm is awful."

"Just hang out until it's over," I urged, wincing as lightning struck close by.

Okay, so I was definitely using her a little, too. "Look." I sighed. "I'll help you with the test somehow, okay? I'll make sure you pass."

Becca turned to me, smiling again, like she'd already gotten what she wanted. "Thanks, Jilly."

But I *wouldn't* cheat.

As I put more blue on my brush, Becca started to wander around my room, absently picking up the stuff on my dresser, then setting things back down, obviously bored. "You wanna do something?"

30

"We could keep studying," I suggested.

"Or better yet, we could pierce your ears," Becca announced like she'd been struck by a brilliant idea. "That would be fun!"

"What?" I looked up to see her staring at my naked earlobes. "You're not serious," I said, picturing blood, and infection, and my mom's expression when she saw that I'd violated her rule against piercing anything before I was eighteen.

"Why not?" she asked, grinning more broadly. "I did Angela Sloan's last summer, and she didn't even cry. The ice—and the vodka—numbed everything."

"Vodka?" I kind of yelped. I knew Becca partied but . . . *vodka?* And needles going through *flesh?* "I don't think so," I said, dipping my blue brush into a waiting jar of turpentine. The liquid swirled greenish black, like pus from an infected ear. "No!"

Becca sighed—a "you're so boring" sigh—and plopped down at my desk, shaking the mouse to bring my laptop's screen to life. Opening the Internet, she started typing, and I watched warily, hoping that she wasn't going to call up sites I wasn't supposed to visit.

Cheating, piercing, porn . . . it would be too much for one night. And if Mom came home early and walked in . . . "What are you looking for?" I asked, wiping my paint-spattered hands with a rag.

"I'm going on my MySpace," Becca said.

I felt a moment of relief—until she added, "I'm checking out Tristen Hyde's page."

I didn't know why I wanted to object to that, too. Why I didn't want to look at Tristen . . . especially not with Becca.

But even on a computer, Becca was socially adept, and of course it took her only a second to get to Tristen's page, and before I could say anything to stop her, she announced, with triumph in her voice, "Well, well, well . . . here's something interesting about the mysterious Mr. Hyde!"

Chapter 6

Jill

"TRISTEN IS, LIKE, A COMPOSER," Becca said, sounding impressed. "He writes *classical* music."

I left my easel and sank down on my bed, surprised and maybe skeptical about a MySpace boast. "Really?"

"He has audio links," Becca confirmed. She clicked a lacquered nail against the mouse, and my bedroom filled with the sound of a piano. "He says it's his stuff."

I wasn't sure what I expected to hear as the file opened. Maybe something that was so good that I'd know Tristen hadn't really written it, and was, like most people, exaggerating online. Or maybe a simple, decent song like a teenage guy might actually write.

But the melody that came forth . . . it was incredible. And yet I also believed that Tristen Hyde really did create it, because it somehow reminded me of Tristen himself.

I cocked my head, listening closer and easily picturing him. Confident, kind of enigmatic . . . and comfortable at the edge of a grave. Although my computer's speakers were cheap and tinny, the song was undeniably powerful. Dark and ominous, yet . . . *majestic,* like the storm that had finally broken in earnest outside.

"That's amazing," I said, forgetting that I'd been reluctant to look at Tristen's online persona, as his composition continued to play. "Really beautiful."

Becca wrinkled her nose, though, and ended the music with another quick tap of her fingernail. "Kind of gloomy, I think."

Wishing we'd heard more, I watched as Becca navigated to some photos of Tristen, and my stomach got ticklish again, like when she'd first announced her intention to check out his page. Although obviously MySpace was public, I felt like we were trespassing, spying on him.

Becca clearly didn't feel the same way. She clicked on an image, making it bigger, and whistled under her breath. "Wow . . . He is so hot, don't you think?" she asked, eyes trained on the screen.

I didn't say anything. I just stared at Tristen's photo, feeling even more uncomfortable, like he had actually joined us in my bedroom, although the picture had clearly been taken at a concert. Tristen was seated at a glossy black piano, his thick hair falling over his forehead, and he wore a tux, which made him look much older than a teenager—even more so than the tie I'd seen him wear. He must have been playing, but the photographer had captured a moment when Tristen had glanced up from the keys, his brown eyes directly meeting the lens, and the intensity I saw there . . .

I felt myself blushing again, and I was glad Becca was also looking at Tristen and not at me.

"It's not just how he looks, but the way he talks, with that accent," Becca added over her shoulder. "You know he went to this super-exclusive school in England, right?"

"No, I didn't know that," I said, although I wasn't surprised by the news. Tristen spoke more like a teacher than . . . well, most of the actual teachers at Supplee Mill. I peered harder at the photo, thinking that Tristen definitely was intriguing, in a way.

Suddenly Becca swung around to face me, laughing. Maybe *at* me. "You *know* you think he's hot, Jill," she teased, like that would be the funniest thing in the world—if it had been true. "I saw you checking him out in chem!"

"No, I wasn't!" *I wasn't* . . .

"But a guy like Tristen," Becca said, twisting one of her curls around her finger. "He wouldn't be good for somebody like you, Jill—no offense!"

My cheeks caught on fire then, both at the unfair accusation that I liked Tristen . . . and at the insult I was perceiving. "What does *that* mean?"

"You're sweet," Becca said in a way that didn't exactly sound like a compliment. "And Tristen . . . Well, he talks really smooth, but he's got a rough side, too."

I sort of rolled my eyes. "Come on, Becca . . ." I honestly couldn't believe Tristen Hyde would be anything but well-mannered, maybe even kind of . . . proper.

"Well, he beat Todd Flick to within an inch of his life!" Becca defended her assertion. "That's pretty rough!"

I jolted, nearly slipping off my mattress. "Tristen *beat up* Todd?"

"Yeah." Becca seemed genuinely surprised by my ignorance. "Didn't you hear?"

"No." Jill Jekel was last on the gossip phone tree. "What happened?"

Becca dismissed motive with a wave of her pink-tipped fingers. "Something about Tristen hitting on Darcy, which is ridiculous, because she is *not* his type."

I studied Becca's delicate, pretty face, wondering how she knew Tristen even had a "type." I also fought against a terrible urge to take twisted delight in Todd Flick, who'd teased me for years, getting a beating. Nobody deserved violence. I hated violence. "Tristen didn't really hurt Todd, did he?"

Becca had clearly been relishing the gossip, but the smile she hadn't quite been able to hide slowly disappeared, and her eyes clouded. "Tris broke Todd's arm."

"No . . ." My eyes darted to Tristen's photo. *He couldn't, could he?*

When I looked back to Becca, I saw that she'd gotten not just solemn but almost . . . spooked. And although we were alone, she lowered her voice, so I could barely hear her above the rain pounding the house. "I . . . I kind of know a secret about Tristen, too," she added. "Something from last summer. A story that I never told anybody."

"Really?" I swallowed thickly, suddenly not sure I wanted to hear any more. Not from Becca. Not about *Tristen,* who'd once held me. "Um, maybe you shouldn't . . ."

But Becca continued confiding in me, with a strange expression that I'd never seen before, not in all our years as friends. "I kind of . . . *saw* Tris, over the summer," she said. "And this *thing* happened . . ."

My fingers curled around the edge of my mattress, and I searched my friend's expression for some clue as to what she meant by that word "saw." Like, she *saw* Tristen with her eyes? Or had Becca Wright *gone out* with the only guy I'd ever come even close to kissing? I *really* didn't want to hear more. Yet I found myself asking, "So . . . what happened?"

I never got to hear the end of Becca's story that night, though, because, before she could tell the rest, my bedroom door swung open, causing us both to jump nearly out of our skins. "Mom!" I cried. "I didn't hear you come in!"

My mother stood in the doorway, wet from the rain, looking so grim and tired that, without even being told to go, Becca slipped on her sequined flip-flops, gathered her stuff, and slunk out, muttering, "See you," to both of us before darting down the stairs.

Mom didn't say a word until we heard the front door shut. Then she brushed her damp, graying hair from her forehead and announced, "We need to talk, Jill. I have some bad news."

"Of course," I agreed.

That was the first reply that sprang to mind, and although the words seemed very matter-of-fact, very resigned, in my thoughts, they sounded surprisingly bitter, almost angry when I heard them blurted out loud.

Of course Mom had bad news.

Would there ever be news of any other kind, in the cursed old Jekel house?

Chapter 7

Jill

MY MOTHER SAT HUNCHED at the kitchen table, shivering a little in her damp scrubs, which clung to her frame. I found myself staring at her shoulders, two bony knobs jutting through the thin cotton fabric. "I'll make you some tea," I offered. "And something to eat while we talk."

"Just tea," Mom said, not even sounding interested in that. "I'm not hungry."

"But you should eat," I told her, a cold knot forming in the pit of my stomach. She'd stopped eating, dropping to nearly one hundred pounds, before her breakdown. "Just a little something."

"No, Jill."

I couldn't force her, so I went to make the tea, putting the kettle on the stove and taking a china cup from the shelf. "So, what's up?" I asked, although I had my suspicions. Bad news . . . that was usually about Dad. "Did the police find something?"

"No, Jill. Nothing."

"Oh." Although Mom certainly hadn't led me to expect anything good, I was still a little foolishly disappointed that there was no news at all about my father.

Ever since we'd learned about the grainy videos captured by Carson Pharmaceuticals' security cameras that showed my dad working at three and four a.m., sometimes with a man whose face was indistinct because they kept the lights so low . . . Ever since then I'd clung to the hope that someday the mysterious man would be identified, and not only would the police solve the case and bring Dad's killer to justice, but Dad would somehow be vindicated.

Silly me.

The kettle whistled, and I reached for it, filling the cup. "So, it's nothing about Dad? Or the other man?"

"Jill."

I turned around to see my mom staring at me, looking more steely than she had in months. "What?" I asked, not sure what I'd done wrong.

"The police are never going to solve the case," Mom said, *sounding* more forceful, too. Sounding angry. "They lost interest when they learned that your father was a *criminal,* too, as surely as his killer!"

I'd known that my excitement was ill-advised, and yet when Mom said that, snuffing out my hope, and calling my dad a criminal, a flash of anger tore through me, too. A wave of fury that bordered on rage. *Mom was giving up on Dad, too* . . . My fingers wrapped around the teacup, and for just a second I had this crazy urge to hurl it across the room so it would shatter against the wall in a million pieces.

But of course I couldn't do that. Couldn't *break* things. Instead, my eyes filled with tears. Crying . . . that was the pathetic way *I* expressed rage. "Mom, please don't call him a criminal."

My defense of Dad, weak as it was, only seemed to make her more mad, though.

"Your father *lied* to us, Jill," she said through gritted teeth. "He stole out of the house in the middle of the night while I was working and you were sleeping! He stole chemicals from his employer!" She paused, then dropped the bomb she'd been holding all along. "He stole your *college fund*, Jill! Nearly every cent!"

I froze in place, stunned into mute silence. "What?" I finally asked.

"Your college money," Mom repeated, her own anger seeming to dissolve closer to tears. Her eyes got wide, miserable, like suddenly she couldn't believe what she was telling me, either. "He withdrew it from the bank in the months before his murder. I don't know why, and I tried to work extra shifts to replace some of the money, but I'm so tired . . ."

Mom closed her eyes again then, anger seeming spent, and buried her face in her hands, like she couldn't bear to face me when she added, "I'm so sorry . . . but I don't know if you can go to school next year. Even with loans—I just don't think we can afford it right away."

The teacup that I held did shatter then, but not in a satisfying way, as it slipped from my fingers, which seemed to have gone numb. "No." My voice sounded strangled in my ears. "Dad wouldn't have done that. Not to me."

Mom still didn't look at me, and it seemed like the room started to spin. I reached for the kitchen counter to steady myself.

My college fund . . . I had a shot at valedictorian, but I might not even *go* to school? My father had stolen my future?

All at once, as I stood in that puddle of tea, I *hated* my dad, just like I suspected Mom did. For a split second I was *glad* that my father was dead.

"I'm sorry, Jill," Mom mumbled again.

"Yeah. Me, too." *Silly, silly me . . .*

There was nothing else to say after that. Not much left to feel, even. So I got a rag and cleaned up the mess I'd made. Mom sat at the table, not even trying to help, like she was too exhausted to move.

When the kitchen was clean, I went back upstairs and climbed into my bed, where I stared straight into space, into the darkness, for about an hour, my mind just blank. Completely numb, like somebody had jammed a needle full of Novocain deep, deep into the cortex of my brain.

Then, when the room was pitch black—it must have been almost midnight—I noticed that the green light on the bottom of my laptop's monitor was glowing. I got up, went to my desk, and shook the mouse, thinking I should shut down the computer for the night. Heaven knew we Jekels couldn't afford to waste power!

But when I rattled the mouse and the screen came to life, I jumped a little.

Because there, staring straight out at me, was none other than Tristen Hyde, whose MySpace page Becca had never closed.

Tristen, the guy who'd come to my rescue the first time I'd hit rock bottom.

I slid down into my desk chair, studying Tristen's face. Studying him and wondering, with a growing flicker of excitement.

Was there a chance he might be able to help me again?

Maybe. If I could just convince him . . .

But the rules we'd have to break, the *locks* we'd have to pick . . . Was I really ready for that kind of trespass, even to right the huge wrongs done to me?

I leaned closer, staring hard into those intense, brown eyes.

And was I ready to do those things with . . . *him?*

Chapter 8

Tristen

"TRIS, THIS ISN'T THE ROUTE coach mapped," someone griped as I led the cross-country team off the paved streets and onto the path that ran along the Susquehanna River. "Coach said—"

"Coach isn't here," I reminded them over my shoulder. "If someone else wants to lead . . . ?"

I didn't await a response. Of course they would follow me, their captain, because they knew that, should one of them pass me, it would be only a temporary state. I would let my lungs burst before I ceded my spot in front.

"I hate this trail," I heard a loud complaint from the back.

"Me, too," I muttered. But I had to take that route again and again. Needed to see the spot. Face it down.

As we ran deeper into the forest, the canopy of trees grew denser, blocking the September sun, and shadows dappled the path. The path in my nightmares. The dreams where I held the knife.

Stop it, Tristen, I told myself. *Get control.*

Yet I subtly picked up our pace, trying to outrace the images that were already bubbling up from my troubled subconscious. Of course, my thoughts matched me stride for stride—threatening to overtake me, hurrying faster than my footsteps.

This is the way I approach her . . .

I stretched out my legs, running harder.

"Geez, Tris." I heard another protest, called loudly. "It's just practice!"

Practice. Was the dream a form of "practice," as Grandfather had predicted? Rehearsal for the crimes, the violence, to come . . . ?

Ahead of me the path veered nearer to the river, widening at the spot, the clearing, where I'd actually been with the girl that evening in July. The place that I also conjured again and again in the nightmare.

I'd nearly lost control with her. She'd been willing—and then something had happened, something I couldn't recall. And I'd come back to myself to find her pushing me away, terror in her eyes. Just like in the dream.

And what had happened in England? Was there a chance I had really . . . ?

Behind me my teammates fought to keep up, their footsteps falling harder against the dirt, sounding for all the world like a mob chasing me. A lynch mob after Tristen Hyde. *Murderer.*

Pulling even farther ahead of my struggling squad, I began to tear through the clearing at a breakneck pace, mind flashing to London.

Oh, hell.

The *blood . . .*

I actually squeezed my eyes shut, a stupid thing for a runner to do, and of course I stumbled, my foot striking a rock, my ankle twisting sharply, and I went down, hard. Borne by momentum, my teammates did their best to avoid me, veering off the trail and crashing through the brush or leaping over me as I shielded my head with my arms, choking on the dust raised by their feet.

When they had all passed, I sat up, signaling at those who looked back, telling them to continue on. Standing, I coughed and brushed myself off, listening to the wind through the dry, rasping leaves and the trilling of the cicadas as I berated myself.

It was just a path. And the nightmare just a dream, as my father insisted. The missing moments—they could be explained, too, somehow. I wasn't *really* dangerous.

Right?

Taking a deep breath, I continued on and ignoring the pain in my ankle, soon overtook my teammates again. Assuming my place as leader, I guided us out of that hated forest and back into the light.

However, when I arrived back at school, still pushing us all too hard, someone was waiting for me in the bleachers. A timid girl with an innocent suggestion that would eventually plunge me even deeper into the shadows I'd just escaped.

Chapter 9

Jill

I WAS WAITING on the bleachers, trying to figure out what I'd say to Tristen, when the cross-country team came running in from the street and onto the track, finishing practice. Actually, it wasn't so much the *team* that arrived as Tristen, alone. He was so far ahead of the other runners that, although I'd heard he was captain, he didn't even seem like part of his own squad.

As I watched, Tristen finished a lap, literally running circles around the football players who grunted and tackled in the middle of the field—minus *their* leader. Tristen kept a steady and seemingly effortless pace until he reached Coach Parker and pulled up short, bending over and bracing his hands on his knees, taking a few deep breaths before straightening and almost immediately falling into a discussion with the coach, their eyes trained on the other runners, who finally entered the field and finished their own, weaker laps.

From where I sat, Tristen and Coach Parker seemed to be taking stock of the team, like they were co-coaches, not teacher and student. Tristen's hands rested on his narrow hips, and his hair was dark and shiny, soaked with sweat. There was a deep, dark V down the middle of his T-shirt, too, and when he raised his hand to point at a straggler, I saw that although Tristen was lean, like most runners, his biceps were sharply defined, stretching the fabric of his shirt. And was it the sun that cast a shadow under his eye, or could I see, even at that distance, the bruise he'd gotten when he'd shattered Todd's arm?

My fingers wrapped around the bleachers, squeezing. Maybe the whole idea of coming there . . . of the experiment, even . . . was bad . . . wrong.

I was standing up, thinking I should just go home, when I guess my movement caught Tristen's eye. He glanced in my direction and hesitated for a second, like he was surprised to see me there. Then he shaded his eyes against the sun, smiled, and waved. I waved back, feeling like an idiot.

Now what should I do?

I was starting to sheepishly step down off the bleachers when Tristen clapped his hand on his coach's shoulder, apparently excused himself . . . and started loping over in my direction.

Chapter 10

Tristen

I WASN'T SURE why I abandoned cross-country practice to talk with Jill Jekel on a hot September afternoon. Perhaps it was something about the uncertain way that Jill stood—or half stood—alone in a huge stretch of empty seats that reminded me of the day I'd held her at the cemetery, in the heart of an equally vast expanse of headstones. As Jill fidgeted in the bleachers, she looked to me as if she needed help again.

"What brings you here?" I asked, taking the bleachers two by two until I reached her. I jerked my thumb toward the football players, grinning. "Don't tell me you've got your eye on one of them."

Jill's cheeks reddened. "No! I was just . . . I wanted to talk to *you.*"

"Really?" I smiled at the way she blushed. Maybe I was flattered, too, that Jill had come for me—although I'd suspected she was too smart to nurse a "crush" on a football player, which seemed almost mandatory for other girls at Supplee Mill. "What's up?"

Jill tucked some wayward strands of brown hair behind her ear, a gesture I'd seen countless times in chemistry class when Messerschmidt would put her on the spot to explain concepts that I suspected baffled him. "It's . . . it's about the chemistry contest," she said. "About maybe working together."

44

I opened my mouth to advise Jill, flatly, that I wasn't interested. After all, I'd had no compunction about turning Darcy down. Or, I *would have* had no compunction if Flick hadn't interrupted our conversation. But Jill—she was looking up at me, the sunlight glinting off her plastic eyeglasses, and I found myself sidetracked, wondering, *What did those eyes hold if one ever managed to look behind the glasses?*

Intelligence, I was certain of that. And pain—I was sure of that, too.

Suddenly I found myself saying, "Sure, Jill. Let's talk."

We both sat down—me keeping a distance, given how the sweat was still pouring down my chest and back.

"Are you sure you're not interested in competing?" Jill began. "Because I have an idea . . . for both of us."

"I honestly hadn't planned to take part," I said. "Chemistry is easy for me, but it's not a real interest."

"Oh."

Jill sounded so disappointed, so defeated already, that I couldn't help but add, "Still, I'd be willing to listen. After all, it is a fair amount of cash."

"Yes," Jill agreed, nodding. "And I think we'd have a good chance of winning. You wouldn't have to work that hard, either, Tristen."

"I do like the sound of that," I admitted. Both the possibility of reward with little effort and perhaps the chance for a partnership with the quiet girl who squirmed on the metal seat. Honestly, what was behind those glasses? So few students at Supplee Mill held any interest for me. They seemed mono-dimensional, disinterested in anything beyond the fight for the pointless goal of popularity.

But Jill—she didn't seem to strive for that at all. On the contrary, she seemed shut off, inaccessible—and that intrigued me. "So, what's the plan?" I asked.

Jill pressed her palms against her knees, taking a deep breath. "Well, you know how people used to tease us about being 'Jekyll and Hyde'?"

"Oh yes, I remember," I said. The jokes—most of which had been completely uninformed by the novel—had nevertheless been an unwelcome reminder of a legend I was trying to forget. For a time, until the topic had grown stale, I'd rather resented Jill just for existing. For having that name.

"Well, I was thinking we could capitalize on our names," Jill said. "Work as a team of chemists . . . Jekel and Hyde . . . on an experiment actually based on the book, *The Strange Case of Dr. Jekyll and Mr. Hyde.*"

I sat up straighter, on guard. "But, Jill, that work is fiction." To everyone but myself and my grandfather . . .

"Not according to my dad," Jill said. "I mean, he believed the *book* is fiction but that it was based on a true story."

I stared at her for a long moment, not believing what I'd just heard. "Really?" I finally asked with deliberate calm. "He did?"

"Yes." Jill nodded. "In fact, Dad said we Jekels are distantly related to *the* Henry Jekyll, the doctor whose true story inspired the novel. My grandfather changed the spelling of our name when he came to the United States. You know, to distance us from the bad stuff that happened in England."

I knew too well the "bad stuff" to which she referred: brutal acts committed by Dr. Jekyll's creation . . . Hyde.

"Go on," I said, hoping she couldn't discern the increasing tension in my muscles, my voice. What she was saying—it was almost too strange to grasp, if only because it was so very, very familiar. "How does this lead to chemistry?" I asked. "To research?"

"Well . . . this will sound weird, but my dad kept this old box

46

in his office. And he swore that it holds the original documents detailing the actual experiments that inspired the novel."

Something like an electric shock tore through me, and I did nearly lose my composure. "Jill," I asked, forcing myself to meet her eyes, expression neutral. "Have you ever actually looked inside this box?"

Jill shook her head. "Oh no! Both my parents agreed that the experiments are too dangerous. I've never been allowed to *touch* the box." She flushed again. "I know it sounds crazy, but Dad especially, honestly *believed* the Jekyll and Hyde story."

I looked out over the football field, crowded with players who probably wished to kill me in retribution for an act I couldn't even recall. Then I turned back to Jill, still trying to seem almost disinterested, although the wheels in my brain were spinning wildly. "And what exactly do you want *us* to do, Jill? For the scholarship?"

"I thought we could open the box and recreate the experiments," she said. "Then, using current knowledge about chemical interactions and brain function, determine whether there really was a chance that one of my ancestors created an evil Mr. Hyde."

I didn't say anything right away, and Jill added nervously, "I mean, don't you think it's a great coincidence: Jekel and Hyde? Our names alone would generate interest."

"But, Jill," I noted, "if your parents expressly forbid you from ever touching the box, why do it now?" If the papers were, against all odds, *real,* Jill couldn't *imagine* how dangerous they might be. I swiped my palm against my shorts, trying to wipe away the sweat, the slickness that made the knife in my dream so slippery. "If this is just about besting Darcy—"

I knew there was rivalry there, but Jill jerked upright defensively. "No! It's not that. I mean, not really."

The caveat was very telling. "If not just Darcy, then why, Jill?"

I was the one on the verge of losing complete control—my grandfather's stories, *confirmed?*—but it was Jill who crumpled right before my eyes.

"My dad," she said, bending and wrapping her thin arms around her knees. "He sort of . . . spent my college savings before he died. I don't have anything left for school."

It was obvious that "spent" was a euphemism for "stole," and if I'd been closer, I might have reached out to give her arm a sympathetic squeeze, not just because I was shocked that her father would do something so cruel, but because it so obviously pained her to share such a private, embarrassing tragedy with me. "I'm really sorry, Jill."

"I need this scholarship," she added. "And I need your help. Not just your name, but your knowledge. You always finish your experiments first . . ."

Oh, god. I wanted to help her. I didn't know much about Dr. Jekel's murder, but I'd heard that he'd been involved in shady dealings at Carson Pharmaceuticals. Poor Jill lived under a cloud of sadness *and* shame, and she seemed like such a sweet girl that I honestly wished I could help her escape both. But I couldn't fall more deeply into the plot of that terrible old novel, and at that moment, when I was close to shuddering—not just because cold sweat was still pouring down my spine—I didn't think Jill should meddle in the past, either.

"Jill," I said, rising, "I'm sorry, truly sorry, but I honestly think that your parents are right. You should leave that old box alone and find another way to pay for your education."

Before Jill could reply, I strode down the bleachers, heading for the showers. When I reached the bottom, I wanted to look back, to offer Jill the farewell I'd forgotten to give her, but I was worried that if I saw her face again—saw that devastated, betrayed, vulnerable expression—I might wrongly change my mind. At the time I really thought I was doing right by Jill to just walk away, even if it hurt her.

That very night, though, I was convinced—compelled—to rethink my decision.

Chapter 11

Tristen

THE NIGHT IS DARK and the river flows sluggishly, putridly at my side. Before me she waits, peering down the path. "Tristen . . . Tristen?" I step behind her, the hilt of the knife hard against my palm. "I'm here, love . . . right here . . ."

Not turning, she leans against my chest, pleased, trusting me. "Oh, Tristen . . ."

I raise the knife . . . She sees it . . . is confused . . .

"Tristen? Tristen? TRISTEN?"

"TRISTEN!"

"What?" I cried, sitting bolt upright, twisting against my damp sheets, which had wound around my legs, binding me. Someone was clutching my shoulder—hard.

"Tristen!" Dad shook me roughly. "Calm down. You're dreaming."

"Stop it!" I yelled, pushing against him. He was grasping me too hard. Hurting me. "Stop it!"

"Easy, son!" He stepped back from my bed, giving me space. "Just relax."

"Oh, god . . ." My shoulders heaved as I struggled to control my breathing. I raked my fingers through soaked hair. "Oh, god . . ."

Dad rested his hand more gently on my shoulder. "It's just a nightmare," he reassured me again. "It's okay, son."

I didn't answer. I was fighting too hard: battling not just for breath but to subdue the trace of the thrill, the desire that I still felt, lingering inside of me. The tingling arousal, the *need*, that continued to rise unbidden from my subconscious, not just for sex with the faceless girl in my dream but for her *blood*. "Oh, god . . ."

Dad kept his hand on my shoulder. "Tristen—don't make too much of this."

"It's getting more vivid," I said, head in my hands. "I can smell the river—"

"That's impossible," he interrupted, stepping back again. "There is no olfactory component to dreams, Tristen. You're in your room now. Safe. Fine."

I looked up at him, and although the room was dark, I realized that my father was still dressed in a shirt and tie. "Dad?" I checked the clock. Nearly two a.m. "What are you—?"

"I want you to sleep now, son," he urged, moving toward the door. "Sleep and don't make too much of this. Promise me that."

"I won't," I said. But I was confused. Why wasn't he in bed? He never worked *that* late. "I'll try not to . . ."

I lay back on my sweat-soaked sheets, trying unsuccessfully to calm my unsettled mind and listening as my father went to his room. Down the hall I heard Dad opening and closing drawers, and when the sound of his running shower finally reached my ears,

I got up and went to my bookshelves, fumbling behind a copy of Carl Jung's *Dreams,* which Dad had loaned me when I'd first begun having nightmares.

"This will reassure you," he'd promised. "Dreams are telling, but they are not the final word."

As Dad had assured me, I had found Jung's ideas comforting at times. That night, however, I shoved *Dreams* aside and dug deeper for a book that I kept hidden. A first edition copy of *The Strange Case of Dr. Jekyll and Mr. Hyde,* which my grandfather had given me on the eve—the actual eve—of his death.

My fingers met the familiar deep gash in the leather cover—as though someone had done violence to the violent work itself—and I pulled down the book. Turning on my lamp, I opened to the first yellowed page, which would have been empty had not Grandfather inscribed it. *To Tristen, with gratitude for being strong when I was weak.*

There was a smudge there, too. A fingerprint. Sometimes I would place my own fingertip against the dark spot, testing the fit, wondering if that finger pointed to Grandfather—or to me. And if my soul did lie at the heart of that swirling, twisted maze, what did that mean for me—and for the girl in my nightmare?

That night by the river with her. That evening with Grandfather. Flick's broken arm. The nightmare, which *was* growing more complete, more tangible, more intense. The documents that Jill Jekel had spoken of . . .

I stared at the dark whorl on the page, recalling Jill's offer—and Jill herself, sitting on the bleachers, so small and timid. And smart. And in possession of what her father swore was a very special artifact.

All at once the fog—the mist from that river—seemed to clear, and I flipped deeper into the novel, fingers mauling the pages as I searched for a passage that suddenly flashed through my mind almost verbatim. Finding it, I read aloud, too excited to keep silent.

"Hurrying back to my cabinet, I once more prepared and drank the cup . . . and came to myself once more . . ."

I shut the book, mind racing.

Jekyll's formula didn't just *create* Hyde . . .

Jill had wanted me to help her, but was there a chance that *she* could help *me?*

It seemed almost absurd. Yet I was ready to grasp at the most fragile straws. For as I stood in my bedroom listening to my father's late-night shower, recalling the desire I'd still felt in the wake of my nightmare, and considering the increasing number of things that I couldn't—or perhaps *wouldn't*—remember, I was convinced suddenly that if salvation didn't lie within a box I hadn't even seen yet, I was doomed.

Chapter 12

Jill

I MOVED MY EASEL closer to the living room window, trying to catch what was left of the daylight. I was kind of stalling, too. The self-portrait that I was trying to paint was the year's biggest assignment and would count for almost 20 percent of my grade.

Holding up my junior year school picture, which I was using as my model, I stepped back, assessing the canvas from a different angle, comparing it to the photo. What was wrong with my face as I'd painted it? Was it my smile? My eyes?

My art teacher, Miss Lampley, agreed that something wasn't right. "As always, your work is technically accurate," she'd mused, standing next to me in the classroom, tapping her index finger against her cheek. "And yet you're not capturing the *essence* of Jill Jekel. There's something missing."

I looked into my eyes rendered in oil paint. I'd worked hard to recreate their tricky green-brown color, even though I didn't like it. But getting the color right hadn't been enough.

What was my "essence"?

With a frustrated sigh, I started to clip the photo to the canvas—but dropped it when my hand jerked at the unexpected sound of a loud knock at the front door.

I spun toward the foyer, surprised and more than a little on guard.

Don't answer it, I told myself. It was getting dark outside, and I'd promised Mom. No unauthorized visitors while she was at work.

The knock came again, though, louder, and I crept to the foyer, thinking I should check the dead bolt just to make sure it was locked. But as I reached out to spin the latch, the person on the porch called, "Jill? Are you there?"

I hesitated another second at the sound of the familiar voice. "No visitors" definitely meant "no boys."

"Jill, I know you're there. I heard you," he said. "So just open up, huh?"

What could I do at that point but listen not to Mom but to Tristen Hyde, who stood on the porch, messenger bag slung over his shoulder, arms crossed, waiting? I stared up at his tall, imposing silhouette. "Um, I'm not supposed to have—"

But Tristen stepped over the threshold, announcing, "I've reconsidered the contest, Jill. I think we should do it." Although I still sort of blocked his way, he sidestepped me and strode into the living room. "Let's talk."

"Tristen, wait." I trailed after him. "My mom's not home and . . ."

But Tristen was oblivious to my concerns, maybe because his attention had been caught by something in the living room.

At first I thought he was looking at my painting, and my heart sank. "I'm still working on that," I blurted, defending my art against criticism that hadn't even been offered yet. "I know there's something wrong with the expression!"

But when Tristen turned to face me, I realized that he wasn't looking at my portrait. Instead he pointed past the easel toward a far corner of the room and asked, with a hint of eagerness in his voice, "Jill—is that what I *think* it is?"

Chapter 13

Jill

EVEN THOUGH *I* wanted to talk about the contest and in spite of the fact that I told Tristen our old piano was out of tune, he couldn't seem to keep himself from moving toward it, walking right past my easel without seeming even to notice my painting. It was almost like he was drawn to the instrument, which Mom and I used as a catchall for all kinds of junk.

"This is a *vintage Steinway*, Jill," he said, ditching his messenger bag on the floor and moving a stack of magazines off the bench.

"Is that good?" I asked, following him. As I passed the easel, I turned it so the portrait faced the wall, hiding my work.

"Oh yes." Tristen lifted a lid to reveal keys that hadn't seen light in years. "I have a Steinway at home. A baby grand. But there's something about these antiques . . ."

He looked to me, questioning, one finger already tapping a key. "Do you mind?"

"No," I said, sort of forgetting about Mom's rules as I recalled the beautiful song I'd heard on my computer. "I'd like to hear you play again."

Tristen arched his eyebrows. "Again?"

My face got hot as I realized my mistake. "I heard you play on your MySpace page," I admitted.

"Really?" A hint of a smile crossed his lips. The same smile I'd seen on the first day of school in Mr. Messerschmidt's class, when Tristen thought I'd been checking him out. "You did?"

"I . . . I mean, Becca was surfing around and found your page," I backtracked, cheeks getting warmer.

"Ah, yes. Becca." His smile faded, and he turned away from me, facing the piano.

I remembered suddenly what Becca had said about seeing Tristen over the summer. The story she hadn't finished. What had happened between them?

"Well, let's see how this neglected instrument performs," Tristen said, changing the subject, stepping over the bench and taking a seat.

I stood in the middle of the room, an awkward audience of one, waiting to hear Tristen make the beautiful music I'd heard before. But what I didn't expect was the way Tristen himself seemed to transform before my eyes.

He closed his eyes and poised his hands over the keyboard, fingers arched high, assuming a position that was obviously familiar to him. And when he actually played, his fingers lightly striking the keys, creating a sweet, soft melody like he was greeting the piano, making friends, right away I knew that I was watching somebody special doing something that was like . . . magic.

The instrument was definitely out of tune, and some of the notes rang sour even to my untrained ears, but somehow it didn't matter. As I listened, captivated, Tristen began to draw out of that old piano the saddest, most beautiful sounds I'd ever heard. It was almost like the sour notes were right—like he was a chef adding bitter herbs to a sweet dish so it all balanced out and was perfect.

I edged closer, mesmerized, as Tristen took the already morose melody to an even darker place, his hands moving to the lower register of keys and his shoulders tensing. But he was relaxed, too. I could see that his face was at peace.

His gorgeous, gorgeous face.

Becca had been right. On any given day Tristen was hot. But when he played piano, there was no word for him except gorgeous. He was beyond just handsome, or compelling, or beautiful, even. That aura of power that seemed natural to him, it was concentrated around him when he played, like he was under a spotlight even in a living room.

I found myself stepping even closer as Tristen dragged that sweet, bitter song toward a conclusion that was as powerful and commanding as the way he'd strode across Mr. Messerschmidt's classroom on the first day of school. His fingers tore across the keys, and the song got faster and louder, rumbling against our thick plaster walls as he began to pound the piano, guiding the song to a breathtaking, furious crescendo. A climax that shook the rafters even harder than the thunderstorm had done a few days before.

Then, just when I thought there was nothing more Tristen

56

could wring out of that old instrument, when I thought the song had been carried as far as it could go, he swept his hand the length of the keyboard and wrecked the whole thing, with an expression of satisfaction that came close to bliss. When I saw him draw back his hand, I almost cried out in dismay, like I could have somehow saved the whole experience. But Tristen . . . the corners of his mouth actually lifted to hear the whole thing destroyed.

I stood dumbstruck. I'd never seen anybody revel in *ruin*. Especially not the destruction of something so magnificent.

When the house was quiet again, Tristen turned to face me, opening his eyes, and I saw the dark black bruise . . . and maybe a glimpse of the dark place where that song had come from. A place that the photograph of Tristen hadn't been able to quite capture.

"Wow . . . Tristen . . ." I didn't know what else to say. Not about the music or that part of him I'd just seen in his eyes. "Wow."

Tristen seemed to accept that as a compliment, though. "Thanks." He nodded toward the easel. "I like your work, too."

I felt my cheeks getting warm again, and I glanced toward the portrait, which looked conspicuously ill-concealed, pushed to the wall. "I didn't think you saw that."

"It looked very accurate," Tristen said, and I saw that he was laughing at me yet again. "At least, I thought it looked just like you—although I barely glimpsed it before you hid it away."

So, he'd noticed that, too. My cheeks got hotter. "It's not done yet."

I was embarrassed not only because I'd been caught trying to hide the painting but because I knew that my work paled in comparison to Tristen's. Nobody would ever laugh at what he'd just created or say that it didn't capture who Tristen was. I barely knew Tristen, but both times I'd heard his music, I knew that I was seeing *him.* Including the stuff that might be beautiful in a way but which wasn't exactly pretty.

I found myself looking to my easel again, confused.

Was that what was missing in my own work? In my eyes? The darkness that I sometimes saw there now when I looked in the mirror? Darkness that wouldn't be reflected in my junior year portrait, taken before Dad's murder . . . and the flashes of utter *blackness* that I tried to force away since learning about his theft from me.

But who wanted to see *that* in a painting? The loss that I always felt and the newer rage . . . they were ugly. Weren't they? Aspects of myself that I shouldn't just hide but banish. Exorcise, even.

"Jill." Tristen called me back to reality, standing up and stepping away from the piano bench.

I turned to him and nervously tucked my hair behind my ear, surprised to find that he had grown very serious while I'd been staring at the back of my painting. "Yes?"

"Enough about art," he said, moving toward me. "Let's see that box."

Chapter 14

Jill

"I HAVEN'T BEEN inside this office since my dad died," I confessed, trying to insert the key, which I'd borrowed from my mom's jewelry box, into the lock. But my hand jerked a little. What would it feel like to see Dad's stuff?

"Why not?" Tristen asked, standing close behind me in the dim hallway. "Why is the room off limits?"

"I don't know," I admitted, kind of wishing he'd give me room. "It just is." My fingers kept fumbling with the key. What would I see in there? Was this a mistake? Why had Tristen changed his mind about the contest, anyway?

"Jill." Tristen sounded impatient. "Here." He reached around me and folded his fingers around mine, compelling me to insert the key into the lock and twisting my wrist, firmly but gently. I felt his hard chest pressing against my back, pushing me forward, opening the door.

And the first thing I saw as the door swung open, illuminated in a shaft of moonlight, was my father, smiling at me.

Chapter 15

Jill

"DADDY . . ."

The childish name that I hadn't used since I was maybe six years old sounded loud in the musty room. I probably should have been embarrassed to have said that in front of Tristen, but I'd kind of forgotten he was there as I walked woodenly toward my dad's desk and then picked up the picture in the black frame.

My parents and I squinting into the sunlight, the Atlantic Ocean in the background. Dad had his arm around my shoulders.

I traced his shape under the glass. *Daddy . . .*

That had been the day he'd gotten stung by a jellyfish, and he'd come tearing out of the surf howling and laughing, because he'd known he looked silly, with his red trunks flapping around his legs, skinny and pale like mine. We'd walked to a nearby store, and Dad had bought vinegar to pour on the wound, telling me how the acid would neutralize the toxins. I smiled a little at the memory, even as a tear splashed on the glass.

Dad . . . always a chemist, a teacher, even in pain. What a wonderful day that had been . . .

"Are you okay, Jill?" Tristen asked, coming up behind me and resting a hand on my shoulder, squeezing.

I took off my glasses and swiped a finger under my eye. "I don't know . . ."

"You three look happy together," he noted. His hand felt warm even through my shirt.

"We were," I said, eyes fixed on the picture, fighting a new, stronger wave of tears. My body shook as I struggled against a sob. Why had Dad changed? Done terrible things at work, and to me?

Tristen stepped directly behind me, wrapping his hands around both my shoulders like he was shoring me up again. "Jill," he said softly. "I told you that it gets better, and I didn't lie. But it takes time. When my mother vanished, it was nearly two years before I could go a day, now and then, without thinking of her. And that's hellish, too, in its own way, to think that I've started to forget her. But you have to carry on, right?"

I spun slowly to face him, forgetting for a second my own grief. "Your mother . . . vanished?"

"Yes," Tristen confirmed, still holding me. "About three years ago."

Vanished. It was like a magic word. It made me think of red velvet curtains and men in black capes and ladies in spangled outfits who disappeared into tall boxes . . . and came back. Slipping my glasses back onto my nose, I searched Tristen's face, wanting to see some hope there for his mother. "Do you think . . . ?"

"She's dead." Tristen was matter-of-fact. "Murdered, I'm convinced, although my father disagrees and the case remains officially unsolved."

"I'm so sorry," I whispered, horrified. "So, so sorry."

It all made sense suddenly. Tristen's presence at the cemetery, and the way he'd understood when I was about to fall apart.

"It's okay, Jill," he said, like he was comforting me about his own misery when I should have been consoling him. "It's okay."

We were face-to-face, closer than we'd been even at Dad's funeral, and I felt at once warm, and soothed, and nervous, too. Finally somebody understood my grief. Somebody strong. Very strong. In fact, all of the qualities that made Tristen Hyde seem powerful and compelling from a distance were magnified up close. His height, the way he stood, the mature planes of his face . . .

Although the room was lit only by the moon shining through the dusty windowpanes, I could see a trace of dark stubble on Tristen's jaw, darker than the shock of dirty blond hair that fell over his forehead. A lot of guys in my school still had curving, boyish cheeks, but Tristen's cheekbones were angular and defined. I looked into his eyes again and saw that, although one was framed by the dark bruise, they were an unusual shade of deep brown, and warm, warmer than I would have expected, but shadowed with sadness. Troubled but beautiful, like his music.

My fingers tightened around the picture in my hands, and I remembered my dad, and suddenly felt like a traitor again. I was mourning but feeling something else, too . . .

Tristen's eyes stayed trained on mine for another long minute, like we shared a communion of misery. He was the first to break away, looking past me and squeezing my shoulders a little harder. Like maybe he was excited. "Is that . . . ?"

I turned and followed his gaze right to the box, on a high shelf in the corner of the room.

Chapter 16

Jill

"YES, THAT'S IT," I told Tristen.

But he was already tossing down his messenger bag, which he'd brought upstairs with us, and walking across the room. He reached high and took down the forbidden battered metal container. When he had it in his hands, he stood in the middle of the room, looking down at it almost like I'd just looked at my dad's picture, which I set back on the desk, turning on the lamp.

Tristen still didn't move. His eyes were fixed on the box. He stroked the sides with his thumbs, seeming lost in thought.

"Tristen?"

He looked up, and for the first time since I'd met him, *he* looked a little uncertain. But he quickly shook it off. "Do you have a paper clip, Jill?"

"What?"

"To pick the padlock," Tristen said, bringing the box to the desk. He pulled out the chair and sat down, and I had a momentary urge to protest. That was Dad's seat . . .

Pushing away the impulse, I joined him, standing at his side. "Do you know *how* to pick locks?"

"Of course," Tristen said, like it was a skill everybody should have. "It's not difficult, especially with padlocks. The Internet is filled with demonstrations."

"Are we going to open it *now?*" I asked as Tristen pulled open the top desk drawer, fingers searching the interior. "Right now?"

"Yes." Tristen dug deeper. "Why not?"

"Tristen, stop," I said. He was going too fast, touching too much of Dad's stuff . . .

But he'd already found what he wanted. Fingers moving surely, as confidently as they'd moved across the piano keys, he uncurled a clip, bent one end to form an angle, and inserted this into the lock, moving the makeshift tool in what looked like a systematic way.

"Tristen . . ." Should we be doing this? I needed time to think. Maybe rethink.

It was too late, though. Even Tristen seemed surprised—jumping a little—as the lock popped. And it was Tristen who seemed taken aback, muttering, "Oh, shit, Jill," as he slipped off the padlock and opened the lid to reveal the contents of that small space—which was even more off-limits than Dad's office.

"Hell," Tristen muttered as we both peered inside. *"Bloody, bloody hell."*

Chapter 17

Tristen

ALTHOUGH I'D HAD no reason to doubt that Jill had told me the truth when she'd described her family's artifact, I was nevertheless taken aback—shaken?—when I opened the dented metal container to discover curled, yellowed papers covered with cramped, faded writing.

Experiment dated 7 October in the year 1856 . . . Addition of phosphorous, 3 grams . . .

"Oh, god," I muttered, scanning the notes. "Son of a—"

"It really looks like what Dad said," Jill noted, sounding uneasy, too. "Experiments."

"Yes," I agreed, unable to tear my eyes away.

Consumed half litre . . .

"Could it be?" I mumbled, shaking my head. "Could it really be?"

Although I didn't want to get excited, I knew that I seemed overly eager as I advised Jill, not even looking at her, "We'll need to begin work immediately. But we will have to do so in secret, after school hours. And there's no need to tell that idiot Messerschmidt anything. He'll only interfere and possibly try to stop us."

"What?" Jill asked, sounding puzzled. "Tristen . . ."

But I was barely aware of her at my side.

"We can meet tomorrow night, at the school," I said. I reached in the box to remove a fat stack of papers, with fingers that threatened to tremble. There was so much to do . . . "We'll want to transcribe each experiment, and there are so many . . ."

I began reading more closely, my excitement spiking as I noted the writing on the top left corner of the first page. *Experimental Log—H. Jekyll.*

The name that my grandfather had so often cursed, right there, in smudged but legible script.

Forcing my impatient fingers to be more gentle with the fragile paper, I opened to a sheet about halfway through the stack. *Addition of .2 grams sodium produces no discernible change in demeanor . . .*

I read the words again, not trusting my eyes. *Discernible change.*

Was it possible that Jill's father really had told the truth? Was there a chance that I held the actual roots of my twisted family tree in my hands?

"Tristen?"

I didn't answer, absorbed in my thoughts, my plans.

"Tristen?"

My name was spoken again, accompanied by a tentative tap on my shoulder, and I looked up to recall that I wasn't alone. Jill Jekel was watching me, with a very curious—and *extremely* uncertain— look in her unusual hazel eyes, which I'd finally really seen as I'd revealed, to the first person in America, the story of my mother's disappearance. Pretty, intelligent eyes.

"Um, Tristen?" she ventured, sounding almost frightened. "Why *really* do you want to enter the contest? Why are you here?"

I'd expected that Jill would ask that question at some point if her father's old box actually held what he'd claimed, and if she and I began to use it as I intended. Jill was a smart girl and certainly wouldn't do the things I planned to do without questioning my motives. Unlike Todd Flick with Darcy Gray, Jill—though shy— would expect to be a partner, not an assistant. Moreover, my obvious excitement right then and there must have seemed very strange to her.

Making my decision, I reached for the messenger bag at my feet and searched inside, retrieving my first edition of *The Strange Case of Dr. Jekyll and Mr. Hyde.* I held it up for Jill to see, thinking how uncanny it was, me meeting the one person on this earth who might possess the key to saving my sanity, and asking, not quite rhetorically, "Do you believe in coincidence, Jill? Or *fate?*"

Chapter 18

Jill

"COINCIDENCE OR FATE? I don't really know, Tristen," I said, confused—and a little scared. He was talking about working in secret at school, maybe after hours, without telling our teacher anything. I couldn't do that. I glanced at the clock on Dad's desk. And Mom would be home soon. "What are you talking about? Why did you bring that book?"

I reached out to take the novel from his hands, but Tristen moved it smoothly out of reach. Another forbidden object, apparently. At least for me.

"This, Jill," Tristen said, "is a gift from my grandfather Hyde. The man who instilled in me the love of music and who first taught me to play piano. The man who set the course for my future—and who insisted that this novel is my past."

"What?" I was even more baffled and sank down in the guest chair next to Dad's desk. "I don't understand."

"Just as your father believed that you are distantly related to Dr. Henry Jekyll, my grandfather insisted that I am a *direct* descendant of the 'evil Mr. Hyde,' to use your own words."

Tristen was one of the most articulate people I'd ever met, and he enunciated clearly, in his very precise British accent . . . but I still didn't quite follow. "So you're saying we're, like, related? Because Dad said Henry Jekyll didn't have any children. That's one of the reasons we ended up with the old papers . . ."

Tristen smiled, but it was a joyless, bitter grin. "No, Jill, we're not related. Don't ever wish that upon yourself!"

I must have still looked very confused, because Tristen lost the smile and tried to explain more seriously. "If you've read the book, you know that Dr. Jekyll believed he altered his very *soul* when he drank the formula. That he created in Hyde a *new being*—a 'new life,' Stevenson called it."

"Yes. I read the book," I said. "But—"

"This new life," Tristen continued, "was completely different, even in size and stature, from its creator. And it was this being, this *beast*, that procreated, beginning *my* family."

I studied Tristen's handsome face, thinking he was about as far, physically at least, from a "beast" as I could imagine. What he was saying, it was laughable. A weird joke. "You can't be telling me that you're descended from a . . . monster?" I asked.

"Yes, that is exactly what I'm saying." Tristen tapped a finger against the novel. "Grandfather gave me this on his deathbed. He called it both 'our hellish genealogy' and 'the horrible map of our future.'"

I drew back slightly, not liking what he said or the ominous tone of his voice. He clearly wasn't joking. "Why a map, Tristen? What does *that* mean?"

"According to my grandfather, all of the Hyde men—down through the generations—are corrupted by the formula that *your* ancestor first drank, creating *my* lineage. Grandfather swore that we all—just like the first Mr. Hyde—eventually succumb to our darker natures and commit terrible acts." His brown eyes clouded over. "At first we aren't even aware of what we do. But eventually, try as we might to control the beast inside . . ."

As Tristen trailed off, I felt my eyes widening and fought the urge to stand up and run away. It was crazy. Tristen . . . He couldn't be *evil*. He'd held me, comforted me. We'd just shared that moment . . . And his eyes. They were so warm and beautiful. I didn't want him to be evil. Or crazy. But I found my gaze drifting to the dark mark under his left eye. "You don't really think *you* . . . ?"

"Yes," Tristen confirmed. "What happened with Todd—that wasn't me. And I've started to dream, as Grandfather promised. Nightmares, which are growing more vivid."

"Nightmares." I kept staring at the bruise under his eye and my voice sounded squeaky as I asked, "What kind of nightmares?"

All at once Tristen was no longer explaining; he was confessing. Spilling secrets that I think he just couldn't bear anymore. His eyes were miserable. "I . . . this thing inside of me," he said. "In my dreams it attempts to kill a girl . . . and *likes* it. *Relishes* the slaughter."

I jumped out of the chair, terrified. "Tristen!" I had to get away. He *was* crazy. But he caught my wrist, and I stared down at his hand. "Let go . . . please!"

"Jill," he said quietly, soothing me. "I won't hurt you. I promise. It's not you that the beast I harbor wants. The dream is very specific."

My eyes were still locked on Tristen's hand, but I sat back down, not sure what else I could do. He was too strong to break away from. "What do you want from me?" I asked, voice still shaky. Although I already guessed the answer, I asked again, "Why are you here?"

"I want to perform the experiments documented in this box." He nodded to the desk, still clasping my wrist. His grip was strong, but not harsh. "And I want you to help me. You are the only person I would trust to be in the lab when I start drinking the solutions. You would know how to counteract toxins if necessary."

I shook my head, too horrified and petrified to be flattered. "You can't drink the formulas . . ."

Tristen raised the novel, which he still held in one hand. "The book is very clear. The formula both creates—and banishes—the

68

beast. That is how Jekyll changed back and forth—by drinking it."

The "monster." The "beast." It was insane. What Tristen was saying was completely insane. "I won't help you," I said. "I can't." My gaze darted to the box. "I won't let you have the papers. You need counseling . . ."

"I am the son of the world's *best* psychotherapist," Tristen advised me, boring into my eyes. "I don't need to lie on a couch. I need to work in a lab. *We* need to work. Together."

"Tristen, no." How could his gaze seem so clear when he was obviously delusional?

"Jill." He *locked* his eyes to mine. His compelling, warm, intelligent, *seemingly* sane eyes. "The nightmares are coming more frequently and vividly. I fear the monster inside of me is gaining power. I've already lost control to it too many times."

My eyes snapped wider. "What? Not just with Todd?"

Tristen closed off to me then. The confession was over. But I'd seen the flash of surprise and self-reproach in his eyes and knew that he'd revealed more than he'd intended. "I am still in control," he said, ignoring my question. "But I don't know for how long. The dream about the girl—I awake sometimes not sure if it was *real*. What if the beast inside of me finally wrests control not only of my brain but of my body, and makes the nightmare reality?"

"Tristen . . ." I twisted against his grip. "Please. This is crazy."

He squeezed my wrist more tightly, but it was a strangely calming touch, as if he was trying to focus me and force me to listen carefully when he announced, very clearly and gravely, "If you don't help me, Jill, and if I can't cure myself, I will *kill* myself before the beast acts upon its nastiest impulses."

Tristen released my wrist then, like he knew that I wouldn't run away . . . which I didn't do. I just sat there, staring at him. And shaking.

I didn't know if I believed any of what he had just said about a beast lurking inside of him thanks to a formula created over one hundred years ago. But looking into his eyes, meeting his unwavering gaze, I did believe in that moment that he would commit suicide before he really hurt someone else. Me, or somebody like Todd Flick, or the girl in his dream, whoever she was.

Still, I found myself saying, "Tristen . . . I don't think so."

He thumped his novel down next to my family's box of documents, putting them close together and turning from me to observe them both. "Your father and my grandfather believed the same thing," he said quietly. Ominously. "The past and the future for me—they seem to be commingling here, Jill."

When he looked to me again, his gaze was commanding but his voice was imploring. "I am asking you to help me. And in return I will help you develop a contest entry. Do my best to see that you walk away with a thirty thousand dollar scholarship. All of it yours. I don't care about the cash."

I stared at him, in doubt about . . . everything. "I . . . I . . ."

I had no idea what I was about to say and no chance to say it because, suddenly, downstairs, I heard my mom enter the kitchen. We'd completely lost track of time.

"You have to go, Tristen! My mom is home!" I searched the room, desperate. We were on the second floor, and the only closet was tiny. "You have to hide somewhere!" I cried, eyes darting everywhere. "And I have to get out of here!"

Tristen didn't seem to share my concern. He calmly packed up the box, replaced it on the shelf, stuck the novel into his messenger bag, and walked to a window, which he unlatched and opened with one powerful shove. He paused and looked to me as

I heard my mother's footsteps coming up the stairs.

"Go, Tristen! Please."

"Think about what I've offered, Jill," he said, stepping over the sill. "It's a good bargain."

Then Tristen Hyde slipped out the window and pulled it shut behind him. I heard his footsteps cross the porch roof and disappear, leaving me to turn and face my mother, who stood in the doorway looking very tired and very, very unhappy.

Chapter 19

Jill

"MOM . . . I WAS JUST . . ."

What was I doing? My eyes darted around the room again, to the box and the window that Tristen had just shut, and the photograph of me with my parents. "I just remembered this, and I really wanted it," I lied, snatching the picture off the desk.

"You're not to be in here, Jill," Mom said, through gritted teeth. "I've told you!"

"But Mom . . ." I wanted to defend myself and say that it wasn't so bad, was it? To be there with Dad's stuff? But the look on Mom's face stopped me. She wasn't just upset. She looked almost beyond anger. Her eyes were getting empty again, like after Dad's funeral.

"I'm sorry," I mumbled, hanging my head with guilt and so I wouldn't have to look at Mom's face. Those flashes of vacantness . . . they were scarier than anger. "I didn't mean to upset you," I added, cradling the picture against my chest.

"Go to your room, Jill." Mom stepped back from the door so I could pass. "Now."

"Yes, Mom." I stared at the floor as I brushed past her. She smelled like hospital disinfectant, but I caught a faint whiff of staleness, too, like maybe she hadn't showered that day. "Good night."

She didn't answer. As I walked to my room, I heard her slam the office door shut, and the faint click of the lock slipping back into place. I closed my own bedroom door behind myself and stared at the photo I'd taken on impulse. Did I even want it, really? Did I want to look at Dad?

Tucking the picture in a drawer, I put on my pajamas and climbed into bed. I couldn't sleep, though. I just kept thinking about madness and money and bargains.

Dad had stolen from me . . . Mom seemed to be losing touch again . . . Tristen might *kill* himself . . . Thirty thousand dollars, all for me . . .

Was it a good bargain?

Yes. No. *Maybe?*

I tossed and turned for hours, and by the time my alarm went off in the morning, I had made my decision.

Chapter 20

Tristen

I WAS AT MY LAB STATION, rotely completing a very basic experiment, when Jill approached me, face pale and drawn, as if she hadn't slept the night before.

"I'll do it, Tristen," she said, her pink lips crushed into a white line. "I'll help you if you help me."

Although it was *my* deal on the table, I took a long moment to consider Jill's offer, regretting that I'd told her so many of my secrets—and sorry at the same time that she would enter into this arrangement without knowing all of them. She probably deserved to know everything—even the terrible thing that I feared had happened in London—but she was already too scared. "Are you sure?" I asked, lowering my voice. "Because we *will* have to work in secret. My way, according to my rules."

Even through her glasses, I caught the flicker of hesitancy in Jill's hazel eyes. "Why in secret?" Her voice dropped to the merest whisper, too. "Can't we at least tell Mr. Messerschmidt?"

"*I* am the lab rat, here," I reminded her. "I told you, there will come a point when I begin *drinking* things. Do you think Messerschmidt will stand by and let me sip from beakers? And more to the point, don't you think he'd wonder why I was doing it? What would we say?"

She tucked her hair behind her ear. "But—"

"We *will* enter the contest," I added. "At the last minute, regardless of what we learn on my behalf. We will record our work, develop a presentation, and have an entry in time to win you thirty thousand dollars."

Her financial situation must have been desperate, because at the reminder of the money, she hesitated just one more moment, then took a deep breath and actually extended her small hand. "Okay. We'll do it your way. In secret."

I took Jill's hand, clasping her fingers, amused by her attempt to seem mature and businesslike. Amused and somehow touched. "It's a deal," I said. "We'll start tonight. Say, nine?"

She nodded, and although I saw that she was still uncertain, agreed. "Okay. I think my mom will be working then."

"Meet me behind the school near the cafeteria," I said, recalling a place where smokers sometimes congregated. "There's a padlocked metal door, used to bring in kitchen supplies. We can probably get in through there."

Jill's fair cheeks blanched, but she kept nodding. "Sure. See you there."

As she returned to her lab station, I watched her ponytail swinging in time to her steps, and I kept thinking that she was not only smart but also a good person. Genuinely good to help me after the insane, truly insane, things that I'd told her. I was fortunate, indeed, to have her as a partner.

I also couldn't help but notice that Messerschmidt, Darcy Gray, Todd Flick, and Becca Wright were all trying hard to pretend that they hadn't just watched what had passed between Jill and myself.

Chapter 21

Jill

"TRISTEN, I DON'T THINK I want to do this," I whispered, touching his sleeve in a weak attempt to stop his hand and an even weaker attempt to reassure myself that I wasn't alone in the pitch-black parking lot behind the school. My other arm squeezed tighter around the box I'd taken after sneaking again into Dad's office.

"Just be patient, Jill," he said. "It's fine."

As Tristen picked the lock, I stole a look over my shoulder. My dad had been stabbed to death in a lonely parking lot, and his killer had never been caught . . .

"One more moment," Tristen said, jiggling the lock. "I've almost got it."

And before I could object again, he drew up to his full six-foot-something height, tugged on the lock, and we were in.

Or not quite in, because I didn't move.

I stood rooted to the ground behind Tristen—the inky silhouette of Tristen, who held open the door with one long arm, waiting for me to walk past him into even more profound darkness.

If we went inside that empty school, what would happen? We would pick another lock and enter Mr. Messerschmidt's room, where we'd break into the stores of chemicals, too. Two doors would close behind me. Behind *us*.

No one knew where I was or who I was with.

"Jill." Tristen's voice was low, deep, inviting . . . and tinged with a hint of warning. I knew what he meant just with that single word. *You promised. We made a bargain.* But Tristen had confided that nightmare to me, too. *This thing inside of me attempts to kill a girl* . . . Relishes *the slaughter.*

"I don't dream of you," Tristen said softly, like he'd read my thoughts. "I swear, Jill, you're safe with me."

I stayed stuck to the spot, throat tight. "Who . . . who is it, Tristen? The girl?"

"No one," he whispered, still holding the door. "A girl I was with briefly over the summer. Not you. Just come inside."

He meant to reassure me, but the reminder made me even less willing to join him. *Over the summer* . . . "No, Tristen." I backed away, clutching the box. "I don't want to."

Then I turned and ran all the way home, leaving him standing alone in the dark doorway without the documents he hoped could save him.

Chapter 22

Jill

IT STARTED TO RAIN while I was running home, and after I locked the door behind me, I went straight to my room. Straight to my mirror, actually. Standing in front of my full-length reflection, I stared at my face; my wet, bedraggled hair; and my shivering body, thinking about Tristen, who I'd left waiting at an open door.

Tristen . . . And Becca.

Becca had mentioned seeing Tristen over the summer, knew "his type" of girl, and had been salivating to tell me some story about him.

As I studied myself in the mirror, I could practically see my friend's reflection standing shoulder-to-shoulder with mine, and I envied everything about her. Her thick hair, her gleaming white teeth, and her full lips, always red and glossy. There was a good chance that Tristen had kissed Becca's lips, or wanted to kiss them, not by accident in a graveyard but on purpose. Because he'd *wanted* her.

By comparison everything about me seemed dull and washed out. My ordinary brown hair, limp from the rain. My eyes like two greenish mud puddles. My pale lips. I was too thin, too. Almost as skinny as my mom. And why had I ever bought the ugly, white collared shirt I wore? Just like its wearer, the blouse had no style.

I was pretty sure that Tristen dreamed of Becca. Yes, they were bad dreams. But that night I envied my friend for inspiring even nightmares. Would anybody *ever* dream about me, bad or good?

Downstairs, I heard my mom open the back door, home from the hospital, and I snapped off the light, plunging my reflection into darkness. I was supposed to be in bed already. Taking off my boring shirt, I pulled on a T-shirt and sweats that were even more shapeless, slid the metal box under the bed, and crawled between my blankets, pulling them to my chin.

How did people like Becca literally *shine?*

I curled up, pretending to sleep and listening for Mom's footsteps on the stairs.

But Mom didn't come upstairs, and after about fifteen minutes of complete silence I started wondering what in the world had happened to her. I didn't even hear her making tea or the sound of the TV. Tossing off the covers, I went to the top of the stairs and listened more closely, getting nervous. "Mom?" I called down.

There was no answer, so I crept downstairs and went into the living room.

And as soon as I saw Mom crumpled on the floor, face buried in her hands, shoulders shaking violently, I knew. That cliff I'd feared she'd been sliding toward . . .

She'd fallen off completely.

Chapter 23

Tristen

I SAT ALONE in the living room of the rented house I shared with my father—on the rare occasions that he was home—eating

77

cold pizza and listening to the rain on the roof, wondering if Jill had gotten caught in the storm as she'd run home.

I knew that I should have chased after her and insisted on giving her a ride, but I'd been frustrated as she'd darted away. Angered at her fear of breaking a small rule. Angered at her fear of *me*.

I'd tried to reassure her that I meant her no harm. Even a monster couldn't hurt someone as gentle, as timid, as Jill Jekel. On the contrary, she sparked in even me a profound desire to *protect*. At times I found it almost impossible not to reach out and steady her, help her.

Tossing the tasteless pizza back into the box, I looked to the end table, where a red light glowed at the base of the cordless telephone.

I should call her. Convince her at least to loan me the documents . . .

I started to reach for the phone—only to jump as it seemed to anticipate me, ringing shrilly in the silence. "Hello?" I grumbled, assuming that Dad was calling, as usual, to advise me not to wait up. However, it wasn't my father's baritone on the other end of the line. It was a soft, scared, but determined soprano asking, "Can you come over, please, Tristen? I need your help. Now."

Although Jill had abandoned *me* earlier that night, I found myself hanging up and getting into my car without even questioning what was wrong.

My primary motive was to get that box while I was inside her house. That, I told myself, was the main reason I jumped so quickly at her summons. However, if I had been honest with myself as I drove through the rainy night, I would have admitted that there was something—*someone*—else in that house that I was starting to want, too.

Chapter 24

Tristen

"THANK YOU for coming, Tristen." Jill swung open the door almost simultaneously with my knock, as though she'd been watching at the window for me. I saw raw anxiety in her eyes and in the way she licked her nearly white lips. "I know you probably don't feel like you owe me anything after the way I left you," she added. "But I just didn't know who else to call."

I stepped into the foyer, following Jill, who was already moving toward the living room. "It's okay," I said, overcoming my last lingering trace of irritation. She was scared, and she *did* sound sorry for leaving me, and the more I thought about it, the less I could blame her. I was a strong, six-foot guy who'd admitted to being half monster, trying to lure a defenseless, tiny girl into a dark, empty school. A girl who'd lost her father to violence. "What's wrong?" I asked.

I didn't need to get an answer. As I entered the room, I saw Jill's mother crouched on the floor, her arms wrapped around herself like a self-imposed straitjacket, rocking slightly.

"Oh, hell," I muttered, stopping short. "How long has she been like that?"

"About an hour," Jill whispered, moving to her mom's side, kneeling and stroking her hair. "I can't even get her to talk."

"Jill," I demurred, "I know I told you that my father is a psychiatrist, but that doesn't make me an expert in a situation like this."

"I know, Tristen." Jill continued to caress her mother's unkempt hair. "But I'm sure you know *something* from being around your dad. Enough not to be scared or freaked out, at least. And what I mainly need is your muscle, anyway."

"My muscle?" I stepped closer and knelt, too, studying Mrs. Jekel's eyes. Her empty, empty eyes. Then I shifted my gaze, wanting to look anywhere but into that void.

Jill was right—and wrong. I did know a bit about psychiatry, as she'd guessed. But her mother frightened me. Was that my destiny that I saw in the abyss of Mrs. Jekel's eyes? The madness to come?

"What do you need my muscle for?" I asked, grateful to look into Jill's very sane, surprisingly steady gaze. She had to be panicking, to see her mother in such a state, but she was mastering it, rising to the occasion.

"I need to get her to bed," Jill explained. "Could you help, please?"

Jill was talking about me lifting—touching—her mother. "Perhaps an ambulance would be better," I suggested.

"No," Jill said firmly. "Mom broke down before, right after my dad died, and I called an ambulance. Our insurance hardly covered anything, and I had to draw from our savings to pay the bills, for *nothing*. Two nights in a hospital and all Mom did was sleep. She can do that here, under my care."

I regarded Jill with surprise. She was prepared to take charge of her mother's care? And perhaps even more impressively, she paid bills? I was fairly independent, but my father still controlled the purse strings. But of course Jill would have had to take control, with her father gone and her mother incapacitated. It wasn't difficult, really, to picture her sitting at a desk, competently writing checks and mailing them in according to schedule.

"Please, Tristen," she asked. "Help me get her upstairs."

"Okay," I agreed, but reluctantly. *Who is the coward now, Tristen? Who wants to run into the night?*

"Thanks." Jill stood and stepped back from her mother, who didn't seem to notice that her daughter no longer comforted her. Mrs. Jekel just kept rocking and staring.

Rising, too, I bent over Jill's mother and slipped one arm around her back, wriggling the other beneath her bent knees. She smelled of stale sweat and I again turned my face away, not wanting to breathe her in.

"Let's go, Mrs. Jekel," I muttered, straightening and stumbling backwards, she was so unexpectedly light in my arms. Shockingly frail. As I settled her body against mine, her sharp hipbone stabbed at my stomach, and I caught a whiff of her hot breath, which was sour, like the smell of her skin. I exhaled sharply. "Show me her room," I said over my shoulder, heading toward the stairs.

Jill darted ahead, leading the way upstairs and down the hallway. "Here." She opened a door near the end of the corridor. "This is Mom's room."

I carried Mrs. Jekel across the threshold—a gagging groom with his catatonic bride—and placed her on the bed, which also smelled of sweat. Sweat and . . . insanity, it seemed to me. Would I reek of madness someday, too? Someday soon?

Stepping away, I coughed into the crook of my arm.

"Could you lift her again?" Jill asked. "So I could pull back the covers?"

No. Yet of course I agreed, saying, "Sure, sure," as I again slipped my arms around Mrs. Jekel's bony frame. When I did so, Jill's mother began to mumble, startling me. Her head rolled back and forth, and she muttered softly, "The list . . . bloody . . . in the compartment . . . his last list . . ."

I stiffened, not sure if I should put her down again. "Jill?"

"It's nothing," she reassured me. "She did that about a half hour ago. Just lift her, okay?"

"Okay." I raised Mrs. Jekel enough for Jill to pull back the sheets, averting my face again and holding my breath.

"You can put her down now," Jill directed.

I rested Mrs. Jekel's head on her pillow this time, and Jill arranged the covers over her mother's skeletal body. Mrs. Jekel continued speaking, more quietly, so I couldn't make out the words, and Jill crawled onto the bed and lay next to her mother, stroking her hair again. "What, Mom?" she whispered. "What are you trying to say?"

In that moment I thought Jill Jekel one of the bravest people I'd ever known. All I could think about was getting the hell away from Mrs. Jekel—and Jill had found it in herself to draw even closer to those empty eyes.

I waited at the foot of the bed, not sure if I should stay, and soon Mrs. Jekel fell silent again. As silent as a corpse. Or a corpse *to be*, for surely Jill's mother was close to oblivion. My father had described patients like Mrs. Jekel. Too often they met their ends in institutions—or early graves if they found the strength, the means, to end their own misery.

Sitting upright, Jill readjusted the covers around her mother's shoulders and crawled off the bed, joining me at the foot.

"Jill," I ventured quietly as we both watched Mrs. Jekel's inert form. "I've provided the muscle; now you need to avail yourself of a professionally trained brain."

"I know, Tristen," Jill agreed, touching my sleeve, indicating that I should follow her out of the room. We moved into the hallway—where I immediately breathed easier—and she pulled the door shut. "You said your father is the best, right?"

I shook my head, thinking *Jill* had lost her mind, too. "You're not saying you want *my* father to treat *your* mother?"

"Yes," she said, again with surprising firmness. "That's exactly what I'm saying."

I rested my hand on her shoulder, prepared to shake some sense into her. "I've told you what I believe about myself. And if it's true, my father almost certainly shares the legacy."

"We don't *know* if you or your father are corrupted," Jill countered. "But we do know that my mom is suffering from mental illness. You just saw her. Heard her."

Saw, heard, and *smelled* her. That smell of insanity. Death coming soon.

Still, adding potential madness to madness didn't seem like a good idea to me. "You could get someone else to treat her," I suggested. "There are plenty of therapists around."

"But your dad is the best. You said so, Tristen."

I sighed, regretting my words. "That might be so," I agreed. "But I honestly believe that one Jekel-Hyde pairing is enough for such a small town. And you yourself seemed to feel tonight that I present a risk," I reminded her. "Enough of a threat that you wouldn't go into the school with me."

"I'll do it," Jill declared. "If you'll get your father to help my mother, I promise I won't run away again. I'll even give you the box tonight. You can take it with you."

I lowered my head, not wanting Jill to see the guilt in my eyes. I had come to the house with designs on getting the old papers. But

I'd forgotten all about that as I'd tried to help Jill and her mother. And I certainly hadn't intended to blackmail Jill into doing my bidding in a chemistry lab. "I wasn't trying to strike another bargain," I said. "I didn't intend to use my father to pressure you."

"It doesn't matter, Tristen," she said. "Just please . . . ask your dad to see my mom. For me."

For me.

I'm pretty sure that's what got me in the end. That desperate appeal and Jill's eyes. Even in the gloomy corridor I could see those big hazel eyes watching me with hope. And, God help me—or forgive me—I found myself reluctantly agreeing. "All right, Jill. I'll ask Dad. But I can't promise that he'll see her."

Even that weak assurance was enough for her, though. She uttered a soft cry of relief and gratitude and to my complete surprise, hopped on her toes and flung her arms around my neck. "Thank you, Tristen," she whispered. "I won't forget this. I promise. I'll repay the favor."

I wrapped my arms around her tiny waist, almost as tentatively as I'd first touched her mother. But the sensation that coursed through me as Jill's heart beat against my chest and her smooth hair grazed the bottom of my jaw and my hand stroked the small of her back—it was completely different from what I'd felt holding her mother. The polar opposite of revulsion—and somehow more than mere *sexual* attraction.

What I felt holding Jill was almost like surrender. The cutting away of a barrier that I'd put up years ago. A wall that I needed to maintain. A bit unsettled, I stepped back, releasing her and getting hold of myself. "I'll ask Dad tomorrow," I promised.

"Let me get the box for you," she offered.

I snared her arm, stopping her. "No," I said, wanting her to know that I really hadn't intended to barter my father's services in exchange for the documents. Wanting to convince myself, too, that the assistance I'd provided had been pure, without strings attached. "Just bring it to the school tomorrow night. If you can leave your mother, of course."

"Okay," she agreed, turning to lead us downstairs. "I'll do my best to be there."

Jill saw me out onto the porch, following me into the chilly night, shivering in a thin T-shirt. "Thank you, again, Tristen," she said, rubbing her arms to stay warm.

"Don't thank me yet," I mumbled, taking all three steps at once and thudding to the sidewalk.

Hyde treating Jekel? It still sounded like a terrible idea to me. But the girl who stood on the porch hugging herself and venturing a small wave as I walked into the night—she was definitely getting to me. Jill looked so alone standing there, with so much to face inside that gloomy old house, that I nearly turned back and volunteered to sit with her all night, even though it would mean angering my father, who would not like arriving home to find me gone. Yet I kept thinking about Jill's mother. What if Mrs. Jekel started babbling again or thrashing? Jill would need someone to help her. Perhaps to hold her again, reassuring her.

I hesitated on the sidewalk and actually turned around, having decided that I would go back. But Jill had gone inside and the porch was empty, so I got into my car to drive home.

Yes, Jill Jekel was getting to me.

Unfortunately, through me—just as I'd feared—worse things were destined to get to *her.*

Chapter 25

Jill

I MADE GOOD on my promise to meet Tristen the next night, even later than planned, because I had to make sure my mom was sound asleep for the night. Although Mom had slept most of the day, it was almost eleven o'clock before I was convinced that her breathing was deep and steady enough for me to leave her alone.

I got to the school first and tucked myself against the building in the shadows. The parking lot was still dark, and I was still scared—scared to be by myself and at the prospect of being alone with Tristen, too. But I was even more desperate than before. I'd called the nursing supervisor to say that Mom was sick, promising that she'd try to make it to work in a day or two, but I was pretty sure that wasn't going to happen. And if Mom missed a bunch of work again . . . maybe even got fired . . . How would I pay the bills?

I clutched the box to my side, shivering, wishing that Tristen would hurry up. And then I saw him pass under a streetlight, coming toward me. He strode across the parking lot, purposeful, and I realized that I was at least less scared of Tristen than I was of empty parking lots. Maybe I was even a little eager to see him. Or maybe my heart just beat faster because we were about to trespass again.

"Sorry I'm late," he said when I stepped out of the shadows. "I decided to hitchhike so my father wouldn't find my car gone if he arrived home before me."

"You shouldn't hitchhike," I told him as he bent to pick the lock. "It's dangerous."

"I won't hurt a random stranger," he said. "I told you. My dream is specific."

I honestly wasn't sure if Tristen was joking, so I didn't say anything. When the lock gave, he stood back and opened the door, and once again the black hallway yawned ahead of me, and I hesitated.

"I spoke to my father, Jill," Tristen said, voice soft in the still night. "He'll meet with your mother if you can get her to his office at Severin tomorrow at five o'clock."

"I'll have her there," I said, grateful, relieved . . . and completely aware of what Tristen meant when he said that. We *had* struck yet another bargain. "Thank you."

I stepped past him then and trespassed into the school. As I walked by, he took the box from me, smoothly but decisively, and I knew the deal was really sealed, and there would be no turning back.

Chapter 26

Jill

"MAKE SURE YOU cap the ethyl alcohol before lighting the burner," I reminded Becca, who was distracted by Seth Lanier's stupid miming of *drinking* his share of alcohol at the station behind us. "It's really flammable."

"I told you that station is dangerous," Darcy Gray chimed in, turning to give us a pointed look.

"It's not really the burner . . ." I started to object, but Darcy had already turned back around, ignoring me. Todd had caught the exchange, though, and he glanced back, smirking until Darcy flicked his arm.

"Todd, get the filtration flask."

"Okay, Darce," he grumbled. "You don't have to boss me so much." But I noticed that he did as he was told.

"Becca—the alcohol?" I reminded my own partner, tapping her shoulder.

"This is so boring," Becca groaned, reluctantly rejoining our experiment. She capped the alcohol. "I don't know how you stand this stuff."

"It's interesting to me," I said with a shrug. "I like to think about how we can control the smallest things in the universe and get reactions or make new substances."

"Yawn," Becca said as I handed her the water I'd measured. She poured it into our flask, but her eyes shifted toward me. "You know, Jill, that test is coming up."

I stiffened, bracing myself. I couldn't cheat. It was bad enough that I was sneaking into the school every night with Tristen, dodging the custodial staff if they fell behind schedule and worked late. "Becca—"

I was spared answering when I felt a hand clamp down on my shoulder. "Jill."

I spun to face Tristen, blushing and nearly knocking over the whole apparatus of our experiment. How was it that, although we were partners, Tristen still flustered me? "What's up?" I asked.

"Can you study this evening?"

"Yes, I guess so," I agreed, understanding the veiled invitation.

"Good," Tristen said with a glance at Becca.

"Hey, Tris." She greeted him with a toss of her auburn hair. "How's it going?"

Was there a slight flush on Becca's cheeks, too? Or was that just my imagination?

I stood between them, feeling very plain again. And stupidly, pointlessly *jealous*. Had something really happened between them? Was Becca really the girl in Tristen's nightmares? If so, she had no idea the lengths that he—that *we*—were going to, in order to supposedly protect her. And she wanted me to *cheat* for her on top of that.

"We should get back to work," I said, surprised by the irritation I heard in my voice. "I mean, time's running out," I added in a more normal tone.

"Of course," Tristen agreed. He looked to me. "See you tonight, Jill."

I sort of avoided his eyes. "Yeah, sure."

But before Tristen could walk away, Mr. Messerschmidt called to us. "Hyde—stay there." As we watched, he lumbered toward us, threading his wide body through the narrow rows of lab tables. "I want to talk to you all."

"What's up?" Tristen inquired in a way that suggested our teacher was overstepping his bounds by asking for a moment of time. "What do you need?"

"Darcy, this involves you, too," Mr. Messerschmidt said.

"Todd, finish up," Darcy directed her partner. Then she turned to smile at our teacher. "Yes?"

"I just wondered if you're all entering the Foreman Foundation contest," Mr. Messerschmidt said, looking from face to face.

"No," Tristen said, shooting me a warning look. "I'm not."

"Me neither," I said, following his lead. But I looked to the floor, afraid that everyone would see the lie in my eyes. We were in that very room almost every night, transcribing notes, mixing chemicals, working on our contest entry—and Tristen's personal project. Most nights he would leave with a bottle filled with solution, in preparation for the time we'd meet and he would begin drinking the variations. We were stealing chemicals like my dad had done.

"Well, I'm in," Darcy announced. "I'm doing my initial research now."

"Good girl, Darcy." Mr. Messerschmidt smiled at his star pupil. Then he frowned at me. "Jill, why not?"

I tucked my hair behind my ear, still averting my eyes. "I don't know. I'm just really busy now."

Very smooth, as usual, Jill.

"And you, Hyde," Mr. Messerschmidt added. "I suppose you're busy, too?"

"No, just lazy," Tristen said. "I told you. I completely lack ambition." Then Tristen walked away, not waiting for Mr. Messerschmidt's dismissal.

"I hope you'll reconsider," our teacher addressed me again. "And if you could convince Hyde to team up like I suggested, I really think you'd have a good shot at winning the money. Especially if you could somehow focus on the intersection of chemistry and brain function. Actually play off the old Jekyll-Hyde story!"

"Oh, I don't think Tristen's interested," I said, getting a little sweaty. I wasn't a good liar, and Mr. Messerschmidt was hitting too close to the actual deception. "I'll talk to him, though," I promised, just wanting my teacher to drop the subject.

"Excellent!" Mr. Messerschmidt beamed, seeming really pleased. "I could help you define your research agenda, bounce around ideas—anything you needed."

"Don't bother." Darcy laughed, interrupting us. I hadn't realized she was still listening, and I looked over to see her watching us while Todd struggled with decantation, one arm hampered by his cast and his big fingers, so adept with footballs, fumbling with the delicate equipment. "I've got a lock on this thing," Darcy boasted.

"Yes, I'm sure you'll do well," Mr. Messerschmidt agreed, like he always did with Darcy. "I just want to inspire some healthy competition. Maybe Supplee Mill could take first and second place."

"I guess they could shoot for second," Darcy said with a shrug. Then she turned back to her lab station and resumed directing Todd.

I stared at Darcy's straight spine, frustrated and powerless to fight back even if for once I had real ammunition. Tristen and I *could* beat her. Darcy Gray couldn't just assume I was a loser. But of course I just stood there, unable to defend myself.

"Talk to Tristen," Mr. Messerschmidt urged. "And remember, I'm here to offer guidance and support."

I met my teacher's eyes, thinking his enthusiasm was starting to border on pushiness. "Um, sure. Thanks," I finally said.

There was an awkward silence, then Mr. Messerschmidt wandered off, leaving me and Becca together again. I continued our experiment, lighting the faulty burner, which sputtered, just like Darcy had warned.

"Are you and Tristen really just studying?" Becca broke into my thoughts.

"Yes," I said. "Why?"

Becca shrugged. "No reason."

I turned around and saw that Tristen had finished his experiment and was leaning back on his seat staring out the window, safety glasses shoved up into his thick hair. Completely oblivious to me.

"Well, we *are* just studying," I repeated, still watching him.

"Good," Becca said.

It was a weird response, maybe as strange as Mr. Messerschmidt's eagerness to see me take part in a contest that wouldn't win *him* any money, but for some reason, I didn't want to think about why Becca might be glad that Tristen and I were nothing more than study partners, so I didn't ask her what she'd meant.

Chapter 27

Jill

"ARE YOU COMFORTABLE, MOM?" I asked, handing her a small amber bottle and a glass of water. "I could turn the heat up."

"No, Jill." She shook her head, dumping pills into her palm. "I'm warm under the covers."

"Okay." Although the night was cold, I didn't press the issue. Our electric bill, which I'd paid that morning from our shrinking checking account, was high enough without cranking the heat. I watched as Mom swallowed her medication, eyes closed, like she was already falling under its spell.

"Dr. Hyde," I ventured, accepting the glass, "does he really seem to be helping?"

Mom nodded, eyes still closed. "Yes, Jill. The medication seems to help. And Dr. Hyde seems to understand me when we talk."

"Oh, good."

I was glad that Mom found Dr. Hyde comforting, because he'd seemed imposing to me the times I'd dropped Mom off at his office. He was tall like Tristen. And his voice was an older, even deeper version of his son's. They shared the same angular cheek-bones and full lower lip. But Dr. Hyde was dark while Tristen was fair. Like his mother?

And what else did Dr. Hyde and Tristen share? That corrupted gene, or broken synapse, or whatever it was that Tristen was afraid lurked inside himself?

"You're sure he's helping?" I asked again.

"Yes." Mom crawled deeper under the covers. "Enough that I'm going to the hospital this week. I called and asked to work a day shift."

"Mom, don't rush it," I urged, although I wanted to jump with relief. *Thank you, Dr. Hyde.* "Just take your time and get well, okay? You've only been in treatment a few weeks."

"I'll be fine," Mom promised with a yawn. "Dr. Hyde thinks I should start getting out of the house. He's reduced my dosage during the day so I can be more alert."

The glass slipped in my hand. "Oh? Just during the day?"

Even as I was blurting out the question, I realized how awful it was, because I wasn't asking out of concern for her. I was worried about how I would sneak out to meet Tristen if Dr. Hyde decided Mom could go without sedation at night, too.

But she was so sleepy that my question didn't even seem to register. She was already breathing in a fairly steady rhythm, her eyes closed and her mouth slightly open.

Dr. Hyde's medicine had done its work.

As I tiptoed out of the room, I reminded myself that it was okay to hope Mom would stay *safely* sedated at night for a little while longer. The scholarship was worth *thirty thousand dollars.* Surely that much money, the way it would ease our family's financial burdens, made everything I was doing right.

Right?

Chapter 28

Jill

"POTASSIUM," TRISTEN MUTTERED, head resting in his left hand as his right scrawled notes in his bold, heavy script. "Potassium."

"What?" I asked, glancing up from my own tedious transcription of Dr. Jekyll's notes. Tristen and I worked side by side by the light of a single flashlight that we kept propped on a pile of books. "What did you say?"

"Potassium," Tristen grumbled, head still in his hand. Dropping his pen, he shoved the paper clip that he used to pick locks across the table in my direction. "Do me a favor. See if there's any in the cabinet? I seem to recall that it was running low, and this formulation requires a significant amount if I'm reading it correctly."

"But I don't know how to pick the lock," I said, not reaching for the paper clip. Tristen—he was our official trespasser. Not me.

"It's simple." Tristen started writing again. He seemed irritated as he directed, "Just jam the clip in the lock and probe around until it gives. It's not rocket science."

I was hurt by his tone and didn't like being ordered, but I reached for the clip, not wanting to worsen the bad mood he'd been in all evening. "Okay."

Heading to the storage cabinet, I stuck the paper clip in the lock and wriggled it like I'd seen Tristen do. A few seconds later I swung open the door. I turned, about to tell him that it really had been pretty easy, but something about the way he was hunched over his notebook made me think he wouldn't really care. "There's plenty of potassium," I said, checking the container and closing the cabinet.

Tristen didn't respond, and I climbed back onto my stool, tapping him. "Tristen? There's plenty."

He still didn't answer. He just kept transcribing, his hand jerking rapidly across his notebook.

"What's wrong?" I asked, not sure if I should be excited or alarmed. "Did you find something?"

He shook his head, still writing. "No," he grumbled. "Quite the opposite."

"What do you mean?"

"This isn't *chemistry*, Jill," Tristen snapped, abruptly slapping down his pen. He sat upright, jamming his hand into his hair. "It's a . . . a . . . *cookbook*. Your ancestor was a fucking Victorian Betty Crocker!"

"Tristen!" I chided him. "Stop it!" The rebuke came out automatically, and I immediately cringed. Tristen wasn't the type of person *anyone* would normally bark at, let alone me. "Sorry."

"No, no. *I'm* sorry." Tristen sighed, seeming to have vented the worst of his frustration. He rubbed his hands across his face. "I just don't understand, Jill. It seems as if Dr. Jekyll was primarily combining kitchen ingredients. The occasional dash of phosphorous or lithium aside, he's mainly dabbling in vinegars and other weak acids and common bases. Not elements that would seem to hold promise for changing a soul, temporarily or permanently."

The more Tristen and I had worked together, the easier it had become to forget that our project wasn't just about me. That night's show of temper aside, the Tristen I was coming to know as a collaborator was kind and considerate of me, and when he smiled, it was impossible to believe that a monster—the thing he called a beast—lurked inside of him. But his exasperation was a sharp reminder of his stake in our project. Of what he had threatened to do if we didn't succeed in creating a formula to "cure" him.

"We haven't reached the end of the papers," I reminded him, suddenly worried on his behalf. "There are still a few pages left. We might still find something."

"No, Jill." Tristen shook his head. Then he fell into a glum silence, staring into the distance and mumbling, "Something is missing. Something . . ."

"Let's keep working," I suggested.

"I suppose so," he agreed, but he didn't sound hopeful. Still, he tore a few pages from his notebook and handed me another stack of the old notes. "Here. Why don't you check my latest transcription against the original? Perhaps you'll find something I've missed or misread."

"Sure," I agreed, bending to read by the dim light. Even squinting, it was hard to read Dr. Jekyll's bad handwriting, made worse by the way the ink had faded over time.

Seeing my difficulty, Tristen reached down and grabbed the edge of my stool, pulling me closer to the light and to himself, so we were practically shoulder-to-shoulder. As he bent over his notebook, I studied his profile. His straight nose, his full lower lip like his dad's, his intelligent, troubled eyes . . .

He looked sideways at me, mouth twitching with his first smile of the night. "What?" he asked, eyebrows raised. "Are you preparing another scolding on outbursts, or the evils of profanity? Is that what's stalling you?"

No, not a scolding. What had stalled me was *Tristen*. I hadn't even realized I'd been watching him for so long. "I—I was just . . ."

"What, Jill?" he prompted, mischief in his eyes. "What *are* you thinking, in that formidable, lovely mind of yours?"

"Um . . ." I noticed that Tristen's smile was slowly vanishing. He was growing serious again. But a different kind of serious. His eyes still gleamed but with a gentle curiosity, a softer amusement.

I flushed under his attention. Could a mind be "lovely"? Attractive? But, no, Tristen didn't think of me that way.

Yet the look in his eyes . . . I didn't have any experience with boys, but I almost thought . . .

"Tell me, Jill," he urged, and we were so close—had he leaned closer?—that I could feel his warm breath on my cheeks. I inhaled the scent of him, which was slowly growing familiar as our lives became more entangled. Tristen always smelled like he'd just showered. Clean and masculine. And his eyes . . .

"What's going on in that beautiful brain?" he asked again.

Lovely. Beautiful. Not me but my *mind.*

What would a truly beautiful girl, like Becca, think of such a strange compliment? Would she laugh at it?

Probably.

Suddenly it was like Becca was standing with us again, tossing her shiny, auburn hair. Becca, who definitely intrigued guys. Who probably intrigued Tristen . . .

"Nothing," I said, breaking our gaze and needlessly shuffling the papers piled in front of me. "I'm just thinking we should get to work. I shouldn't stay out too late. My mom might wake up and wonder where I am."

"Yes," Tristen agreed, clearing his throat and edging his stool away from mine, just an inch or so. And he sounded aloof, almost like we were business partners—which we sort of were—when he added, "And how *is* your mother?"

"Pretty sedated most of the time," I said, tapping the papers back into order. I dared to look at him. "Is that normal for most of your father's patients?"

"I don't know too much about Dad's methods," he said. "But, yes, I understand that the initial phase—'stabilization,' as he calls it—involves heavy sedation. It's meant to keep patients from doing themselves harm while the brilliant Dr. Hyde probes their psyches looking for more practical, lasting solutions."

I had planned to ask Tristen just how long "stabilization" lasted, but the sarcasm I heard when he assessed his father's work surprised me. "Don't you think he's really brilliant? You said he's the best."

Tristen smiled wryly, resuming writing. "Yes, Jill. I suppose he is brilliant. *He* certainly thinks so."

I decided to let the subject go, just happy for the reassurance that my mother was getting care from a top psychiatrist. One whose methods enabled me to come to the lab at night—and who didn't seem in any hurry to add to the growing pile of bills that I kept arranged by order of urgency in a box in our kitchen.

Tristen and I worked in silence for a while, the only sound in the room the scratch of his pen and the crackle of stiff paper when I turned the pages, checking his work.

Addition 5 ml hydrochloric acid to . . .

I swallowed hard, imagining how the acid would feel going down someone's throat. Had one of my old relations actually *drunk* that? Would *Tristen?*

I kept reading. *Increased HCl to 10 ml . . .*

Yes, the first Dr. Jekyll had used a lot of common pantry ingredients. But there was dangerous stuff in there, too.

"Does your mother ever say those things anymore?" Tristen eventually broke the silence, interrupting my worried thoughts:

images of him drinking a deadly concoction, writhing in agony . . .
I shook the pictures out of my head.

"Things?" I asked. "What things?"

"About the 'bloody list.' In the 'compartment.' The things she mumbled as I lifted her."

"No," I said. "For a while it was like a mantra . . . the whole thing about the 'altered salts.' But I guess the medicine kicked in—"

"Jill?"

I looked up to see him staring at me, a strange look on his face like I'd startled him. "What?"

"What did you just say?"

"The medicine kicked in—"

"Before that. About the salts."

"Mom kept mumbling about 'altered salts.' You remember."

"No." Tristen shook his head. "I couldn't hear everything she said."

"She kept talking about a list of altered salts in a compartment," I said, not sure why he found Mom's delusional ramblings so interesting. "Why are you looking at me like that?"

"The book, Jill. The book . . ."

"What book?" He was losing me completely.

"Oh, hell," he muttered, rising from the stool and reaching for his messenger bag, rummaging deep inside. "Oh, hell."

"Tristen, what book?"

"*Jekyll and Hyde,*" he said with impatience, pulling an object from his bag. I recognized the first edition novel that his grandfather had given him. Tristen sat on the stool again and grew distant, talking to himself, clearly agitated. His face was pale. "How could I have forgotten the 'altered salt'? Grandfather told me—read the novel. 'If there is a chance for salvation, the clues are in the novel.'"

But Tristen didn't open the book he'd retrieved. He slammed it onto the table like he was punishing it and buried his face in his hands. "Oh, hell. Bloody, fucking *hell!*"

I didn't scold him for swearing that time. His despair was so raw that I rested a tentative hand on his shoulder. His muscle was hard, tense under my fingers. "Tristen? What's wrong?"

He looked up, misery in his eyes, and I wished I had the courage to be even bolder, maybe take his hand. He was scaring me.

"Oh, Jill," he groaned. "It's all pointless. The experiment can't cure me."

My heart jumped at the unexpected announcement. He said he'd *kill* himself . . . Whether or not I believed in the "beast" we had to at least try . . . "Why not?" I asked, mouth dry.

Tristen picked up the book again, leafing through, fingers tearing at the pages until he was almost at the end of the novel. "Listen," he said, reading. "'My provision of the salt, which had never been renewed since the date of the first experiment, began to run low. I sent out for a fresh supply, and mixed the draught; the ebullition followed, and the first change of colour, not the second; I drank it, and it was without efficiency . . . I have had London ransacked; it was in vain; and I am now persuaded that my first supply was impure, and that it was that unknown impurity which lent efficacy to the draught.'"

Tristen slammed the cover shut. "Jekyll tried to recreate the formula to kill Hyde once and for all, only to learn that the original potion contained a *tainted* salt. The formula could never be repeated. That's why he could never destroy Hyde. It's such a brief passage . . ." He gestured to the box. "But it means this is all worthless for me." He buried his face again, his voice muffled by his hands. "How could I have forgotten *that?* I suppose I got so excited by the idea that the formula even existed . . . I'm such an idiot. It's all *pointless.*"

"No, Tristen," I said with more conviction than I felt. "We'll find an answer. We can read the passage again. Maybe you're wrong—"

"No. I'm correct." He dropped his hands and fell silent, staring into the distance.

I started to reach out to him again, but he seemed so distant, so isolated, that I let my hand fall to the table.

Yet a few seconds later Tristen turned and reached out to *me*, grabbing my wrist and squeezing it. "Jill," he said, and I saw that his brown eyes were gleaming again—almost fevered, like Mom's had been. "The list of altered salts . . . *his last* list?"

"Yes?"

"What if . . . What if your father was working on the formula, too?" he suggested. "I thought the old lock on the box gave too easily. What if your mother saw some list he was keeping just before he died . . . ?"

"But why?" I asked, confused. He was grasping at straws. "Why would *Dad* work with the formula?"

"I'm not sure," Tristen admitted. His eyes clouded. "Perhaps . . ."

I waited, but he seemed to change his mind about speculating, saying only, "Who knows? But the coincidence is a strange one, isn't it?"

"Yes, but . . ." There *was* an element of coincidence—tainted salts in the book, my mom's talk of altered salts—but it was thin at best. "I don't think you should get too excited," I cautioned.

"Perhaps." Tristen absently rubbed my wrist, too hard, because in spite of my warning he *was* excited. "We need to find that list," he said. "We need to find that 'compartment.'" He met my eyes, shaking my arm. "You've got to ask your mother if she recalls what she said."

I shook my head. "No."

Tristen released my wrist, incredulous. "Jill, this is life or death for me."

I rubbed the spot he'd clutched, feeling sick to my stomach. "I don't have to ask, Tristen, because I already know."

If a list of altered salts existed, I was pretty sure where it was hidden.

Oh, but I didn't want to go to that terrible place.

Even though it was right in my own backyard.

Chapter 29

Jill

"MOM ALWAYS COMPLAINED about Dad's messy car," I said as Tristen pulled the school door shut then replaced the padlock. "He never carried a briefcase, so he just threw loose papers on the seats." I smiled a little at the memory of my dad's "filing system," adding, "Unless it was important. Then he would jam it in the glove compartment 'for safekeeping.'"

"So you really think this list—"

"If it exists," I cautioned, "which I doubt."

"If it exists," Tristen conceded, leading us across the parking lot and toward the sidewalk, "it might be in the car?"

"Yes." The night was chilly, and I rubbed my arms, wishing I'd brought a jacket. "But this is such a long shot, Tristen—"

"Are you cold?" he interrupted, looking down at me.

My teeth chattered. "A little."

"Here." Before I could object or even grasp what he was doing, he stopped walking and shrugged off an old striped dress shirt that he wore unbuttoned over a T-shirt almost like a jacket and held it out. "Wear this." Tristen taking control as usual.

"No." I raised my hands, pushing the offering away. "I can't take your shirt!"

"Just wear it, Jill." He sidestepped me and draped it over my shoulders. "Put this on and let's get moving."

"Okay . . . thanks," I agreed. As we started walking again, I put my arms in the sleeves, which dangled past my fingertips. The shirt still held the warmth of Tristen's body and smelled like the soap I associated with him. Wrapping myself inside, I inhaled, feeling not just warmer but somehow braver, like I'd donned armor or borrowed some of Tristen's swagger.

Maybe I could do this: face my Dad's car . . .

"Wouldn't someone have noticed this list?" Tristen mused aloud as we moved across the parking lot side-by-side. "Surely you've used the car since your father died?"

"No, we haven't," I said. "We had it cleaned to get rid of the blood on the seats." I flinched to say that out loud and kept talking to erase the image. "And then Mom parked it in the garage, threw a tarp over it, and never drove it again. It's like we don't know what to do with it. I mean, who would even buy it?"

Tristen halted again, seeming taken aback. "Your father was murdered *in the car?*"

"Yes, I thought you knew. It was all over the news."

"I seldom watch news," he said grimly. "Especially not that type. The grief others suffer is not my entertainment. I've misery enough of my own to keep me quite diverted."

We continued walking again in silence, Tristen probably lost in the past, in thoughts of his mom, and me trying to face the future, where the interior of that car waited. It had been detailed, but what if it somehow *smelled* like blood? Like . . . *murder?*

We passed under a canopy of trees, both staring at the shadowed pavement when a voice broke the silence of the sleepy street.

"Tristen? Jill? Is that *you?*"

Chapter 30

Jill

"WELL, WELL, WELL." Todd Flick laughed, strolling up with Darcy, who had called to us. "What's going on *here?*"

"What do you want, Flick?" Tristen demanded, already sort of squaring off against Todd, who still wore a soft blue cast on his arm. "We're busy."

"Doing what?" Darcy asked, clearly suspicious. "Why were you in school after hours?"

My heart sank. We were busted. In so much trouble.

But Tristen didn't seem nervous. "What we do in or out of school is not your business," he said levelly.

"It is if you just broke into a locked building," Darcy said, but with a hint of laughter, like she thought the idea was ridiculous. "That's illegal!"

Oh, we were going to jail . . .

"You're here, too," Tristen pointed out with a shrug.

"Walking *past,*" Darcy countered, "on the way to my house. But you guys came *out of* the school. I saw you."

"Yeah." Todd draped his broken arm around his girlfriend's shoulders. "If I didn't know better, I'd think you two were fooling around in there or something. A little action on the wrestling mats, maybe?"

"You're pushing your luck again, Todd," Tristen cautioned. "Don't go there."

Todd ignored the warning, snorting a laugh. "Hey, Hyde, if you're hoping Jekel will put out, you're gonna be disappointed." He withdrew his arm from around Darcy, smirking. "Good luck getting those skinny legs apart!"

"Todd," Darcy snapped at him. "Stop it."

I wasn't sure if she was defending me or trying to save her boyfriend. If it was the latter, she was too late, because Tristen's hand had already darted out, and before I knew what was happening, he'd grabbed Todd's shirt and was twisting it in his fist, dragging Todd toward him, so in a split second they were nose-to-nose, Todd up on his toes, Tristen glaring down at the shorter quarterback. "Talk about Jill like that again, and I won't bother with breaking your arm," he snarled. "I'll rip your whole damned, empty head off."

There was something so menacing in Tristen's voice that even Todd suddenly looked nervous. And I was scared, too. Terrified and flattered at the same time. Tristen was defending me. But was this the *other* side of him? Was I seeing it right there? He'd changed so abruptly, seemed so different. "Tristen?" I squeaked. "Um . . . Tristen?"

"Come on, Todd." Darcy intervened more forcibly, tugging at Flick's sleeve. She appealed to Tristen. "Tristen, let go. Please. This is stupid."

I stood by, mutely helpless. *Please, Tristen. Please . . .*

Tristen remained tense, clutching Todd's shirt, jaw set, eyes fixed on Flick's. Then he suddenly shoved Todd away, stepped back, and to my complete shock, sought my arm, slipping his hand up under the long sleeve of his own shirt, twining his fingers in mine, and pulling us both back a step.

"Don't ever make a crack like that again, Flick," Tristen warned more calmly. "Not unless you want to answer to me." He paused, then his voice dropped back to a low growl. "And god help you if you ever *touch* a hair on Jill's head. They'll find yours in a gutter somewhere."

Without waiting to see if Todd replied—and I thought even Flick was smart enough to keep silent—Tristen pulled us both down the sidewalk, clasping my hand. I could feel Darcy's and Todd's eyes on us following our progress, probably staring at the point where we were joined: the hot, hot press of Tristen's palm against mine.

I should have been terrified. Maybe horrified. Did I hold the hand of a . . . *beast?* Was it possible?

Tristen's fingers clenched around mine.

But I wasn't really scared. Mostly confused. Why did we hold hands at all?

When we reached the corner of Pine Street and turned toward my house, Tristen let go of me, and I realized that my palm was soaked with sweat. I wiped my hand on my jeans, wanting to ask what had just happened.

Had Tristen felt the monster that he swore lurked inside of him coming out?

And just as much, I wanted to know why he'd defended me at all.

But of course I already knew that answer. He'd protected me because I had the potential to help save him. I was *serviceable,* just like I was to Becca in the lab.

Jill Jekel: always needed, never really wanted. I should have had that pathetic slogan tattooed across my body—assuming I was ever allowed to alter my un-pierced, untouched flesh in any way.

We were still about a block from my house, but I pulled my arms out of Tristen's shirt and held it out to him, forcing a smile. "Here. I'm not really cold anymore."

"Are you sure, Jill?" He seemed distracted, already accepting the shirt before I even answered.

"Yes," I assured him anyway, shivering.

We walked along shoulder-to-shoulder, me and a boy who might have just become part monster, until we reached the garage behind my house. The dark, dark garage where the bloodstained car, and so many old hurts and fears . . . and maybe one soul's long shot for salvation . . . waited.

Chapter 31

Jill

"YOU'VE HEARD OF BROOMS, right, Jill?" Tristen asked after I'd switched on the single bare bulb that struggled to light our big sway-backed barn of a garage. "This place is in desperate need of a cleaning—or better yet a bulldozing."

I didn't bother to remind Tristen that maybe I'd have more time for sweeping garages if I wasn't trying to *save his life*. I was too busy staring at the hulking silhouette of my dad's old Volvo hunkered under the dirty tarp like a gruesome gift in filthy wrapping. I didn't want to go any closer.

"Jill?" Tristen asked, checking my face. "It was just a joke . . . gallows humor . . ."

"This is even harder than going into his office," I said, eyeing that vehicle like the killer might still be hiding inside. "Dad *died* in there, Tristen. He suffered."

I expected Tristen to sympathize like he'd done in the past. But he didn't. He just stepped past me and, like a magician unveiling his latest trick, stripped the paint-spattered canvas right off the car, tossing the tarp to the ground.

And there it was. The car in which my dad had been butchered, looking surprisingly normal.

"Like ripping off a Band-Aid, Jill." Tristen clapped some dust off his palms. "Best to get these things over with. After you've sat inside, perhaps you'll want to drive it."

I stared at him, incredulous, not moving toward the car. *"Drive it?"*

"Why not?" He shrugged. "You don't have a car." He tapped the side of the Volvo. "And yet you do."

"Tristen . . . I don't even want to open the door."

"Then I will," he said, opening the driver's side. He nodded toward the passenger side. "Your turn."

I hesitated.

"Jill, I am *very* impatient to look in the glove box and will do so myself in about ten seconds," he said. "But I honestly believe you should open the door. This effort to hide, to pretend the murder never happened, it's not healthy. You've been in your father's office. You know you can face this."

I got a little upset with him then. "I thought you said you weren't a psychiatrist like your dad," I reminded him. "Maybe my mom and I are just dealing with things in our own way."

"Your mother fell apart, Jill," Tristen said.

I got *really* angry when he said that. "You don't know what caused her breakdown!"

We stared at each other by the light of the bare bulb, Tristen resting one hand on the Volvo, me standing near the door of the garage. A part of me suspected that he was right. What Mom and I were doing—locking Dad away, pretending he didn't exist—probably wasn't healthy. But I didn't have the courage to do anything else. How we dealt with Dad's murder—it was like another rule, an unspoken code, that I followed.

The autumn wind blew, the rafters creaked, and Tristen ended the standoff, moving not toward the passenger door, which I knew he was itching to open, but toward me. He leaned down so we were eye-to-eye, and I saw again the soft side of him that I liked. Too much.

"Jill," he said, "I've never told a soul this, but when my mother disappeared—when I *knew* that she was dead—I forced myself to go into my parents' bedroom, and I lay down on her side of the bed, my head on her pillow, breathing in her perfume. The scent that she'd worn my entire life. I stayed there, choking on what had once been comforting and pondering what hell Mom might have suffered in her last moments. All the awful scenarios that had played around the edges of my imagination—I faced them head-on. And the strange thing is when I smell that perfume now, it's okay again. Almost . . . welcome." His gaze flicked to the car. "If you take this out in the sunlight a few times, you'll get past the murder and start moving on to the good memories."

I didn't know what to say. I still wasn't even sure how I wanted to remember my dad. My horror over his murder was mingled with my outrage over his deception, like oil and water that kept mixing and separating again and again.

What I did know was that I didn't want to move. And not only because I didn't want to enter that four-door chamber of horrors that crouched on deflating tires just a few feet away.

No, I didn't want to break the moment that Tristen and I were sharing. That communion of grief, it was getting stronger. And for me going beyond a shared misery. He was so strong. Not just physically but emotionally. He would kill himself if he had to . . .

I stared into his eyes and he watched mine, and for a split second I could have sworn, for the second time that night, that I saw my own growing feelings for him reflected there. Or maybe I was mistaken, because the wind blew again, the rafters groaned, and Tristen slowly straightened, distancing us. "Do it now, Jill," he said. "Don't hesitate longer."

Listen to him, Jill. He understands this . . .

Taking a deep, ragged breath, I inched toward the Volvo, aware of Tristen trailing behind me, practically feeling his renewed eagerness as I fought my profound reluctance.

When I reached the side of the car, my hand stretched toward the door handle, and images, horrible images, began to chase through my brain. Dad . . . The flash of a knife blade . . . My father screaming . . . Blood coursing from a wound in his throat as he was dragged from the car . . .

But I kept moving, tugging on the handle, swinging open the door, my eyes darting around the interior, hunting for flecks of blood by the glow of the dim dome light.

Nothing. There was nothing.

I slid into the once-familiar vinyl passenger seat and snapped open the glove compartment. Papers and napkins spilled out, and Tristen, who had been looming above me, hands braced on the door frame and the roof, couldn't check his impatience any longer.

"Well, Jill? Well?"

"I . . . I don't see"—my hands flew through the mess. Why had Dad kept so much junk?—"anything."

But then I noticed it.

The blood that I'd dreaded. Old and black but somehow distinctive, like only blood can be. A stain on a creased and crumpled and worn paper. A sheet that looked like it had been crammed into the compartment by somebody in a hurry.

My hands shook as I unfolded and smoothed the paper on my lap, eyes squinting to read Dad's cramped handwriting.

"Well?" Tristen repeated. "Is it there?"

"Tristen . . ." My voice shook harder than my hands. "Look," I said, turning to offer him the stained paper.

The bloody list.

Of systematically altered.

Salts.

Chapter 32

Tristen

"'$K_2CR_2O_7$ PLUS . . .'?" I pored over Dr. Jekel's list, confused. Jill's father *had* been tinkering with salts, yes. But what he had added—the notations made no sense. The abbreviations didn't even signify elements on the periodic table. Nor could I discern a *private* system of abbreviation. Half of each formula seemed to be meaningless. Yet there was a pattern, too.

I was so absorbed in my thoughts that I didn't even hear my father enter my bedroom.

"Tristen? You're working late."

I spun around in my chair, startled, eyes darting to check the clock. It was nearly two in the morning. I'd completely lost track of time.

"I'm just finishing an assignment," I said, facing him—but trying to slip the bloodstained list beneath a chemistry reference, which was, thank god, open before me, too: the *Inorganic Materials Chemistry Desk Reference*, in which I'd been seeking information on all types of salts. "Senior year, you know?" I added, trying to sound casual. "I'm quite buried, between running and classes."

Dad drew closer, stepping into the puddle of light cast by my desk lamp. "Is this anything that I can help with? I've a few academic degrees under my belt, you know."

"No, thank you." I managed a smile, even as I tried to position my arm over the list, a good portion of which stuck out from beneath the book. "This is chemistry," I added, joking, "*my* strong suit."

"Now, Tristen," Dad said, sitting on the edge of my desk, "I'm not ignorant of chemistry. You wouldn't call your father *ignorant,* would you?"

"No, sir, never," I agreed, regretting my attempt at humor.

"Let's see . . ." Dad reached out and ran his finger across the open pages of the reference book, his hand just inches from the list, and sweat began to trickle down my back. He gave me a quizzical look. "I thought you're studying organic chemistry this year."

"Yes . . ."

"But you're using an inorganic reference?"

"Just looking something up." I shrugged. But the blood was pounding in my ears.

Dad knew that I was lying to him. Although the light glinted off his silver-rimmed spectacles, I could see by the curve of his mouth that he was laughing inside.

Oh, hell.

"Well, if I can help, just call down the hall." He rose and moved toward the door and away from the hidden list.

Had he seen it?

"I'll do so," I promised. *Leave, just leave . . .*

But Dad wasn't quite finished with me. "Tristen?" he noted, pausing in the doorway. "You're not working late because you're distracted from your studies by something other than running, are you?"

"No, sir. I am quite focused," I promised, tensing again. Did Dad somehow know about my late-night forays into the school? My extracurricular project?

But, no, my father wasn't talking about that type of diversion. "I just thought perhaps there might be a young lady," he said. "After all, you've never lacked for girlfriends—until lately."

"No," I said, and for the first time since he'd entered the room, I heard my casual façade crack. "No one," I repeated with deliberate calm. "I'm too busy right now."

"Oh." My father sounded almost disappointed. "Given your eagerness to help her mother, I thought perhaps you fancied the Jekel girl."

My mouth tasted curiously metallic as I said, "Jill? No. She's just a friend."

Dad frowned. "That's too bad, Tristen. Because Mrs. Jekel, although fragile right now, shows flashes of sweetness and charm." He rested one hand on the doorknob, that queer smile flitting across his lips again. "And you know what they say. Like mother, like daughter." He laughed. "And of course, like father, like son."

With that, Dad left me, closing the door without even saying good night.

My hands shook almost as badly as Jill's had done as she'd handed me the list, which I now folded and hid inside a Hemingway novel that I'd been assigned to read junior year. Then I shrugged off my jeans, shut off the light, and lay down on my bed.

Sleep proved elusive, though.

Like mother, like daughter. Like father, like son.

Had Jill suspected back in the garage what I had believed with near certainty the moment I'd laid eyes on the "last, bloody list" of "altered salts"? Had it even crossed her mind that my father had, in all probability, *killed hers*—or at the very least been involved, somehow? That perhaps it really was no accident, Jekel meeting Hyde in the heart of Pennsylvania?

I felt sure that Dad had come here not just to teach but to confer with Dr. Jekel. I wasn't sure why, or how, they'd come together, but the coincidence was too great to be ignored. There must have been some sort of collaboration. A partnership that had gone terribly wrong at some point . . .

My father—who was he now? Who—*what*—did I live with?

I closed my eyes, willing myself to sleep, needing to escape my thoughts, which of course pursued me even in slumber, and I woke up less than two hours later, thrashing in the throes of the nightmare.

She was so close to turning, revealing her face—although I'd already guessed her identity.

Becca Wright. But why did I want to kill *her*?

That night by the river had meant nothing to me—nor to her. Becca wasn't faceless just in the dream. Although I saw her nearly every day, she barely registered with me. She was a blur of self-consciously styled hair, slave-to-fashion clothes, and bright eyes that managed to be dim at the very same time. Why was this thing inside of me obsessed with slaying such an innocuous girl?

"Oh, god," I groaned aloud.

I was close to a solution. I could feel it. But I was close to destruction, too.

Something had happened again with Todd Flick, outside the school. There were moments that I didn't recall, and I'd come back to myself to find Jill's hand in mine.

I sat up in bed and ground my palms against my eyes, sick, frustrated, and confused. Because of all the things that disturbed me that night, the one that bothered me most was the lie I'd told my father when he'd asked me if there was anyone special in my life.

Oh, Jill . . .

Twice I'd stood close to her in the shadow cast by her murdered father, and the second time I'd wanted desperately to *kiss* her. Perhaps it was my own slide toward total corruption, but sometime over the course of the last few weeks, the innocence that I'd once found amusing had become touching, and then compelling, and then I'd recognized in it a strength that I lacked. A sweetness and a moral force that I needed.

If ever there were two opposites ripe for attraction, it was Jill Jekel and I. Beauty and the literal beast. Yin and yang. Pure light and pitch black.

I groaned again in the dark room.

How unlucky it would be for Jill if she were ever to start feeling the same powerful, insistent need for me that I had begun to experience for her.

Not just unlucky but tragic. For although I had the promise of rescue tucked away on my bookshelf, the clock was ticking. And even if I earned salvation, I was nowhere near redemption. No, as the pieces of my life's puzzle began to click into place, I was increasingly certain that I had committed a sin back in London that a good girl like Jill Jekel would *never* forgive.

Hell, I couldn't imagine ever forgiving *myself.*

Chapter 33

Jill

"JILL?"

I looked up from my sociology book to see Darcy Gray standing across from me with her arms braced on the cafeteria table.

I swallowed my bite of peanut butter sandwich and tried to greet her, but it came out too nervous, almost like a question. "Hi?"

Darcy never sought me out. She was going to turn me in for breaking into the school . . .

"I've been thinking about last night." Darcy seemed to confirm my worst fears, narrowing her eyes. With her sharp-edged haircut and designer clothes, she looked like an angry boss about to dress down me, her employee. "Thinking about what I saw."

The peanut butter stuck in my throat. "You—you have?"

Darcy glanced around herself, making sure we were alone. Which, of course, we were. I almost always ate by myself in a far corner of the caf, using the time to study. Satisfied that we had privacy, Darcy leaned closer. "Look, Jill," she said in a quiet but warning tone, "I *saw* you and Tristen come out of the school, and unlike Todd, I don't think you two were screwing on the wrestling mats."

I stared up at Darcy, scared—and curious about this second

reference to the mats. Was that something people actually *did?* Was sneaking into the gym another part of sex, a local mating ritual that I didn't know about? "Darcy, we weren't—"

I had no idea what I was about to say.

Darcy didn't wait to hear excuses, anyway. "I think you two are teaming up for that scholarship and hiding your work."

I choked harder on the peanut butter that I was *still* trying to get down my throat. "What?"

Darcy leaned down even farther, crouching like a wolf about to pounce, her blue eyes icier than I'd ever seen them. "I think it's pathetic that you're afraid to compete with me in the open," she growled. "It's totally underhanded, teaming up behind my back. Did you think I would steal your ideas? Or that you'd lull me into doing less than my best because the *brilliant* Jill Jekel and Tristen Hyde are forming some powerhouse brain trust? Because if you remember, I told you from the start that I didn't want to work with you or your violent, loner *boyfriend.*"

"No, it's not like that . . ." We weren't working against her. Not maliciously. And Tristen *wasn't* my boyfriend. "We . . . We . . ." What could I tell her?

"You're just like your criminal father," Darcy spat, rising and crossing her arms. "Sneaking around late at night, working in secret. It's uncanny! Unbelievable! You'd think you of all people would have learned a lesson from what happened to *him!*"

I sat in stunned silence, ears ringing with Darcy's words.

"And with Tristen Hyde's propensity for violence," she added, "you'd better watch that you don't end up like your dad."

With that, Darcy spun on her heel and stalked away, leaving me sitting alone, my open book and my half-eaten sandwich in front of me, not quite sure what to do. Run and cry? Act like nothing had happened, even though it felt like the walls were closing in?

How could Darcy have said those things? Thrown my dad's *murder* in my face?

I got up the courage to look around the crowded room, sure that the whole school must have heard. That Darcy's words must have been projected over the loudspeaker. But everybody else just kept eating and talking and enjoying their blissfully normal lives.

Everybody, that is, except Tristen, who I spotted at the opposite corner of the caf. He was alone, too, but as usual solitude didn't seem to bother him. He was leaning back, balancing his chair on two legs, his long legs propped on another seat, seeming absorbed in a book, his hand absently reaching now and then for a tall Styrofoam cup of coffee that featured the logo of a nearby gas station.

Darcy had called Tristen my boyfriend. But she was wrong. He didn't want me that way.

As I watched, he yawned and stretched, which made him seem even taller, more imposing.

Violent loner. Darcy had called Tristen that, too.

Although I knew a different side of Tristen, a sweet side, I hadn't been able to defend him against her charge. And as for Darcy's prediction about me ending up like my father . . .

I watched as Tristen flipped his coffee cup into a nearby trash can, remembering the feel of his hot palm against mine on the night he'd threatened to tear off Todd Flick's head. I'd felt safe with him in the school. But then he'd snapped.

Tristen stood now, stuffing the book into his messenger bag, which seemed like a bottomless pit for possessions that were treated with the same casual disregard he offered Mr. Messerschmidt and all authority.

Tristen and I were distant . . . but getting closer, in a weird way. He didn't lust after me, but we had a connection. A connection rooted in bloodshed and grief.

Darcy's words echoed again in my brain. *With Tristen Hyde's propensity for violence, you'd better watch that you don't end up like your dad.*

Feeling suddenly hotter, queasier, I turned my back on Tristen and wadded up my uneaten sandwich in a napkin, not hungry anymore. Because, as I knew all too well from years of fighting for academic supremacy, Darcy Gray was rarely wrong twice in one day. She'd been mistaken about Tristen and me being together—would she be right about how I'd "end up"?

And to make matters worse, even though Tristen didn't have feelings for me, even though I was afraid he really might harbor a monster inside, I turned around one more time, unable to keep my eyes off him. Unable to stop wishing that the gorgeous, talented, complicated, potentially murderous guy who was shouldering his battered messenger bag then sauntering out of the cafeteria like he owned the whole school really was my boyfriend.

Chapter 34

Jill

"TRISTEN, WHAT ARE YOU doing here?" I asked, pulling my robe around myself, not because my pajamas were revealing but because they were so ugly. "It's almost midnight!"

"I know." Tristen pushed past me into the foyer. "I need to show you what I've discovered."

"Can't this wait until morning?"

"No." He walked into the living room and switched on a lamp. I saw then that his brown eyes were bright with excitement. I also noticed what he held in his hand.

The list. Which I hadn't seen since that night in the garage.

"My mom . . . ," I said, eyes fixed on the paper. "You shouldn't even be here, and if she sees *that* . . . I told you, she hasn't mentioned the list since that night she broke down. I don't know how she'd react."

"She's sedated, right?" Tristen guessed, taking a seat on the couch and smoothing the list on the coffee table. "And we'll be quiet."

He was right: my mother was sleeping soundly. Still . . .

"Come sit down." He patted the cushion next to him. "I need to show you. Then I'll be gone. I promise."

"Okay," I agreed, stepping around the table to join him. By the light of the single lamp I could barely make out the words on the paper, but the bloodstains looked like fingerprints marked in dark ink. I looked away.

"Jill, look," Tristen directed, edging closer, shoving the list under my nose, so that I was crowded both by the strange things I was feeling in the present and a recent, horrific past. It got a little hard to breathe. Dad . . . Tristen . . . Two powerful presences, hemming me in . . .

Tristen was so excited that he didn't seem to notice how I was squirming. "At first I thought your father was irrational," he said. "I could see that he was systematically manipulating salts but with nothing recognizable." He jabbed a finger at one of Dad's notes. Dad's familiar handwriting next to those terrible stains . . . "Still, there's a clear pattern. And when I started thinking about patterns, I thought of *codes*."

I forced myself to ignore the blood and follow Tristen's finger as he traced down the list. "$CaCl_2$ plus R . . ." Calcium chloride plus . . . what? Yes, clearly Dad had been marking something in code, adding another layer of secrecy to his hidden life. "Do you think we can crack it?" I asked, not sure if I wanted the answer to be yes or no.

Did I really want to know the truth about my father when the few facts that *had* been pieced together were so damning? What if there was more ugly reality hidden, encrypted, on that sheet of paper?

"I've already done it," Tristen informed me, ending my inner debate. "It was a very unsophisticated code—no offense to your father." We both turned to the list again, Tristen edging even closer, so we were practically collapsed on each other on the sagging cushions. "See?" he said, pointing. "He simply divided the alphabet in half and transposed 'A' for 'M' and vice versa. Very simple. A half-hearted attempt at subterfuge at best."

"But why even try?"

Tristen was too focused on his goals to worry about the mysteries that interested me. "Who knows?" he asked. "The point is, when you match this list to Dr. Jekyll's notes, it's very clear that your father was working from the basic formulas and systematically tainting salts—seemingly with materials that would have been common in a pharmacy or laboratory in the nineteenth century."

"It seems like you've thought everything through," I said, pushing his hand away. The list . . . the *blood* was too close to my face. "But are you sure you're right? How do you know about the historical part?"

"The Internet," he said. "We may live in a rural backwater, but I can still access cyberspace."

"Still . . ."

"I'm right, Jill," he said firmly. "This is about my life—and death. I am *positive* I'm correct."

I looked down at the "last, bloody list."

"It's about my father, too," I muttered, more to myself than Tristen. "And me."

Tristen got quiet then and placed the paper on the coffee table, turning to face me. "Jill," he said softly, "I haven't forgotten that this list raises even more questions about your father." He seemed pained as he added, "Believe me, I've thought long and hard about what role this document might have played in his last moments. But you must forgive my excitement for myself. I promise, if I manage to save myself, I'll devote my energy to winning the contest—and helping you solve your father's mysteries, too, if that is what you want. I promise. Just let me do this first."

I stared into Tristen Hyde's brown eyes, just inches from my own. He wasn't violent. Right then, I couldn't believe it. He was warm. Kind. Gentle. He *would* help me. If only he felt more . . . felt what I did at that moment . . .

And then, as we sat face-to-face, it was almost like my wish came true, because I saw something change in Tristen's eyes. Not the frightening change that I'd seen when he'd gotten angry with Todd. This was the change I'd seen in the lab on that same night.

I thought I'd seen a new kind of warmth in his eyes back in the classroom and maybe again in the garage, but I was *sure* right then. *Almost* sure . . .

We searched each other's face, like Tristen was looking for clues to my feelings, too—although I was sure my emotions must have been obvious, written large in my eyes, whether I really wanted him to know or not.

"Jill," he finally murmured, raising his hand and brushing my ever-wayward lock of hair behind my ear.

I sat stiffly, spine rigid, even as something deep inside of me started melting, tingling. I was afraid that if I moved, Tristen would move, too, and take away the hand that lingered behind my ear, and the melting would stop.

He kept studying me, eyes moving to my cheeks, my nose, down my throat to my hideous pajamas, and when he raised his eyes to mine, he seemed almost confused. Yet I was certain, absolutely certain, that I heard desire in his voice when he whispered, "You're such a *good* girl, Jill."

I was used to hearing that word in a mocking way. Jill Jekel the goody two-shoes, always good. But when Tristen said it . . . it sounded like the most beautiful compliment in the world.

His words barely registered, though. All I could think about was the feel of Tristen's fingertips against my ear, and the warmth that was spreading, radiating from the very core of my body, as he drew the back of his index finger against my cheek and down along the line of my jaw with the same slow, deliberate confidence that had enabled him to wordlessly wrest control of a chemistry class or an out-of-tune keyboard.

My heart was pounding with anticipation—and fear.

I'd wanted this. I *did* want this. With him. A part of me had wanted it since that day in the graveyard . . .

But I'd never been kissed before. Would Tristen know? I knew that he had experience.

And he said he was *dangerous*. Darcy said it, too. Warned me . . . *You'll end up like your father* . . .

The blood on the list so close to us . . .

I pulled back, just slightly.

"Jill," Tristen repeated, voice huskier in his throat, his hand more firm as his fingers slipped around the back of my neck, drawing me closer. "Such a nice girl."

"Tristen . . ." I knew I should stop him, *had* to stop him . . . Yet

I allowed myself to be pulled, willingly lured. "Tristen . . ."

He didn't answer me. He just continued to caress my throat in a way that gently but surely brought us even closer together. I smelled the familiar soap on his skin, heard tenderness in his voice . . .

Just one kiss. Then I'd push him away . . .

I closed my eyes just as Tristen's rough, warm lips barely brushed against mine, the sensation nearly imperceptible and yet overwhelmingly powerful, causing me to melt and freeze and panic and press my hands against his chest.

No, it was wrong . . . The timing was wrong . . . *He* was wrong . . .

Had Becca hesitated? *Becca of his dreams?*

"Stop this instant!"

I thought I'd cried out.

But when Tristen and I abruptly jerked apart, I opened my eyes to see my mom standing behind the sofa, arms crossed, looking horrified and angry—and more alert than she had in weeks.

Chapter 35

Jill

"WHAT'S GOING ON HERE?" Mom demanded. "Explain this, Jill!"

My face reddened in shame. "It's—it's nothing!" I stammered.

Had it been nothing?

I glanced to Tristen but couldn't read anything on his face. "It's my fault, Mrs. Jekel," he said, rising. "I came over to talk with Jill, and I'm afraid . . ." He shrugged, with a smile that was probably as close to "sheepish" as Tristen Hyde ever got. "What can I say except that I like your daughter? And I'm certain I'm not the first to try to kiss her."

My face grew hotter, and I prayed that my mom wouldn't contradict him. She knew I'd never had a boyfriend. Not even a real date. He *was* the first.

And did Tristen mean that about liking me? Or was he just placating Mom? What had happened—or nearly happened— between us?

"That's all it was," Tristen added more seriously. "One visit, one kiss—and barely that."

Yes, barely that. Could I even say that I'd been kissed?

"Is this true, Jill?" Mom asked me. "Is this the first time he's been here?"

I could tell that she was upset to think that something had been going on while she slept, drugged, upstairs. "Yes, Mom," I fibbed. "Just tonight. And it wasn't like we'd *planned* anything."

But my mother's attention had already returned to Tristen. She cocked her head. "You look very familiar. And sound familiar."

"Yes," Tristen said. "I've been told that I strongly resemble my father."

Mom's shoulders relaxed a little, as did the set of her mouth, and she nodded slightly in recognition. "Of course. You're Tristen. Your father speaks of you often."

"Complains about me, I'm sure," Tristen ventured a joke.

"No, he seems very proud of you." Mom tucked her hands into the pockets of her worn chenille robe and looked Tristen up and down, no doubt trying to reconcile the unwanted guest with the boy she'd apparently heard praised by Dr. Hyde. "Your father says you're an accomplished pianist," she noted. "That you show great promise as a composer."

For once *Tristen* seemed uncertain, and I suspected he was surprised to hear that his father had bragged about him. "That's nice to hear," he finally said. "Although I'm afraid Dad wouldn't be happy to learn that I've upset you tonight. Again—my apologies."

Mom paused, seeming to consider her next move. "I suppose I might have overreacted. Especially given who you are, Tristen. I know you went out of your way to help us."

"It was nothing," Tristen said.

"No, it was very kind, what you did for me—and Jill. I—I should have thanked you sooner."

When Mom actually *thanked* Tristen, I realized that he had seized control of even this situation like he always did.

My mother looked to me, eyes sad and weary. "I know it's difficult for you, Jill," she admitted. "I'm sure you're trying to follow the rules, and I suppose I was home, technically . . ." She seemed to grow more unsure, and adjusted her disheveled hair with a shaky hand, an echo of my own habit. "I know your life isn't normal right now, with boys and dating, like other girls. It's . . ."

Mom seemed unable to finish the thought, and Tristen and I shared a worried glance. "Mrs. Jekel?" he asked, moving to Mom's side. "Are you all right?"

"Just tired," Mom said. "I came down for my medicine . . ."

"Here," Tristen offered, taking Mom's elbow and leading her around to the sofa. She sank down next to me, and as Tristen backed away, he smoothly swept up the list, which had been in plain view, folded it, and tucked it back into his pocket.

But Mom had seen it. "What was that?" she asked, suddenly sharply alert again. "That paper?"

My heart jumped into my throat. I wasn't sure if Mom even remembered talking about the list, but I was afraid that if she saw my dad's blood again, she might go into a tailspin. Get completely catatonic. That couldn't happen. I looked to Tristen for rescue. *Tell her something. Distract her again. Take control.*

"It's a school project," Tristen said coolly. "That's why I initially came here. To ask Jill for help."

Mom eyes narrowed, like she was trying to remember something. "It looked like—"

"You said you came down for your medicine," Tristen noted, interrupting her. "Can I get it for you? Just tell me where it is and what you need. I'm actually quite familiar with the regimen and the importance of following the schedule."

I looked at Tristen with surprise. He was familiar with the medicine? But he'd said back in the school that he didn't know much about his father's methods . . .

Mom started to rise, but weakly. "I should do it."

"No." Tristen pressed her gently back down with a hand on her shoulder. "Let me. Please."

"Thank you," Mom agreed. "The bottles are on the counter. I need two of the generic benzodiazepines and one Atarax."

"Keep your mother company," Tristen told me. "I'll be right back—then on my way, of course."

When Tristen disappeared into the kitchen, Mom rested her head back on the sofa. "He seems nice, Jill," she said quietly. "I suppose it would be silly to think you'd never have boyfriends. That you'd always be the innocent little girl who hid behind my skirt on the first day of kindergarten, too shy to play with other kids."

She was starting to sound so melancholy, like I was abandoning her, that I felt a lump rise in my throat. "I'm still pretty innocent, Mom."

"I know, Jill." She gave a faint smile and patted my hand. "You're a good girl. I do trust you."

Tristen returned then, interrupting us to offer Mom a handful of medicine and a mug of water. "Here."

Mom looked into her palm, counting the pills, wisely not trusting a high school boy to dose her, even one descended from Dr. Frederick Hyde. But Tristen must have followed her directions, because Mom popped her hand to her mouth, raised the mug to her lips, and swallowed.

"Drink it all," Tristen advised. "That's recommended."

I shot him a curious look. How did he know that, too?

But Tristen didn't meet my eyes. He was watching my mother drain that mug. Watching intently.

Seconds later, before she was even finished, the mug dropped from Mom's hands and rolled to the floor, spilling water on both of us. Her head lolled sideways, and she slumped against me. "Tristen?" I cried, alarmed, shaking my mother.

She didn't respond.

"I had to do it, Jill," Tristen said miserably. "For all of us."

Chapter 36

Jill

"YOU *DRUGGED* MY MOTHER?" I yelled, snatching at her wrist, feeling for a pulse. I raised my eyes to him, hurt and betrayed and terrified. We'd almost *kissed*. But he'd done this . . . "Why, Tris-ten?" I demanded. "Why?"

Why had any of this happened? The near kiss, the assertion that he liked me—the *attack* on my mom?

"She's fine," Tristen promised, kneeling next to us and taking her other wrist. "Her heartbeat is steady. The dose was completely safe. Just a little extra Atarax crushed in her water."

Seeing his hand on Mom, I felt a protective, almost maternal instinct come over me, and I shoved hard at his shoulder, pushing him away, sending him sprawling backward on the floor. "Get away from her! Don't touch her!"

I *loathed* Tristen at that moment. Loathed and feared him. How could he? He *was* a monster.

Tristen rose off the floor, dusting himself off, and I was sud-denly very aware of his height and the muscle that I'd felt those two times he'd held me. The strength that had once seemed comforting, now menacing.

"Get out," I ordered him. Or maybe I begged. "Please, get out!"

"Your mother saw the list, Jill," Tristen said, sounding guilty and wretched even as he tried to justify what he'd done.

But he couldn't, because he was a terrible, evil beast—just like he'd said he was.

"She didn't just see it," he clarified. "She *recognized* it."

"So what, Tristen?" I cried, all at once sick of secrets.

"*So what?*" he asked, incredulous. "What if she'd demanded it *back,* taken it away from me? Just as I'm on the brink of performing an experiment that might save my life!"

"It's *my family's* list," I reminded him, voice shaking with fear and anger. I kept my fingers wrapped around Mom's wrist, reassuring myself that her pulse beat steadily. "Not yours! The list isn't yours, and the box isn't yours. You act like they are! But they aren't!"

Tristen didn't say anything for a few seconds. He just stared at me.

And when he finally spoke, he no longer sounded remorseful. He sounded angry. "The list, the box—those are *my* legacies, too," Tristen advised me in a low growl. *"Mine."*

I shook my head. "No, Tristen! They belong to my family!"

"Your *family?*" Tristen spat the word. He started to pace but stared steadily at me. "Do you want to talk about your *precious* family?"

I wasn't sure. I held Mom's arm . . . but followed Tristen with my eyes.

"You *Jekels* ruined my whole life and the lives of my ancestors," he continued, voice rising. "Created a monster that kills, *breeds,* and kills some more!"

"Tristen . . ."

He was losing control. But not like he had with Todd. No, what I saw before me was just Tristen Hyde . . . mad as hell.

He stopped pacing and faced me directly, eyes narrowed, voice getting quieter, but in a way that only made his words that much more ominous. "Did you ever stop to think, Jill, that any blood the *Hydes* may have shed is on the hands of the *Jekels,* too? Did you ever think that perhaps YOUR ENTIRE FAMILY owes me? And that perhaps, just perhaps, I have a right to do what I must do in order to fix everything that one of *your* ancestors wrought? All of the *mayhem?*"

Tristen was loud again, digging his fingers into his hair, practically roaring, like he was releasing years of pent-up frustration and anger. "All of the HORROR, Jill! The HELL that I live with every day INSIDE MY FUCKING HEAD! And you, Jill. Did you ever stop to think that maybe YOU are as corrupted as ME?" He laughed, a harsh, almost choking sound. "You come across so innocent, but your blood is as tainted as mine in its own, perhaps *worse,* way! Your family *created* a line of killers! Have you ever thought of that since we started this whole effort to save MY FUCKING SOUL?"

I swallowed thickly, rubbing my mother's wrist, where the blood . . . our Jekel blood by birth and bond of marriage . . . pulsed through her veins.

No. I'd never thought about guilt, complicity. My family couldn't be responsible for the corruption of an entire bloodline. We were *victims* of violence. And like I'd just said to my mother, I was innocent. Innocent . . .

Tristen stopped talking—stopped accusing—and stood facing me, breathing hard, shoulders rising and falling, glaring at me. When it must have become obvious that I had nothing to say, that I didn't intend to defend myself, he moved to the sofa and slipped his arms under my mom's still body.

"Tristen?" I clung to Mom's wrist more tightly. "What are you—?"

"I'm taking her upstairs," he interrupted gruffly, avoiding my eyes. "If she doesn't wake up in bed, she might recall that something went wrong tonight. I want her to awake rested and oblivious to everything that happened here." He looked to me then, but his eyes were hard, impenetrable. "What we were doing. The list. Everything."

What we were doing . . . I thought he meant the kiss. And the way Tristen said it, the look on his face, the bitterness I saw . . . I knew that we would never come close to touching like that again.

Which was the way it should be.

I hated him. *Monster.*

"Take her upstairs and get out," I said, voice flat with defeat. He'd do what he wanted, anyway. "Just go, then get out. Please."

Tristen lifted Mom, her arms dangling loosely and her head lolling backwards as he cradled her against his chest.

I looked away, staring into the black, empty fireplace. "You know where the bedroom is."

"Yes." I heard Tristen take a few steps then pause. "She'll be fine, Jill," he said quietly. "I really do know the safe dosage, and she didn't even drink it all."

Squeezing my eyes tightly shut, like against the glare of blinding snow, I thought back yet again to that day in the cemetery.

Trust me, Tristen had urged.

Yeah. Sure. *Right.*

"Just put her in bed—gently—and go," I said, eyes still closed.

Tristen didn't answer. I just heard his footsteps moving toward and up the stairs.

I sat alone in the heart of a house that suddenly seemed spent of energy, like all the rage, and fear, and desire or whatever Tristen and I had just shared, had been snuffed out. Sort of suffocating in this vacuum, I listened to his footsteps fade down the corridor, and the sound of Mom's mattress squeaking as he placed her on the bed.

Burying my face in my arms, I listened, too, as Tristen came back downstairs and moved almost soundlessly through the living room and into the foyer, letting himself out, the door creaking softly shut behind him.

He didn't say good-bye, which was fine by me. I didn't want to see his face or hear his voice.

Besides, I was crying too hard to answer, anyway.

Chapter 37

Tristen

THE NIGHT IS STEAMY, and the river that pulses sluggishly at my side smells of decay: the wilt and rot that accompany the fecund height of summer. Smiling, I turn my face to the black sky and see the Man in the Moon leering down with approval, his round, disembodied head swinging from a gibbet of stars.

"Watch," I want to tell him. "Watch what happens next. The slick, sick trick that I will pull."

"Tristen?" the girl calls softly, bending to peer down the dark path from which she expects me to emerge. "Are you there?" She sounds nervous. "It's very dark!"

I wait a moment, enjoying the sight of her before me, her slender form so thin that her shoulder blades jut out, two angel wings waiting to be snatched before she can even think to fly away . . .

I lick my lips and clasp the knife more tightly. My palm is wet against the hilt, as if her blood is already spilling across my fists.

"Tristen," she whispers again. "Where are you?"

Her voice is musical, a siren song to my ears. But I won't be the one to crash upon the river rocks at our feet.

I step up behind her, unable to wait a moment longer for the satisfaction that I seek. "Hello, love," I whisper directly into her ear. "Boo!"

She starts, nearly screaming, but I stifle her cry, not with my hand across her mouth, but with a firm, reassuring palm upon her trembling stomach, and a soft, nuzzling kiss to her throat: a kiss that makes her groan in dismay and laughter and relief—and desire. "Oh, Tristen . . ."

She relaxes back against my chest, and I can feel her smile as I run my lips up to her ear, teasing her. "Did you wait long? Did you start to wonder if I would arrive?"

"No, Tristen," she says, those angel wings pressing against my chest. "No, I trusted you. I trust you."

"As you should, love," I tell her, withdrawing my other hand from behind my back and swinging the blade slowly around until it presses against her throat. Another surprise! "As you should."

"Tristen?" She is confused at first. She does not understand. "What . . . ?"

"Trust me," I whisper to her, lips twitching with mirth, like the jerking legs of a hanged man in his last moments. "This . . . this will be beautiful. Beautiful like you."

"Tristen!" she wails, realizing my betrayal, fighting in my arms. "Tristen? This isn't funny. Tristen!"

Tristen, Tristen, twisting against Tristen. The harmonious words play in my mind, pleasing me further. Making a wonderful moment even more delicious.

She continues her pointless struggle, writhing against me, fighting to spin, and I yield slightly, wanting the pleasure of seeing her face as she dies.

"Tristen!" she screams, turning to confront me, accuse me, implore me—and her eyes, her unusual hazel eyes, are so wide, so round, as I plunge the knife deep, deep inside of her, loving her for her sacrifice, for sharing the blood that flows across my hand, dripping down my wrist.

"Tristen!" she cries, using her last few breaths to call my name, collapsing into my embrace. I hold her body, which is growing limp, and watch the life drain from her chest and her eyes. Still, on the brink of oblivion, she needs to know.

"Why, Tristen? Why?"

I awoke at dawn exhausted, spent, and shoved my hands deep under my pillow, too terrified to look at them, because I wasn't really sure, not until I'd finally summoned the courage to withdraw them, shaking, my whole body wracked with tremors . . .

Until I saw that my palms were wet with sweat and not blood . . .

Until that moment I wasn't really sure if I'd murdered Jill Jekel. I'd been at her house. *Drugged* her mother to save myself. Yelled at Jill, unfairly. Destroyed that kiss I'd wanted so badly.

I rolled onto my side, unable to look away from my clean hands, the only proof of what little innocence I had left.

Jill.

It had never been Becca Wright, as I'd believed. Of course it hadn't been. All along the beast inside me had wanted *Jill.* Just as I did.

I swung my feet to the floor and pulled on my clothes, not bothering to shower.

If I didn't cure myself that night—if the experiment didn't work—well, I didn't think anyone would give a damn about how my lifeless body *smelled* when it was discovered on the floor of Mr. Messerschmidt's chemistry lab.

After a moment's consideration, I assembled my textbooks, deciding to attend classes. School would provide a diversion—a sense of normalcy—while I waited for the day to pass so I could enter the empty building again, alone, at night.

Still, as I shoved the books into my bag, I thought that I was curiously calm for a man who was probably destined to die that day.

Perhaps I was composed because, as I'd awakened from the dream of Jill Jekel's murder, I'd realized, with dead certainty, that I *loved* her. Maybe *we* loved her, I and the beast that I harbored. We were both drawn to Jill's innocence, her wide-eyed trust, the fragile way she yielded to us—and the subtle strength that held us both accountable for our varying degrees of sin.

The difference was the beast wanted to shed Jill's blood: consummation by destruction. But I—I had awakened more than willing to shed my *own* blood on her behalf.

I slung my messenger bag over my shoulder and left the house, striding into the morning sunlight. It was really just a matter of who would act first.

Chapter 38

Jill

I FOUND TRISTEN AT LUNCH sitting on the bleachers, just far enough from the usual crowd of stoners and hard cases to define himself as the loneliest of the loners. Or more accurately, the king of the loners. A monarch too proud to sit with commoners. As I picked my way across the seats, he watched me, and raised his hand. I thought he was about to wave, then realized he was putting a *cigarette* to his mouth.

"I didn't know you smoked," I said when we were close enough to speak.

"Every prep school kid in England smokes now and then," he said, taking a deep drag then exhaling into the brisk, chilly air. "Are you going to lecture me? Is this worse than swearing?"

"It doesn't seem good for a runner," I said, thinking Tristen seemed in a strange mood, even given the terrible events of the night before. Or maybe it was his sunglasses, which obscured his eyes, that made him seem remote. I shaded my own eyes, trying to see him better. "You'll let your team down, won't you? You're their leader—"

"I might not be running much longer," he interrupted with a shrug.

"Not running?" Although I was done with Tristen and had sought him out only to get back the *Jekels'* documents, I felt uneasy on his behalf. I sat down, the metal chilly against my legs. "Why not?"

He didn't answer me. Instead he held out the cigarette. "Drag?"

I recoiled, holding up a hand. "No, thanks."

"Good girl," he said with a small smile. "Don't succumb to vice."

I studied his face, wishing he'd take off the sunglasses. "Tristen . . ." Where should we start?

"How's your mother?" he asked, stubbing out the cigarette.

"She was groggy, but okay when I left."

"Did she mention—?"

"No," I said. "It was like you predicted. She doesn't seem to remember anything."

"Good."

We gazed out over the empty football field, where Todd Flick would have played his final glorious games if Tristen hadn't ended Todd's season before it had hardly started. "Tristen," I said, "I need the box back. And the list."

"Sure, Jill." He surprised me by agreeing. Of course, there was a caveat. "Tomorrow."

"I—I'd like them today. Please."

"Everything will be yours tomorrow," Tristen said. "Just be patient for one more day."

Tomorrow? "Tristen, what are you doing tonight?" I asked.

"You're a smart girl, Jill," he said. "One of the smartest people I've had the pleasure of knowing. Surely you can guess."

"You're going to start drinking the solutions."

"The *last* solution," he clarified, still staring out across the field. Then he turned to me and smiled, and I saw a hint of his usual wry humor. "Solution. I never thought how appropriate the word is, did you? Might it really be the solution for me?"

"Tristen," I said, growing alarmed—even though I never wanted to see or talk to him again after I got the box and list back. "If nothing happens, if you don't feel anything, how will you even know . . . ?"

I couldn't seem to express all the thoughts that were whirling through my head. If he drank a solution and *survived,* how would he know if he was cured? And if he didn't feel cured, what would that mean? What would he do?

"Don't worry," he said. "I've got a plan of action. And I promise you, as of tomorrow, all of the things that do rightly belong to the Jekels will be back in your possession."

He stood up, brushing the cold cigarette to the ground under the bleachers, where it joined about a thousand dead comrades. "Now I've really got to go."

"Where?"

Tristen didn't answer. He took wide steps down across the bleacher seats, and when he reached the bottom, I couldn't help but call after him, even though I *didn't* care what happened to him. "Tristen?"

He turned. "Yes, Jill?"

"The last formula . . . what is the salt tainted with?"

Tristen smiled, white teeth flashing in the bright sunlight. "Don't worry. It's nothing *too* deadly."

He was making a joke. But I'd come to know the mysterious Tristen Hyde just well enough to know that he wasn't really *joking*.

I watched as he walked, seeming completely relaxed, across the football field, headed away from school and toward who knew where.

When he was about fifty yards away, I noticed that Tristen had left a nearly full pack of cigarettes on the bleachers where he'd been sitting.

One last cigarette . . . Through with running . . . I'd get the box back tomorrow . . .

I realized, then, that I was watching a guy who was pretty sure he was doomed. A person who was prepared to do desperate things. I clambered down the bleachers, thinking I should chase after him and beg him to be reasonable.

When my feet hit the ground, though, I thought about my mom lying drugged on the couch, her heart just barely beating, and I stopped following him.

Turning back toward school, I told myself that I wasn't responsible for anything Tristen Hyde might do. My family and I, none of us Jekels could be blamed for the history or the fate of the Hydes.

Chapter 39

Tristen

AS THE SUN SET, I emptied my school books from my bag and replaced them with the box and my notes—and one last item I'd purchased at a hardware store on the way home from school. Inside myself, deep within my brain—my soul—the beast wriggled, clearly understanding that something was happening to both of us. It was the first time I'd consciously ever felt us coexist, and the sensation was at once alarming and reassuring.

The thing inside of me was growing stronger, asserting itself—which meant that I was right to stop it, even if that meant ending my life.

I'd never thought much about heaven and hell, but as I closed my bag with the vial of rat poison—deadly strychnine—inside, I wondered, briefly, what the verdict would be if I stood in judgment that night. Some people believed suicide doomed a soul to hell. But Christ himself had been born to sacrifice his life.

I hoisted my bag, thinking the point was moot, anyway. I would do what I needed to do.

Walking down the hallway, I passed my father's office. The door was open, and the room dark. Dad was at the university as usual. His home computer, at which he used to work so often, sat abandoned on his desk.

I hesitated, thinking that I would probably die without ever knowing just who he was, how much of Dad was left—and how much the beast controlled.

On a whim I set down everything that I carried and went to his computer, thinking that perhaps I'd drop him a line. A farewell note explaining what I'd done and what I knew for certain about both of us. Logging onto his machine, which clicked and whirred in the dark room, I called up the word processing program and actually started to smile, mentally composing my message.

Dear Dad . . . Guess what your insubordinate son's done now!

I actually typed that line and hit "save," not wanting my work to disappear inadvertently like its author. The prompt popped up asking me what I wanted to call the letter. I smiled more broadly, nearly laughing at the absurdity. What else but "suicide note"?

I typed "su," and the computer automatically began to file alphabetically. And what should I notice but a document in my father's personal files entitled "SubjugateHydeJrnl1.doc."

Curiosity piqued by the strange title, so relevant to my own plans for the evening, I saved and temporarily abandoned my note, then opened my father's work.

Scrolling and skimming, with increasing speed and heightening amazement, I leaned toward the screen, unable to believe my eyes.

Chapter 40

Jill

"HOW'S THE SOUP, MOM?" I asked, sitting down on the edge of her bed.

She rested against a nest of pillows, spooning broth into her mouth in a steady rhythm. "It tastes good. Thank you, Jill."

I smiled, thinking that even that simple comment was another breakthrough. Mom wasn't starving herself anymore, and some food even tasted *good*. "You look better tonight," I said. "You have more color."

"I feel better." Mom set the empty bowl on her nightstand and closed her eyes. "Tired from a full day at the hospital, but stronger overall."

"Good." I reached for the sedatives she still took at night. As I uncapped the bottle, I looked closely at her face.

My mother was still pale and slept a lot. But whatever Dr. Hyde was doing, it really was working. Not only was Mom lucid all day, but she even smiled now and then. Not the forced, pained grimace I'd gotten used to but a real, if tentative, *smile.*

I handed her the pills, and as I reached for her water glass, I noticed the clock on her nightstand.

It was just after ten o'clock. Would Tristen be at the school yet? Would he be getting ready . . . ?

It didn't matter, I reminded myself, offering Mom the water. It was his life and his problem. There was nothing I could or should do.

"Jill." Mom interrupted my thoughts.

I looked over to see that she was holding out the empty glass, which I accepted. "Yes?"

"Dr. Hyde . . ." She closed her eyes, preparing to drift off to sleep. "He's really helping me. We've sorted so much out. And I realize now how much I've let you down since your father died."

"No, Mom." I set down the glass and took her hand. "You've been sick."

"Yes, that's what Frederick says," Mom agreed. "But still, I feel awful to think how much you've had to handle."

"It's no big deal," I reassured her. Yet a part of me was thinking, *"Frederick"? Not "Dr. Hyde"?* Was that weird or did most patients address their therapists so informally? "Just keep getting better, Mom," I said. "Don't worry about me. I'm fine."

"You're a strong girl, Jill." Mom squeezed my hand, starting to sound groggy. "Thank you for taking such good care of me. And please say thank you, too, to Frederick's son . . ."

"Tristen," I reminded her. Had Tristen drugged her so effectively that she'd forgotten his name, even?

"Yes, Tristen." Mom choked a little, and I was surprised to see a tear run down her cheek. "If it wasn't for you asking him and his intervention . . . I don't know if I'd even be here today," she said, voice thick with emotion. "You have no idea how close I was to giving up . . ."

"Don't say that, Mom," I cried. "You wouldn't have—"

"I don't know," she said. "But you shouldn't worry now. The last few months are starting to seem like a bad dream. I would never hurt myself, not now."

All at once, I felt myself starting to choke, my throat tightening.

Mom wouldn't do anything crazy. But Tristen might—that very night. At that very *moment*, he might be ingesting something dangerous . . .

My eyes darted to the clock again. Almost ten fifteen.

"Tell him when you see him, Jill," Mom added, in the sleepy voice that always told me when the medicine was taking effect, "that I will never forget what he did for me. Frederick said that Tristen spoke so powerfully on our behalf that he felt compelled to take my case . . ." Her voice trailed off, the pills and warm soup and the effort of confiding so much taking their toll.

"I will, Mom," I promised, forgetting in that moment everything that Tristen had done *to* her. I stood up, feeling sick and filled with terror and remorse. If I didn't try to stop him, his blood *would* be on my hands. "I have to go."

"Where, Jill?" Mom murmured. But she sounded barely awake.

"Out," I said. "I need to thank Tristen—right now!"

Mom was already dozing, though, and I didn't think she knew that I'd left her. Closing her bedroom door behind me, I darted down the hallway, pausing only to grab my backpack and a paper clip from my desk, and praying that I wasn't too late.

Chapter 41

Tristen

I HAD DIFFICULTY picking the lock at the school. My hands shook almost uncontrollably—not in anticipation of the fate that I probably faced, but due to what I'd just read on my father's computer.

A draft of a journal article. A piece that he'd obviously planned as his magnum opus. An exploration into the troubled psyche of none other than Dr. Frederick Hyde. The doctor as patient—and savior, too. An article that convinced me that my father had been overwhelmed and defeated, months ago—that I lived with only the beast.

I jabbed the paper clip into the lock, mastering my fingers and gaining entry.

With typical hubris, my father had been confident that he could vanquish the monster, armed with nothing more than self-analysis and an arsenal of pharmaceuticals.

As I closed the door behind me and walked into the silent school, passages that were burned in my mind came back to me verbatim.

I have come to believe that the Hydes are, indeed, subject to a genetic anomaly . . . The dreams intensify . . . Regression therapy ineffective . . . Yet I remain confident of a solution . . .

The document chronicled months of self-examination and the methods my father had employed to gain control of the nasty soul that fought to emerge. These passages were interrupted by extensive notes on cases that Dad had deemed similar and the long-term, even trans-generational, effects of certain chemical compounds on the human body.

The article was raw, unedited, but in the powerful sweep of Dad's self-assured prose, I could read his excitement, his desire to battle the beast and win. Dad had never once doubted that he would be the victor—even as I could clearly see him losing, in his own words. *Last night—three hours lost—awoke frustrated . . .*

I made my way down the corridor where in just a few hours teachers and students would flood. If I did die, who would be the first to find me? That idiot Messerschmidt? Would he scream to see my body? Would there be blood, given what I was about to drink? Would it pour from my mouth, spilling from my corroded stomach?

I picked the lock on the classroom door, fingers more sure.

My father had also chronicled his excitement upon finding and teaming with an unidentified American collaborator who was so clearly Dr. Jekel. *Have located and begun correspondence with U.S. chemist who believes himself in possession of valuable documentation and taken him into confidence . . . Begun efforts to relocate temporarily in hopes of collaborating . . . If successful, the potential to secure both our reputations is tremendous . . . Implications for treating personality disorders . . . criminal rehabilitation . . . social controls . . .*

My father had written of finding Dr. Jekel through simple genealogical research. And reading between the lines, I could see that Dad had then used a potent combination of guilt and the promise of fame and fortune to convince Jill's father to help him find a cure for his looming madness. Judging from some of the passages, I found that my father had not only expected to save himself; he'd sold Dr. Jekel on grandiose dreams of potentially using their findings to revolutionize the treatment of *everyone* with criminal impulses.

Jekel and Hyde's magic formula for a safer society!

How ironic was *that* fantasy?

I locked myself inside the chemistry room and thumped my bag onto my lab table, not hesitating for fear that the slightest falter would cause me to rethink the whole doomed adventure. For I was all but certain that the formula would never work. The odds were too long—and the potion itself too toxic.

Dad, though, had believed that he and Dr. Jekel were drawing close to an answer. *My collaborator feels confident that a breakthrough . . . that SUCCESS . . . is imminent . . .*

And then, abruptly, the proposed journal article had been abandoned. The last saved date was close to the previous Christmas. Not long before the murder of Dr. Jekel.

Glass clinking against glass, I assembled the implements and ingredients that I needed and moved quickly to mix the chemicals, unable to push away the question that gnawed at my mind: should I kill my father before I risked killing myself?

If I did so, I would almost certainly be avenging Jill's father's death and probably gain retribution for my own mother's murder, not to mention saving future victims. Because the beast that had overtaken Dad *would* kill again.

But, god forgive me, I kept working alone in the school.

Perhaps a small part of me clung to the faint, faint hope that the formula which I hurriedly mixed, which bubbled and seethed in the Erhlenmeyer flask, might actually save me and enable me to bring my father back, too.

Or perhaps I was a coward, unable to murder, along with the beast, the man who had given me life. The stern, demanding, undemonstrative egomaniac who had nevertheless written, at the very start of his most important work, a draft dedication: *For my son, Tristen—that I may save him, too.*

I worked hurriedly but with precision, checking my notes and mixing the chemicals. *Addition half litre filtered water . . .* Messerschmidt would have been in awe had he witnessed my efforts.

And finally, as the modern Dr. Jekel's document indicated, I added the strychnine to the already dangerous potassium dichromate and poured that lethal mix into the flask.

Strychnine. An alkaloid mistakenly believed medicinal back in the nineteenth century. A chemical that would have been commonly found in pharmacies, and which, in the amount that I held, would indeed shake the drinker to his very core.

Refusing to think further, to consider the future, the way the solution might feel as it seared my throat, paralyzed my lungs, I raised the flask before my eyes, toasting my own fate, and was actually about to say "cheers" when I heard my name screamed from the doorway.

"Tristen! Stop!"

Chapter 42

Jill

"TRISTEN, DON'T," I begged when I saw his hand hesitate. My backpack slid from my shoulder, thumping to the floor, and I stepped closer. "Please. Let's talk first."

"How did you even get in here?" he asked, confused, fingers wrapped around the throat of a flask that was filled to the brim. He looked to the door. "I locked that . . ."

"I just picked it," I said, opening my hand to show him the paper clip. "Like you taught me."

"Oh, hell," Tristen groaned. "I should never have shown you—"

"What's in there, Tristen?" I edged even nearer, terrified that he would tilt the flask to his mouth and drain it dry before I could reach him. "What's in the formula? How is the salt altered?"

He didn't answer the question. "I think you should go now, Jill."

A cold knot formed in the pit of my stomach. "Tristen . . . what is in there?"

He still didn't answer but set down the flask and came around the table, stopping me with two firm hands around my upper arms. "Jill," he said, boring into my eyes, "you *really* need to go."

I knew then that whatever Tristen Hyde was about to drink, it wasn't just dangerous; it was probably deadly. He didn't look scared. He looked resigned and determined, and that expression tipped me off more than raw terror would have. I'd seen that look on Tristen's face the day he'd first asked me to help him with the experiment. The day he'd promised to commit suicide if he couldn't cure himself.

"Tristen, you don't really believe this will help you, do you?" I asked, fighting back emotions that were about to overwhelm me and make me irrational. Fear at the prospect of seeing somebody actually die. And something more. Terror at the prospect of losing Tristen. Forever. I wouldn't be able to bear it. Because even if he didn't love me back, I loved him.

Loving him was stupid and pointless and maybe wrong. He was dangerous and arrogant, and he broke every rule that I followed, and lured me to break them, too. But I knew in that moment that it was true: I had somehow fallen in love with a guy who was about to take his own life. "You're killing yourself, aren't you?" I asked, hating that my voice broke.

"Perhaps," Tristen admitted. "Of course, I hope that the formula will save me. But there is a strong chance that I might not survive drinking it."

Although I'd suspected that, hearing him say it made my blood run cold.

"Why now?" I asked, trying to reason with him. "Why not wait, Tristen? You're not even *sure* the beast is real. Not one hundred percent!"

"I'm sure, Jill," he said evenly, still holding my arms. His fingers tightened slightly around me. "I am positive."

I searched his face, almost like I was looking for some hint of the monster in his eyes. But all I saw was Tristen: complicated, sometimes frightening, occasionally violent, even. But also capable of great good, great warmth, a willingness to sacrifice his *life* for others. For Becca, in particular, if my suspicions were right. "How do you know?"

"I dreamed last night," he said.

"You've dreamed before."

"This time I concluded the dream," Tristen confided. "I finally saw the outcome . . . the actual *murder*."

"That doesn't mean anything!"

"I saw her face, Jill," he continued, loosening his grip on my arms, not so much restraining me as just holding me. "I saw her face as she died. As the monster killed her."

"I don't understand . . . You knew all along who it was." Becca. How in that awful moment could I be jealous again? But I was.

"No, Jill," Tristen said, brown eyes miserable, "I was wrong. He didn't kill a silly cheerleader."

"No?" My voice sounded strangled in my throat, because somehow . . . some clue in the way he was looking at me gave me the answer to the question I was about to ask before I could even voice it. "Who—who was it, Tristen?"

"You, Jill," he said. "I—he—murdered *you*."

Not Becca, but me . . .

We stood together in the lonely classroom: me and a guy I loved who swore that something inside of him wanted to kill me. Yet I wasn't afraid of him.

Trust me, Tristen had said.

And somehow I did.

I *was* scared, but not for me. Just for him—even when Tristen, pinning my arms, revealed very matter-of-factly, "He wants to kill you right now, Jill. And not just in fantasy."

And how could I describe the way it felt when Tristen pulled me closer—voice throaty with what I thought were sadness and need—how could I ever capture how it felt when he said, "It's been you all along, Jill. He wants you as much as I do. But I'll be damned, genuinely *damned,* before I let him have you."

It was maybe the world's sickest declaration of affection, complete with a touch of black humor, but it rang as perfect to my ears.

Tristen cupped my chin in one hand then and bent over me, wrapping his other arm around my waist, and I had my first real kiss with a boy—a *man* . . . a monster and a martyr, who might very well be dead in the next few minutes.

Of course Jill Jekel wouldn't have a normal kiss good night at the front door after a movie or a school dance.

Of course a relationship that started at the edge of one grave would culminate on the brink of another.

Of course that first kiss would not just be to say good night but probably goodbye.

Chapter 43

Tristen

OH, HOW THE BEAST INSIDE of me roared and snapped and snarled when I finally kissed Jill Jekel the way I'd wanted to for—how long?

Could I trace my attraction to that night in the diner when she'd walked by the window, her demure lace blouse somehow more intriguing than Becca Wright's skintight T-shirt? Or had it started in chemistry class, where I watched that glossy ponytail swinging in hypnotic rhythm? Was that when she'd first mesmerized me? Or had it been the day I'd held her at her father's funeral, felt her cling to me, so in need of strength, protection?

How ironic that as those soft, pink lips finally pressed against mine, uncertainly, and as Jill's hands fluttered to find their proper place—my shoulders? hips? chest?—and as her mouth yielded to my gentle pressure, opening so I could feel her timid tongue against mine one time before my own mouth was seared and wrecked forever . . . How ironic that a kiss born of a desire to protect was all but overwhelmed by my struggle to control a force within me that wanted nothing less than to destroy Jill herself.

As she hesitantly drew closer into my embrace, resting against me, the beast wriggled in my soul, trying to break free, to take control. *Stop now, Tristen,* I told myself. *Stop before you black out.*

Stop before you do something that can never be undone.

Yet the feel of Jill in my arms, the exhilarating, intoxicating mix of passion and tenderness that she elicited in me—it was like nothing I'd ever felt with any other girl, and I couldn't quite bring myself to make the feeling end. I wanted the kiss to go on and on, fairly certain that it was my last, completely certain that it was the best, and I drew Jill even closer to me, hungry for her, a condemned man trying to savor his last meal even as he hears the construction of the scaffold just outside the cell.

"Oh, Jill," I murmured, wanting to tell her that I loved her. Wanting to say so much but not wanting to pull away long enough to say it. "Jill," I whispered, nuzzling against her soft, soft cheek, hoping she heard everything I wanted to express just in the way I spoke her name.

"Tristen . . ." I heard my emotions echoed in Jill's voice, too. Sad, desperate bliss like my own. Her heart raced against my chest.

And I heard something else, too, intruding upon my thoughts. *"Yes, Tristen . . ."*

Its voice.

As I folded Jill to me, caressing her back, stroking her throat with my thumb, the words echoed softly but clearly from somewhere deep inside of me. A place that I was only beginning to recognize.

I'd felt the beast twisting within. But this was the first time I heard it *speak.*

Stop, Tristen, I told myself—even as I continued kissing Jill. The attraction, the passion, escalating as she ventured to slip her hands around my neck. *Just one more minute, Tristen, and then never touch her again . . .*

I thrust my hand into Jill's hair, nearly dislodging her ponytail, hurrying the kiss, knowing that I couldn't continue much longer.

"Jill, Jill," I groaned when we both wasted a precious moment separating, needing oxygen to fuel an escalating intensity. I wanted her so badly. Wanted more than this before I died. "Oh, Jill . . ."

My own voice sounded strange in my ears. Yet somehow familiar. A voice I'd just heard.

Hurry, I told myself. *Hurry or stop . . .*

"Don't stop . . . Don't stop . . ."

Shutting out the command, silencing my now vocal foe, I tried to focus on Jill, tightening my arm around her waist, my lips grazing her throat. *"Her soft, soft throat . . ."*

"Tristen," Jill murmured, sounding breathy but a little nervous as I nipped at her neck, hearing myself make a low growl of need. "Tristen?"

"Yes, love," I murmured against her ear. "Yes . . ." "Yes, yes . . ."

Yes . . . Just another moment, and I would release her forever. "Oh, Jill . . ."

I didn't mean to be rough or desperate, but time was running out, and I clamped hard upon her mouth, our lips grinding together, my hand digging into her hair.

"Take her, Tristen . . . And what you start I will finish . . ."

No . . . No . . .

My head began to ache from the struggle, a crushing pain, and I sensed that I was losing. Yet I couldn't stop kissing her. This was my last chance . . . I clasped her more firmly, moving her back against the desk, trapping her, pressing our bodies together. Her hips wriggled against mine.

"That's right. She wants this, too. Don't listen, if she protests. She wants this . . ."

"Tristen," Jill cried out softly, her hands no longer uncertain as I crushed her against the table. No, her palms were pressing against my chest, pushing back against me. Against *us*.

"Ignore her. Trap her there. Bend her backwards . . ."

"No, Tristen!" Jill called more loudly. More insistently, as if she knew that I was far away and she was desperate to reach me. "STOP! PLEASE!"

I was so far gone, losing to the beast, that I scarcely heard her. But her plea, the sound of her voice—the voice that I loved—it was enough to reach me even as everything began to grow black.

"Stop, Tristen," Jill whimpered, on the verge of tears. "Please . . . stop . . ."

Like the dream. It was just how she sounded in the dream.

Without a word I snatched my hands away, released her squirming body, and stepped back, dragging the back of my hand across my mouth, which was wet with my saliva, Jill's saliva. We were both breathing hard, almost panting. Her slender shoulders heaved. And her beautiful hazel eyes were wide with fear.

My stomach clenched to see the terror there.

No. I hadn't wanted that. Never. Never to scare her. Or *hurt* her.

"I'm sorry, Jill," I whispered. "So sorry."

I'd almost failed to protect her. I'd wanted to be with her so badly that I'd almost been complicit . . .

Jill stared at me, face pale, hands raised slightly as if to ward me off should I step toward her.

"Oh, god." I buried my face in my hands, afraid that I might break down. Too sickened to face that look in her eyes. "Oh, god, no."

We stood apart in silence—as distant as we'd just been close. Jill didn't try to touch me, and I didn't try to excuse or explain myself, although I longed to tell her that I wasn't like that. I wasn't a guy who would . . . Especially not with her . . .

And yet—I almost had . . .

"Tristen?" Jill finally prompted, voice quiet. I heard the faint sound of the slipperlike shoes that she always wore tapping against the linoleum and then felt a tentative hand on my shoulder, and I nearly did break down.

She was better than me. Braver than me. She should have run screaming for help. Yet she *touched* me.

Dragging my shaking fingers through my hair, I stepped out of her reach and turned my back on her, unworthy of her concern and unable to show my face. "Leave, Jill. Please. Leave."

She didn't listen to me. Instead she stepped closer and stroked my shoulder. "Tristen . . . was that . . . ?" She seemed unable to finish the question. But I understood.

Was that the beast? Or you?

"It doesn't matter," I said. "It doesn't matter now, Jill."

Straightening my shoulders, I went to the lab table, not giving her a moment to protest—if indeed she even thought of protesting. I raised the foul-smelling flask to my lips and without hesitation drank as much as I could, downing the disgusting brew in huge thirsty gulps, heedless of dosage, heedless of the havoc the strychnine would wreak on my body, because at that point I didn't give a damn about a cure, and I wanted the agony. I'd seen the look in Jill's eyes—the betrayal, the terror—and I wanted nothing less than to kill both the beast and *myself.*

Nothing less would do to punish what I'd nearly done.

Beast or no beast—I'd been there, too.

Chapter 44

Jill

HE HAD TO CURE HIMSELF.

I told myself that as I watched Tristen raise the dark concoction in the beaker to his mouth.

I'd felt and heard the beast start to overtake him when we'd kissed. Felt Tristen slipping away from me, becoming somebody, something, completely different. The boy who'd first touched his lips to mine and the *animal* that had tried to pin me against the desk: they were two different beings entirely. They felt, spoke, looked, even *smelled* different. Tristen's skin itself had roughened, and his beautiful, warm brown eyes had taken on a gray, metallic sheen.

The shift had been barely perceptible. If he hadn't been so close to me, pressing against me, breathing on me, I might not have been sure I'd seen it. But I had. The beast was real. And I'd met it.

It was a monster, and it had to be stopped.

If it was killed, I could have Tristen . . . the real Tristen. We could kiss again without being afraid.

Looking back, I think that's why I waited so long before begging him to stop drinking. It was selfish, really, what I did.

I wanted Tristen so badly that I would risk even *Tristen* to have him.

Selfish, selfish, selfish Jill.

I was so caught up in the hope that Tristen would somehow be cured that at first I didn't even realize we'd never talked about dosage. It wasn't until he'd drunk almost half the contents of the flask—drinking so quickly that some liquid spilled over the lip of the vessel, and over Tristen's lips, and poured down his throat, too—only then, when he doubled over clutching his stomach, did I realize that Tristen wasn't trying to cure himself. He was killing himself right before my eyes . . . and I'd let him do it.

"No, Tristen!" I finally screamed, running to him.

But I was too late.

Chapter 45

Jill

"TRISTEN, NO!" I wailed, kneeling next to him, clutching his shuddering shoulder. "You drank too much!" I shook him. "What was it? What was in it?"

Tristen didn't answer. Maybe he couldn't answer. He writhed on the hard linoleum floor, arms wrapped around his stomach, groaning and sort of *growling* like he really struggled not only with the pain but with the monster, too.

"What was it, Tristen?" I begged, shaking him more gently. "Please. Tell me. We could try to neutralize it!"

Tristen only curled more tightly against himself, breathing hard and raggedly, and I jumped up, tearing through the notes, the packets and vials of chemicals— And then I saw it.

A small *half-empty* bottle of strychnine.

"No!" I cried, snatching up the vial. It was *poison*. His muscles would be seizing painfully, and soon his breathing would stop . . .

Tossing aside the bottle, I dropped next to him again, only to see that he'd gotten quiet. A stillness that was worse than his writhing agony. Was he past pain? Past help? "I'll get an ambulance," I promised, choking back tears, feeling for the faint pulse that beat in his wrist. He was dying . . . dying right before my eyes.

I started to crawl away, scrambling for my backpack, where I kept my cell phone—only to be stopped by a firm hand snapping around my ankle with the force of a bear trap.

"Tristen, let go!" I begged, spinning back and tearing at his fingers. He was still curled in a ball, but his grip was remarkably strong, like he'd drawn power from the pain itself. "I have to get help!"

"No," he ordered, sucking ragged breaths. His grasp was strong, but his voice was weak, almost inaudible. "I don't want that . . . and I don't want you . . . involved—"

"But you're . . . you're . . ." I couldn't bring myself to say "dying."

"I know," he said, fingers clutching even more tightly around my ankle as a wave of pain washed over him, causing him to grimace and shudder again more forcefully. "It's what . . . I want, Jill."

"Tristen." I was sobbing by then. "Please . . ."

"Just . . . stay with me. Stay until . . . Then leave me here . . ."

I hesitated, wanting to save him, longing to help him. He was getting weaker, fainter, falling away from me, and I probably could have unwrapped his fingers from around my leg. But Tristen didn't want to be saved. Probably *couldn't* be saved.

And in the end, whether it was right or wrong, I chose to honor his request. Because I loved him, I would let him die on his own terms.

He was still, so still, by the time I made my decision that I twisted easily out of his grasp, crawled back to his side, and cradled his head, trying to give him some small comfort. Not that he probably noticed. I thought Tristen was definitely past pain at that point. Maybe past life—he was so motionless and pale.

I couldn't bring myself to check. I was too scared to take his pulse and confirm the inevitable. Because the moment I did . . . if his heart really didn't beat . . . Tristen Hyde would really be gone.

Forever.

The sobs I'd almost controlled started again, and I sat on the floor, holding his head and weeping over him. Selfishly crying for myself, too.

Selfish, selfish me.

"I'm so sorry, Tristen," I whispered, stroking his hair. "So, so sorry."

Sorry for the awful fate that had been handed to him. Sorry for the terrible end he'd chosen.

Sorry that I felt worse at that moment than I did even at my father's death.

Sorry . . . I was sorry for everything . . . Sorry that we'd kissed only once and even that had been destroyed, stolen from us. From me.

I stroked Tristen's cheek, felt the rough stubble, the sweat that was growing cold, and in a perverse reversal of Snow White, a grotesque twist on all the Disney princess movies I'd daydreamed over as a little girl, I bent to kiss Tristen: part prince, part beast, with no hope of a happy ending.

His skin was stone cold against my lips.

Tristen . . . Tristen was gone . . .

I would bury him just like I'd buried my father. The only two men I'd really loved, in the span of a year.

Grief crashed over me, and I squeezed my eyes shut, but the hot tears wouldn't stop, and they spilled down my face like a river as I sat alone on the floor. Just moments ago I'd been part of a pair. Now I was alone again. Not just alone but broken.

Who would hold me at *Tristen's* funeral? No one . . . No one . . .

Suddenly I couldn't bear to cradle his head any longer, couldn't look at his face so empty and frozen, and I gently rested his head on the floor, certain that he couldn't feel the ground beneath him. Then, like a wounded animal, I crawled to his side and collapsed on him, giving in to my own agony, which felt like poison, too, burning inside of me. I clutched at his shirt, burying my face against his chest, wailing.

Dead . . . He was dead . . .

That was when I felt a hand begin to stroke my back, comforting me.

It didn't sink in at first. Someone was comforting me.

But slowly I realized what was happening, and I raised my face from Tristen's chest, not understanding.

I was alone—except for Tristen's body.

Except for *Tristen*.

Not daring to believe, I swiped one arm across my eyes and slowly turned my face to his, sucking in my breath at the sight of his open eyes. Astonished not just by the fact that Tristen was alive but by the expression on his face.

I heard the wonder, the confusion, in my voice as I dared to say his name.

"Tristen?"

Chapter 46

Jill

TRISTEN SAT UP SLOWLY, still holding his stomach, his face still pale and his breathing still shallow. There was something different about him, too, aside from looking like he'd been to hell and back, as maybe he just had. Something had changed in his eyes. Something was missing, it seemed. The haunted, hunted look that had always been there, even when he laughed.

"Tristen?" I took his arm, helping him slide up straighter so he could rest his back against a lab table. "Are you okay?"

He couldn't be okay. Could he?

He leaned his head back against the table and closed his eyes, obviously exhausted and still hurting. But as I watched his face, wondering if maybe *now* we should get to a hospital, he *smiled*. "I'm fine, Jill," he murmured. "I'm fine."

At first I thought he was still incoherent. Or that maybe this was some calm before a new storm and he might double over again. The suffering he'd just endured . . . He couldn't be "fine."

"Tristen, let's get help now," I urged, gripping his hand.

"No." He shook his head, still beaming that strange, blissful smile. "No, Jill. I just want to rest for a minute."

"What's happening?" I asked, wishing he'd open his eyes again. What was that look I'd seen there? "What . . . what are you feeling? Are you in pain?" Was I about lose him again? Because I didn't think I could bear it.

"What I feel, Jill, is peace," Tristen said. "The first peace I've felt in years."

My own eyes widened in disbelief. Although I'd seen the change in his expression, I couldn't quite grasp what he seemed to be implying. "You're not trying to say that the formula *worked* . . . ?"

He squeezed my fingers, smiling more broadly. Some of the color had returned to his face, and he looked almost *rested*. "Let's not question it right now, Jill. Let me just be at peace for a moment. Okay?"

Tristen tugged my hand, drawing me closer, and I shifted to sit beside him. He let go of my hand and slipped his arm around me, pulling me close in that protective embrace I'd thought I'd never feel again. He opened his eyes then, meeting mine, willing me to look closely at him. It was almost like he knew that he must look different and was showing me, trying to prove to me that he had changed.

Trust me, his eyes said.

As I stared deep into his familiar, yet different, brown eyes, I knew with certainty that whatever had happened to Tristen on the floor of that classroom, whether it had been the formula he'd drunk or by sheer force of will, he had beaten the monster that had tormented him. The dark shadow that had always seemed to lurk inside his eyes was gone. The Tristen who held my gaze was still the boy I loved: confident, smart, and commanding. But he wasn't scary anymore.

He closed his eyes again, leaning his head back, and I rested my head against his chest, feeling his heart beat. Feeling completely happy for the first time I could remember since maybe elementary school—when I'd moved beyond the circumscribed happy sphere of my parents' acceptance of me for who I was. Since before I'd come to realize that being shy and plain were bad qualities in most people's eyes. Tristen's arms recreated, in a very tangible way, that circle of approval I'd known in childhood.

Gradually his heart started to beat even more strongly. He rested his cheek against the top of my head then turned his face to kiss my hair, whispering, "Thank you, Jill." He squeezed me more tightly. "Thank you for coming for me and for staying with me."

"I couldn't leave you," I said. "You drank too much—" I wanted to scold him for being too reckless, but my voice suddenly threatened to break at the memory of him writhing on the floor, growing cold.

"I had to destroy it," Tristen said, alluding, for the first time since waking, to the defeated beast. "It wanted you too badly."

Tristen wanted me, too. I knew that as he again brushed his lips against my hair.

I forced away the image of Tristen shoving me against the desk. That was over now. I was safe. I was wanted. For the first time in my life a boy—one that I was crazy about—actually wanted Jill Jekel.

I turned to see his face, our eyes met again, and I saw then that the new warmth there was burning a little more intensely.

"I want to kiss you, Jill," he said softly. "Just me." He paused, watching my face, maybe seeing my uncertainty, because he added, "Do you still want me? Or has what happened . . . what nearly happened . . . Are you sickened by me? Frightened of me?" A shadow crossed his face, dimming his happiness. "Because *I* am sickened by me. By what could have happened here if I hadn't heard your voice—"

"Nothing happened," I reassured him, even though I flinched again, too. Images of Tristen's eyes turning that scary shade of steel, the rasp of his rough skin against mine, the pressure of his body bending me back over the desk . . . I forced them all out of my mind. "Nothing happened," I repeated, wanting to erase recent history for both our sakes. "And I'm not frightened now," I added truthfully. Because I wasn't afraid of Tristen anymore. The beast was gone.

But . . . I was lying, too. Because I was a little scared. Not of monsters but of the very things I'd wanted for so long: a boyfriend, a love life . . . sex? I needed some kind of instruction or rules. Instruction on what to do and rules about how far we should go. Tristen was obviously experienced. It showed in the way he bent his head to meet my lips again, gently but with confidence. Confidence that I lacked.

Were we boyfriend and girlfriend now?

I loved Tristen, and he'd nearly died for me. What did *I* owe *him,* in life? What did I want to give him? I didn't know.

I wanted him, badly. But I wanted time, too. Even though my stomach tickled with attraction when his fingers stroked my throat, I couldn't help tensing and putting one hand on his shoulder, in case I'd have to stop him again—not because he was a beast, but because he was a *man.*

But suddenly, when Tristen once again somehow opened my tight, nervous lips, as surely and effortlessly as he picked every other lock that blocked his path, and our tongues touched for the second time that night, twining around each other, drinking each other in . . . suddenly a shudder rippled through my entire body.

I didn't shake with fear or cold or tremble with lust or longing or love, even. No, what I felt was all that and more, including a violent stab of pain that was so pure it could only be described as pleasure.

What I experienced was me . . . transforming.

And, oh, did it feel wickedly good.

Chapter 47

Jill

"TRISTEN," I MOANED—pleaded—slipping my hand from his shoulder and wrapping my arm around his neck, pressing our chests together, rubbing against him. "Come on, Tristen, please."

Suddenly I was impatient with him and for him. My side ached, and I held it with my other hand, wanting even more pain, more action.

Too much tenderness . . . not enough friction . . . What is he wait-ing for?

"Jill," Tristen muttered against my roving mouth, my searching lips. *"Jill!"*

Too much talking . . . not enough touching . . .

I slipped around to climb aboard his lap. *Let's see what you've got there . . .*

But he caught my hips and stopped me, pushing back. "Easy, Jill," he said, half laughing but sounding confused, too. "It's not a race. Or a rodeo!"

Oh, but it is a race . . . a race to the finish . . .

I pried at Tristen's fingers, wanting our hips to get better ac-quainted.

In response, he clutched me more firmly, actually lifted me off his lap and set me back on the floor while I struggled to keep our tongues engaged, which only caused us both to sprawl sideways in a tangled, messy heap, and suddenly we weren't kissing anymore; we were wrestling. And not in the way I wanted to wrestle.

"Jill," he said firmly, no longer amused but sounding doubly baffled. He held me at bay with one hand on my shoulder. "Slow down—or at least let me lead a bit, too."

I sat up, staring at him in disbelief. *Is* that *was this is about? Male pride?* "Fine," I agreed, shrugging. "Go ahead. Lead." *As long as we get the deed done, what do I care?*

But apparently Tristen had changed his mind entirely. He sat on the floor looking at me with concern, not desire, in his eyes. "Jill," he said, studying my face and massaging my shoulder. "Let's just stop for a moment, eh? This doesn't feel right to me." He shook his head, clearly puzzled. "Something isn't right."

He's joking, right? Boy. Girl. Dark room. Nothing wrong with that scenario—except that we have our clothes on.

"Come on, Tristen," I begged, reaching out for him. "Let's keep going!"

He caught my wrist with his free hand. "No. Not right now, Jill. I think this whole night has been overwhelming for both of us. You seem a bit . . . frantic."

Yes, frantic. And hot and bothered, for him. What is wrong with that?

"It's getting late," Tristen added, rising. He held out his hand, pulling me up, too. "I need to make some more formula then get you home."

Ahh, the formula. I licked my lips again, distracted from sex. "You do?"

"Yes," Tristen said, moving behind the lab table. He seemed to get edgy. Almost cagey, not meeting my eyes. "I want to mix up more—in case I need it."

"I'll help," I volunteered. *Help and learn.*

"No," Tristen replied too quickly. "I'll do it."

Is he hiding something from me? I watched suspiciously as he arranged the beakers and vials, working fast. "But I could help you," I offered again.

The pain in my side was subsiding, becoming a dull ache, and my head was starting to clear. I felt weird, like the hormones that had just caused me to act so boldly, so *embarrassingly* forward, were filtering out of my brain.

"You could start to clean up, I suppose," Tristen suggested. "If you don't mind? We could get out of here sooner."

I didn't want to be his janitor, but I was really starting to feel sheepish about how I'd just attacked him, so I agreed. "Sure."

"Could you repack my bag?" Tristen requested, nodding toward a pile of papers and books as he poured something that I couldn't identify into a new flask. The mixture bubbled.

Delicious. I shook my head, not sure why such a weird word had popped into my head, and joined Tristen at the lab desk, stacking papers that were scattered across the surface, like in his hurry to mix the formula, he'd dumped his whole bag onto the table. And when I lifted his bent, crumpled lab manual, I saw the novel, which Tristen hadn't allowed me to hold before.

Lifting it, I opened the cover and saw that someone had written inside.

To Tristen . . .

But suddenly *The Strange Case of Dr. Jekyll and Mr. Hyde* snapped shut in my hands, causing me to jump back and drop it to the table, where Tristen scooped it up, stealing it out of reach. "We don't need that anymore, Jill," he said. "I'm done with that."

I watched Tristen's face and saw that his new peace was already shattered. I didn't see the beast anymore, but something definitely haunted him.

He jammed the book into his bag and took over cleaning up the other papers, too. "I'm done mixing," he said. "Would you mind decanting the formula into some smaller containers for me? I'm tired suddenly and want to get out of here."

I wanted to leave, too. With every minute that passed since Tristen had *tossed* me off his lap, I felt more ashamed. I'd spun completely out of control. I'd been so pathetically desperate that he had *stopped* me. Had that ever happened to any other girl in the entire universe? And what had I been thinking? Would I really have had *sex?* On the floor?

No. Never. I would have stopped. Of course I would have stopped.

"Yeah, let's get going," I agreed, finding four smaller beakers with stoppers and pouring the formula into them. I wanted to get home and sleep. Tristen had been right. The whole night must have overwhelmed me. Made me crazy. "I don't think I feel very good," I said, wiping my arm across my forehead, which felt warm.

"I'll hurry and take you home," he said, looking at me with new concern. "I thought you seemed feverish."

"Do you mind if I just go now?" I asked. "I really feel kind of queasy."

He hesitated, wanting to be chivalrous but knowing that we couldn't leave the room looking like it did. The place was a mess. "Are you sure you can't wait?"

"I'll be fine," I promised him.

Tristen seemed torn. "If you're sure you'll be safe . . ."

"I'm sure," I said, moving toward the door. I didn't kiss him good night. I wasn't sure if I was supposed to or if he'd want me to, so I took a path that would keep us separated by the rows of lab tables. But I paused at the door. "I'm . . . I'm happy for you, Tristen," I said. It seemed like a lame thing to say, but nothing else came to mind. "I'm really happy."

Tristen watched me, seeming disappointed at how the night was ending. He sounded almost sad as he said, "Thank you, Jill. Thank you for everything."

"Good night," I said, slipping into the dark hallway.

It wasn't until much later that I wondered why Tristen had seemed so gloomy when I'd left him. As I rushed home in the dark, I was too busy searching my own soul. Trying to figure out why I'd filled four vials . . . and left only three on the lab table.

Yes, I really did feel sick that night.

Running up to my bedroom, I stood by my bed, untucked my shirt from my jeans, and let the fourth vial—the one I'd stolen—fall to the mattress.

If I hadn't been so focused on trying to understand my own behavior, my own motives, maybe I would have figured out why Tristen had gotten so somber.

Maybe I would have guessed at what he was about to do.

And maybe I would have thought more about what I'd seen inside the novel that Tristen had snatched from my hands.

The bloodstain just under his name.

Chapter 48

Tristen

I WOKE EARLY from a sleep that was less troubled but still plagued by dreams. New nightmares in which I—not a faceless girl—suffered and died. And when dawn finally arrived, the sunlight filtering into my room didn't reassure me at all. It only made the shadows—the *foreshadows*—of the previous night seem to grow deeper.

How many times would I need to face death—need to kill or be killed, perhaps—in the course one lifetime? In the course of one *week?* Not to complain, but didn't I deserve a day or two without murder on the mind? Didn't I merit a normal *date* with Jill?

And what had come over her the night before? The sweet, quiet girl I'd thought I might kiss for months before getting so much as a hand under one of those lacy shirts had all but attacked me. Had it just been excitement over my return from what must have looked—and what had definitely felt—like death? Or was Jill just inexperienced, not sure how to behave in a situation that might have been new to her?

That definitely seemed possible.

I stared at my bedroom ceiling, troubled by more than just Jill's behavior as my eyes began to follow a familiar, long and thick crack in the plaster. A fissure I sometimes pictured as one line in a grand staff—the grid upon which musicians compose. My imagination could easily build the rest, and when I couldn't sleep, I often amused myself by mentally arranging notes there, creating dark melodies in my dim room. But that morning all I could see was a crack that desperately needed repair. No melody came, and that made the fracture seem ominous somehow.

Had I ended more than just deviant desires when I'd banished the beast in me?

Down the hall my father stirred, his mattress creaking, and I rolled over to sit upright, thinking that I had no time for pointless worry.

I was the ward of a monster. I had more bloody work to do.

Standing, I pulled on a sweatshirt and went quietly down the hall to the kitchen, where I measured out three scoops of coffee, dumped them into a filter, poured some water into the reservoir, and turned on the machine. Soon the kitchen was filled with the strong aroma of brewing coffee—which effectively masked the fainter smell of the good-sized dose of formula that I poured into my father's usual mug, glancing again and again over my shoulder, worried that the beast might pad silently into the kitchen and find me trying to slay him.

Oh, that would not go well for me.

"You're up early, Tristen."

I had just stashed the empty vial in a high cupboard—was still reaching up to close the door—when I heard him behind me, and I tensed. "Yes, I have an exam today," I said. "I'm going in early to study."

Look at him, Tristen. Act normally.

I turned slowly, relieved to find that he was still groggy, yawning in his robe and pajamas. Apparently neither soul, thank God, functioned well in the morning.

"I made coffee," I said, knowing that I had just a few moments to trick him. He had to drink out of habit, without thinking or even looking. Although the formula was dark, it wasn't as black as coffee. I handed him the mug, handle out, so he wouldn't feel that that the ceramic was cool, lying, "It's piping hot, just as you like it."

He accepted the mug, rubbing his eyes. "Thank you, Tristen."

Drink. Just drink. I turned away and reached for my own cup, not wanting to appear unusually eager to watch him. But my hand fumbled as I poured my share of coffee. *Is he drinking? Is he?*

"Tristen?"

My blood froze, but I set the pot back onto the machine. "Yes?"

"What were you reaching for up in that high cabinet? What do we store there?"

"I was looking for more coffee," I improvised. "I thought we'd bought some, but it seems to have disappeared."

"Oh."

Had he still not taken a sip? Why wasn't he doubled over in pain? I had to see what the hell he was doing . . .

I turned to face him, unable to bear the suspense any longer, certain by then that he was suspicious. That my plan had failed.

When I saw his face, I knew that I was right.

I was also, unfortunately, a split second too late.

Chapter 49

Tristen

"HOW DARE YOU?" the beast roared as the mug full of formula smashed behind my head, which I'd ducked just in time. But having my back turned for so long—it had put me at a disadvantage. Because my face had been averted, I hadn't seen him silently withdraw the knife from the butcher block holder.

"Dad!" I cried as he slammed into me, shoving me against the cabinets with one powerful hand around my throat, banging my head so hard that I felt my skull crack the thin wood. "DAD!"

He wasn't my father. And yet what other name could I use? I writhed as he crushed my windpipe and then shoved back against his shoulders. "Dad, don't!"

The beast squeezed harder, pinning me with astonishing strength.

My father, I was fairly certain that I could have beaten him in a fight. I was younger and stronger. But this thing that I battled, it drew its power from pure evil and held me easily even as I struggled. A struggle that I abandoned entirely when he slowly, deliberately raised the knife, jabbing the point beneath my chin—using the tip first to subdue me and then compel me to turn my face so that we were eye to hideous eye.

Licking his lips, he slid the blade to the tender, defenseless spot close to my throat. A place where it seemed, if he thrust upward, I would feel the metal plunge all the way into my brain.

I remained as still as possible, watching him, battling my ragged breathing, afraid that I might slip and do *myself* in. But my eyes rolled wildly, looking at anything, anything other than his eyes, so fearful was I of what I might see there. Or what he might perceive as missing within me.

"Look at me," he finally snarled, jabbing the knife deeper into my flesh.

Gagging from the pressure, enough that he relented a little, I forced myself to meet his gray eyes. His vicious gray eyes. And when I did, I could not look away again.

In the beast before me there was no trace of my father. No trace of sanity or humanity. How could I not have seen that before? How could the monster have fooled me in the months since my father had typed that last journal entry?

Already, though, I knew the truth. I hadn't *wanted* to see the beast. I had, to some degree, fooled myself. I'd seen glimpses of the reality that stared me down in that kitchen and then, as I had just moments before, averted my gaze.

But the monster that threatened to impale my head on a short pike had no compunction about seeing into *my* soul. He stared hard into my eyes, realization dawning.

"What have you done, Tristen?" he thundered, his hot breath rank and sickening. He shook me with the hand that clutched my throat, allowing me just enough air to survive. "WHAT THE HELL HAVE YOU DONE?"

"You know . . . what I've done." I gasped. "And I could help you, too, Dad."

"Your father is GONE," the beast spat. "Beyond help! I AM HIM!"

"I don't believe it," I said, looking deeper into his eyes, searching for any trace of my father, the slightest hint that Dad still existed, caged somewhere deep within the thing that held me. "I can help you! I've found the cure!"

Later, when the dust had settled, I would always wonder if I had somehow reached Dad and saved my life, because the beast hesitated for a split second, the blade at my throat withdrawing another fraction of an inch, and his eyes shifted, softening.

And then, with a mighty roar, he withdrew the knife completely, drew his hand back, and slashed the blade across my cheek, causing drops of blood to spatter on the white refrigerator before I could press my hand against the wound, nearly falling as he released my throat—only to crack my wrist against the sharp edge of the counter so violently and efficiently that I heard bones snap, and dropped to my knees, forgetting my bleeding face as I clutched at my smashed arm.

How could he . . . ? To me . . . ?

I raised my face to his—the familiar yet completely alien features—betrayed by the obscene violence, irrationally thinking, *But we're blood.*

But of course we weren't blood. The monster that stood over me wasn't my father. And I no longer harbored the beast that *he* had considered his son. His heir.

I had killed *his* child.

"Where is the formula?" he growled, glaring down. "Get it and drink it again! Undo what you've done!"

"I don't have any more," I lied.

"Make more!"

I shook my head. "No. Never."

He still held the knife and drew back that hand, but it was the back of his fist, not the blade, that I felt against my face, snapping my head sideways.

For some reason that was the last straw. The final indignity. "You killed my mother, and I'm going to *slaughter* you," I snarled, trying to rise to my feet. But when I placed weight on my shattered wrist, I nearly buckled, and he easily kicked me back to my knees.

"You'll want the formula again," he said, starting to smile: a warped, triumphant grin. "You're a Hyde, and you will long for that side of you."

"No. Never."

"You will, Tristen," he promised, crooked smile disappearing. "If only I could have fooled you a little longer. If only I could have lured you along until you felt the thrill of a trusting, innocent thing perishing in your arms. You were so close to killing her, Tristen. Killing that girl you love, just as I *did* kill your mother."

Although I already knew that, I nearly puked to hear him finally confess—and with such satisfaction in his voice. I actually felt the vomit rise into my throat. I really had been living with my mother's killer. "No . . ."

"Oh yes, Tristen," he confirmed. "And had you experienced that just once, enjoyed the incomparable sensation of taking your lover's very life, you would have joined me, willingly." He scowled at me, dragging the sleeve of his robe across his mouth, wiping away some spittle that flecked his lips and beard. "You *will* join me . . . *son.*"

No. I wasn't like that. I'd proven it with Jill. I'd stopped the beast *and* myself.

"Never," I insisted again as the kitchen started to grow dim. I could feel the blood coursing down my face, and the bones grinding in my wrist as I struggled again to stand, determined to fight. "I won't . . ."

"I'll give you time to come to your senses, Tristen, because I have long held high hopes for you," he said. "You are the best of our lineage, and I am as yet unwilling to give you up for lost. *As yet.*"

"Never!" I vowed one last time, even as the room grew black around me. "I'll die before I drink it again!"

"You *will* drink again," he said, actually starting to laugh. "And of your own desire and your own free will."

I felt myself swaying on my knees, losing my bearings. "And if I don't?"

I heard him stop laughing, and although his reply seemed to come from far away, I didn't miss the warning, just before I blacked out.

"I will finish what I started here."

Chapter 50

Jill

"JILL, I JUST ASKED YOU what I'm supposed to do with this stuff," Becca nudged me, holding up a beaker. "You're, like, in a fog today."

With effort I dragged my gaze away from Tristen's empty lab station and tried to remember what Becca and I were doing. "Just pour that into the other flask," I said, too distracted to care about being precise.

I couldn't help looking at Tristen's table again. Where was he? Obviously something had gone wrong...

"Jill, will you turn around and help me?" Becca asked, sounding irritated. "Tristen's not here, okay? Just let it go. I'm doing everything, and it's not fair!"

"Sorry," I said, but absently and without moving to help her. I kept staring at the empty spot where Tristen should have been standing, imagining all sorts of awful possibilities. Like Tristen waking up from a nightmare to realize that the beast hadn't really been defeated and stumbling to his bathroom, getting a razor, and holding it to his wrist... Oh, the blood-soaked scenes that I couldn't stop imagining...

Yet I was still unprepared when the whole class gasped, and Becca blurted out, loudly, "Oh, my god! What in the world happened to him?"

Chapter 51

Jill

TRISTEN STRODE THROUGH the classroom in the heart of a silence that rang louder than applause. It was an ovation of shock as he walked toward his lab station with complete self-possession, like he was oblivious to the stares.

I stared, too, in horror at the wide gash across his cheek and at his arm, which was wrapped in what looked like a torn T-shirt. Although his wrist was bound tightly, his hand hung crooked, like a mad doctor had sliced it off and botched its reattachment.

"It's about time somebody finally beat the hell out of him," Flick muttered under his breath, breaking the silence. "I wish it ended *his* damn season."

"Shut up," I snapped, wheeling on Todd.

Flick reared back, seeming more surprised maybe by my outburst than Tristen's injuries. I saw him start to reply, and I kept glaring at him, not caring for once that he was the most popular guy in school. Eventually, Todd shut his mouth, and it crossed my mind that I'd wasted so much time taking crap from him when all along I could have silenced him just with a look. I thought I was smart, but even after months of watching Darcy Gray control Todd like the pretty, plastic Ken doll that he was, I hadn't learned until that moment that I had the same power.

Unfortunately, though, Darcy had to have her say, too. "I told you he was violent," she said to me, sounding like she didn't care about Tristen at all. He might as well have been a broken burner at a lab station. "I warned you, Jill."

I glared at Darcy, too, thinking that she had no idea what had happened to Tristen. He could have been in a car accident for all she knew. But Darcy Gray was so sure that she knew *everything* that she took her assumptions as truth. I hated that, hated that she was right and hated myself because, even though I'd just snapped at Todd, I still couldn't bring myself to contradict Darcy.

I turned around to watch Tristen as he took his seat, wincing when he rested his wrist on the table.

His dad had hurt him; I was sure of it. The whole story seemed so obvious as I looked at the dark slash across his face. Of course Tristen had tried to cure his dad when he'd gone home last night. And somehow it had gone wrong. How could I have not foreseen that? I'd been too busy worrying about my own strange behavior . . .

"That's enough," Mr. Messerschmidt announced, starting to walk toward Tristen. "Stop staring and get back to work."

Following our teacher's instruction, I turned back to my experiment. But I couldn't stop glancing over my shoulder to watch Mr. Messerschmidt conferring with Tristen.

What were they discussing? What in the world would Mr. Messerschmidt say that would actually cause Tristen Hyde to look *interested?*

"Hey, Jill." Becca tapped my shoulder. "This experiment is graded, remember?"

For once I didn't care. Not about my grade or Becca's. I kept watching the conference at the back of the room.

Watching and wondering . . . why wouldn't Tristen look at *me?*

Chapter 52

Tristen

THE LAST THING I wanted to endure, beyond the stares of my classmates, was a lecture from my chemistry instructor. Wasn't I in pain enough?

Yet there he was waddling toward me, a concerned look on his fleshy face. "Tristen," he said, surprising me by using my first name. Since I'd met Messerschmidt the previous year, I'd always been "Mr. Hyde," which he seemed to intend to wield with sarcasm but which always came out gratifyingly deferential. "What happened?" he asked. "Did you fight again?"

"No."

My teacher shook his head. "Tristen . . ."

I struggled to unzip my bag and retrieve my textbook, using only my left hand, but the process was awkward. "It's nothing," I snapped, irritated by Messerschmidt's nosiness and my own clumsy movements. "Nothing."

He wasn't buying it, and leaned closer to me, lowering his voice. "Tristen, I've been teaching for nearly twenty years, and I've seen lots of cases like yours."

In spite of my pain and frustration I nearly smiled. He had? He knew of other chemically-induced half-monsters whose lives were chronicled in classic fiction?

Messerschmidt wasn't talking about my particular predicament, though. He was talking about something more common—and he was almost presciently on target. "I've seen domestic violence," he said very quietly. "Sometimes fathers and sons fight, especially if there's no mother to intervene."

I dropped the textbook to the table with a thud and wheeled on Messerschmidt. "Don't bring up my mother," I warned in a whisper, suddenly defensive. My mother was a victim, and certainly not to *blame* for the male Hydes' struggles. I turned away and began slapping at the pages, looking for the day's experiment, ignoring my teacher. Then I shot him a sharp, accusing—and suspicious—look. "And what do you know about my mother? My home life?"

Messerschmidt fumbled with his tie and cleared his throat. "Um . . . I just . . . I've just heard that you and your father live alone."

"That's not your business," I advised him, staring hard into his dull eyes until he looked away.

I resumed turning pages, not even sure at that point what I was looking for, and Messerschmidt stayed by my side, watching me struggle with the book.

Eventually, exasperated, I looked to him again. "Is there something more? Because I'm falling behind with the day's work."

Mr. Messerschmidt didn't seem insulted by my tone or angry. He didn't make one of his weak attempts at disciplining me. Instead he leaned closer again and said, "I just want you to know, Tristen, that if there is a problem, I could help you. I have room in my house, even, if you need a safe place to stay for a while."

I stared at him, shocked by the suggestion. I couldn't imagine living with Mr. Messerschmidt even for one night, but the offer made me feel a bit guilty for venting my anger on him. "Thanks," I said with grudging gratitude, "but everything is fine at home."

Messerschmidt pulled a pen and small pad from his breast pocket and scrawled a note. "Here's my number and address," he said, holding it out.

I didn't extend my hand. I honestly didn't think I needed a place to stay. I'd awakened to find the beast gone—along with most of my father's clothes, and I took that to mean I was living alone until he decided to confront me again. "No thanks," I declined.

"Take it." Messerschmidt shook the paper at me. "You might need it."

"Fine." I accepted the information, jamming it into my pocket. Then I shoved my book back into my bag and slung that over my shoulder, because I was obviously getting nowhere with my experiment, and—truth be told—I was having a difficult time dealing with Jill's presence in the room. Even more than I'd expected.

I wanted to look to her, but what if I saw pity in her eyes, too? Pity or, worse yet, *love?*

Wouldn't it be cruel to become more deeply involved with a girl who'd just suffered one loss to violence when I knew the odds against my own survival were even at best? I tried to move my wrist and flinched. Perhaps far less than even.

"I'm going to take off," I told Messerschmidt.

He didn't remind me that the bell wasn't close to ringing. "Take care, Tristen," he said. "And use that number if you want. Any time, day or night."

"Perhaps," I said.

"And Tristen," Messerschmidt added with a hand on my good arm.

"What?"

"Don't try to get revenge," he cautioned. "Adding violence to violence . . . it's never a good idea."

I couldn't help but smile at that. Violence to violence to violence, down through the generations. That was the Hyde way. Even finding the cure to the madness couldn't seem to stop the cycle entirely.

"See you around," I told him, walking toward the door.

Some of my classmates actually edged aside as I passed, as if I might beat the hell out of them if they got too close. I didn't check the expression on Jill's face.

Stepping out of the room, I closed the door behind me, shutting them all out, and pulled Messerschmidt's contact information from my pocket, opening it and reading. It had been nice of him to want to help. For just a moment it had felt kind of good, too, to think that I had an ally. Even a weak one.

Then I crumpled the paper, before I could memorize the information, and tossed it to the floor.

What I needed to do, I had to do alone.

Chapter 53

Jill

TRISTEN LEFT CLASS without ever even looking at me, and I somehow managed to help Becca finish our experiment, and eventually the bell rang, ending the longest, most miserable class I could ever remember living through.

"Jill." Becca stopped me as we headed out the door. "Can we talk?"

My eyes darted, checking up and down the corridor, like Tristen might miraculously appear. "I can't right now, Becca."

"It's important," she said, snagging my arm. "It's about you and me and—"

I pulled away, already knowing what she was about to say. She was going to ask about cheating again. Our first big exam was looming fast, and I'd been waiting for her to bring up the subject again. But how could she even think about the test? Hadn't she seen Tristen? Didn't she know somebody had to help him?

"I've gotta go," I said, walking away from her. "We'll talk later, maybe."

I left her standing in the hall, and without even really thinking about what I was doing, I headed for the main door at the front of the building—and I walked right *out,* in the middle of the day, without a pass.

Running home, I dug in the junk drawer in the kitchen until I found an old set of keys. Then I ran out to the garage and yanked the dirty tarp off Dad's Volvo and hopped in and turned over the engine, which took about three tries. The tires, which were low on air, seemed to stick to the garage floor when I first hit what was left of the gas. I pressed harder, they pulled loose, and I backed out into the sunlight.

Tristen had been right. Driving the car . . . it was okay. I hardly thought about what had happened maybe on the very seat where I sat. As much as the crime still haunted me, and would always define my life to some degree, I guess I was too busy worrying about the bloodshed that might be ahead to agonize over blood shed in the past.

Chapter 54

Tristen

I STRETCHED OUT on my bed, eyes closed, trying to concentrate. Was there *anything* that I could do to prepare? To better my odds when the inevitable showdown occurred?

I could think of nothing, so I lay there, resting and aching—and waiting.

I finally managed to sleep, only to be awakened by a light touch on my shoulder. "What?" I started, rolling to my side and pushing myself upright, forgetting my broken bones—until a sharp pain tore through my body.

"Oh, hell," I groaned, resting back, hurt but relieved. And yet dismayed, too, for my visitor wasn't a beast intent on claiming my soul. It was Jill Jekel, the other person I'd wanted to avoid, even though I'd known that meeting was inevitable, too.

In fact, a part of me was almost more scared to face Jill than to grapple with the monster, because the more I thought about it, the more certain I was that Jill and I shouldn't become more deeply involved. It would be wrong, selfish, to draw Jill closer, only to get myself killed, and I knew that I should fight my desire to be with her, lean on her. Yet looking into Jill's worried, warm hazel eyes, I knew the odds of me winning that battle were even worse than my odds of winning against the beast.

Chapter 55

Tristen

"JILL, YOU SHOULDN'T BE HERE," I said, sitting up again, more carefully, and holding my throbbing wrist. "My father might come here, and I'm not sure I can protect you."

"I'm not scared," Jill said softly, kneeling beside me, studying my face, "just worried about you."

Once again I was struck by how brave she was when it really counted. Just a few weeks before she'd been nervous about being alone with me in her own house, almost refused to allow me inside. But now, when I was in trouble and the stakes were truly high— when we might be interrupted by a monster bent on killing at least one of us—Jill had her back to the door, not concerned for her own safety. Worried only about *my* welfare.

"Let me see your wrist, Tristen," she said, gently taking my wrecked arm in her hands. "It doesn't look like it's set right."

I let her cradle and turn the shattered bones. "It was tricky to do on my own with one hand."

She began to unwind my makeshift bandage, working carefully, her touch feather light. "You should have called me or gone to a hospital. Or both."

"I couldn't do either of those things," I said. "I don't want you to be involved. And I don't want any authorities involved, either." My voice grew thick with emotions I'd suppressed. Feelings that I hadn't even known I harbored. "He's my *father*, Jill."

She turned her face up to mine, and I knew that she was thinking about her own dad, who'd betrayed her, leading a double life and stealing her college savings. Yet Jill wouldn't have turned in her father, either. Not until there was literally no other way—if then, even. What a strange but powerful bond of misery and betrayal and loyalty we shared.

After a moment of silent understanding Jill resumed unwinding my bandage, and although I knew that I should order her to leave, I let her stay. I didn't think the Jill Jekel who went wordlessly to the cabinet in my bathroom—returning with alcohol, a washcloth, and a pair of scissors—that girl wouldn't have listened to me, anyway.

Somewhere along the way, as she dabbed the damp cloth against the gash on my cheek, shushing me softly when I muttered a curse but holding my chin firmly in place, I ceded my dominant role in our relationship, and Jill assumed her proper place as full partner. Never again would I call all the shots—and that was all right by me. I had grown tired of self-sufficiency, anyway.

"That looks better," she said, stepping back and observing her work. She glanced around the room. "Do you have something I could cut up to make a new bandage?"

I nodded toward a pile of clothes, heaped in a plastic basket. "Those are clean."

"Okay." She dug in the laundry and chose a white T-shirt. Sitting down next to me, she took the scissors and bent her head, cutting a neat, long strip of fabric. "Give me your arm again," she said, moving my hand to her lap.

"Oh, shit," I complained through gritted teeth as she wound the new bandage around my broken bone.

"Tristen!" she chided me, but softly. And when she turned her face to mine, I saw a trace of amusement in her eyes, in spite of the awful circumstances. "That's enough."

"I'll try harder," I promised, digging the fingers of my good hand into the mattress as Jill returned to caring for me, tenderly but firmly moving my hand until it aligned better with my arm. The pain was almost unbearable, and to keep myself from passing out, I tried to focus on her profile. The faint flush of nervous exertion on her cheek, the way she bit her pale, pink lower lip as she concentrated, the serious furrow of her brow as if she suffered, too, to cause me pain: I focused on all those things, reminding myself that I needed to be alert to protect her if the beast returned and found us there.

"I think we're done, Tristen," Jill finally said, tying off the bandage and standing. "You should rest now."

I didn't argue and lay back on the bed, closing my eyes, thinking that in a few minutes I would feel stronger, and then I really *would* send Jill on her way.

I listened as she cleaned up the bloody cloth and the unused fabric. Then, while my eyes were still closed—before I could tell her to go—the mattress creaked and sagged next to me, and I felt a small warm, strong body lie down next to mine, and a tentative arm drape across my chest so lightly that I barely felt the pressure.

I didn't think it was possible, but I soon found myself drifting toward sleep again, dozing lightly, awakening now and then to feel Jill's arm still resting on me. At least, I thought I merely dozed, and that only minutes passed. Yet when I awoke fully, feeling more rested than I had in a long time, I realized that the room had started to grow dim—and Jill's arm was tighter around me, her body pressed even closer to mine.

How far Jill had come since that night at her house when I'd first tried to kiss her and felt her shyness, her inexperience. And then there had been that strange night in the lab . . .

I shifted and turned to Jill, suddenly uneasy, as if I might find myself face-to-face on the pillow with that frantic creature, whom I nearly hadn't recognized.

But no, I saw nothing more than sweetness in her eyes, which blinked at me, inches away. Sweetness and tenderness and a hint of the uncertainty that I'd expected she would have when the time came for us to be together like this.

Neither of us speaking—both understanding what was happening—I stroked her cheek with my bandaged hand, not really caring that it ached to touch her. At my very subtle pressure against her shoulder, Jill shifted more to her back, and I managed to rise up, relying on my good arm to brace myself but resting a little heavily on her as we began to kiss, lips barely brushing, not rushing, just savoring being together.

This . . . this was how I wanted to be with her. Not the way she'd been on that first night in the lab, when we'd both gone a little insane.

"Tristen," she murmured as I settled more completely against her, sliding my hand under the hem of her blouse, caressing the soft skin just above her hip. "Oh, Tristen." She rested her hand against my bicep, testing my muscle—and tensed beneath me.

"It's okay," I whispered, reassuring her, wondering if she'd flashed back to the terrible, wonderful night when we'd first kissed. "It's okay," I promised again, and felt her relax, soften. She was so, so soft. Her breath against mine, the trace of skin above her hip, her own touch on my skin.

We lay that way for a long time, kissing more deeply, more intensely, Jill slowly gaining confidence, moving her hand into my hair, stroking it as our tongues met again and again, but still I didn't try to go further. Not yet. She would let me know when she was ready. She would give me some small sign, and until that time I would content myself with giving her what she wanted and nothing more. I would never be that monster again, would not even come close to pressuring her.

"Tristen." She murmured my name when our lips parted. "Tristen?"

I drew back, moving my injured hand to stroke her cheek again, and she opened her eyes. "What, Jill?" I whispered, mesmerized by the changeable color of those remarkable eyes. "What is it?"

I waited expectantly.

I wanted to hear her *say* what I saw in those eyes. That she loved me.

I'd thought of saying those words to Jill a dozen times as we'd kissed but ultimately held back. I could tell that Jill, too, was on the verge and—selfish me—I wanted to be told first, not hear my words echoed back to me.

"Tristen," she whispered, caressing my face, too, her eyes filling with tears. Good tears. The kind of tears that Jill Jekel deserved. Not a torrent of stinging salt water into an open grave but the slightest trickle onto *my* pillow. "I . . ."

But before she could give me what I really wanted—as much, if not more, than kissing her, touching her—the telephone shrieked in the hallway, and we both froze, the moment shattered.

Under any other circumstance I would have let that phone scream until dawn. But my father was a hostage, in a sense, and I was awaiting orders from his captor. "I'm sorry, Jill," I whispered, meaning that more than I'd ever meant it in my entire life.

"Get it, Tristen," she urged, seeming to understand what was going on, although I'd never told her exactly what had happened between the beast and me. "Hurry."

I kissed her once more, quickly, not knowing at the time that I should have savored it more, and went to answer the phone, leaving Jill alone in my room.

Chapter 56

Jill

I WAITED IN TRISTEN'S BED, listening to the sound of his voice as he answered the phone.

Me . . . I was *in Tristen's bed.*

What would have happened if the phone hadn't started ringing?

I'd gotten caught up in the moment, so much that I'd almost admitted that I *loved* him. But what we were doing, it scared me as much as it excited me. I'd felt the muscle in Tristen's arm, and when he'd rested more squarely on top of me, I'd felt . . . *him.* Every hard inch of his body pressing against me. The realization, the *reality,* had been wonderful and thrilling and completely terrifying.

I'd been *in bed* with a guy. A guy who was clearly ready to do more than just kiss, which was itself still new to me.

Down the hall Tristen kept talking. I could hear his deep, *masculine* voice.

What would we do when he came back? Kiss some more? Talk about . . . condoms? Did he *have* condoms? Would he ask if I took the pill? Or would he assume that I didn't? Would my obvious inexperience be enough of a clue?

Sitting up, skin hot and prickly, I crawled off the bed.

I hadn't meant for us even to kiss when I'd climbed in next to Tristen. I'd figured he was too hurt and too exhausted to even think about . . . what we'd been doing. But suddenly it had started happening, anyway, when he'd sort of pressed my shoulder back to the mattress—which I'd wanted but . . .

I started moving nervously around his bedroom, not sure what I should do and getting kind of frustrated with myself.

That girl who'd kissed Tristen in the chemistry lab, the one who'd come out when I tasted the formula in his mouth, she wouldn't be tugging down the hem of her blouse like she was trying to stop his fingers from moving up any farther. No, that girl would have taken *off* some clothes. But I wasn't her . . .

I kept pacing, moving to Tristen's desk. That's when I saw, buried under some other books, his first edition copy of *Jekyll and Hyde*. The novel that he obviously wanted to keep out of my reach.

Down the hall, Tristen was still talking. I couldn't make out what he said, but I knew the caller wasn't his father like he'd hoped. Or feared. He was too calm, and he sounded kind of formal, like he was on the line with somebody he didn't know very well.

In front of me the forbidden book sat, tempting me. Why wasn't I supposed to see it? I'd let Tristen *keep* my family's most important things. What was he keeping from me? Didn't I have a right to know everything about him? We were sharing a *bed* . . .

On impulse I darted out my hand and slid the novel from under the other books, flipping it open to the inscription that I'd caught a glimpse of back in the classroom.

To Tristen, with gratitude for being strong when I was weak. Never, ever doubt that your actions were just, despite how the world . . . judge Keep . . . remem . . . me

I couldn't make out some of the words, and the writing, which was faint to begin with, got more scrawling and erratic as it ran across the page. And there were the smudges that I'd noticed before, just under the signature. A wide smear and a smaller fingerprint. I knew that I was looking at blood because I'd seen plenty of it.

I peered more closely. Blood, just like my dad's on the list of salts . . .

"Jill? What are you doing?"

My head snapped up, the book snapped shut in my hands, and I spun around to see Tristen standing in the doorway with his arms crossed, watching me.

"Tristen," I stammered, torn between guilt and a vague, but very real, unease, "what, exactly, did you *do?*"

Chapter 57

Jill

"JILL, I'VE TOLD YOU not to touch that," Tristen said, moving into the room and closing the door behind him. His eyes were a little cold, like he was mad at me. "It's private."

My cheeks flushed with embarrassment over getting caught, but I held my ground and didn't put down the book. "But, Tristen, I've shared *everything* with you." Well, *almost* everything . . .

He came even closer to me and gently but firmly pried the novel out of my fingers. "Jill," he said, and I noticed that his face was pale. "I don't think you want to know everything about me."

I looked up at him, shaking my head. "That's not fair, Tristen. You can't decide that for me."

He was keeping a secret. A bad secret.

Awful secrets were like bloodstains in my life. I knew enough about them to recognize them before they'd even been revealed. The evasive, haunted look in Tristen's eyes told me everything I needed to know—except for the truth itself. "What happened, Tristen?" I demanded. "I deserve to know."

We'd just been in bed together. I'd shared with him the key to banishing his own demons and stayed by him when he'd nearly died. He owed me the truth. Tristen had an obligation to explain the strange dedication . . . and that *bloodstain.*

"Oh, Jill," he said, cracking easily, like maybe he'd secretly longed for a confidant. He set down the novel and dragged his good hand through his hair, eyes no longer cold. On the contrary, he looked guilt ridden and grief stricken. "I don't know how to tell you this," he said. "I wasn't sure if it was even true until recently. I *hoped* it wasn't true, and tried to convince myself . . ."

"It's okay, Tristen," I said. But I felt scared. "Just say it."

His cheeks got even paler, and his lips were a thin, white line, but he met my eyes as he stated, very directly, "I murdered my grandfather, Jill."

Chapter 58

Jill

"WHAT?" I WANTED HIM to repeat that, because I hoped I hadn't heard right. "Tell me again, Tristen."

"I killed my grandfather," he said. "Or the beast did, through me."

We stood facing each other, his body blocking the door that I wanted to run through. "How?" I asked. My voice sounded strangled. "What did you . . . ?"

"A knife." He winced like a blade was slashing *him* again. "That seems to be the way it prefers to kill."

I knew that Tristen wasn't really responsible for whatever had happened to his grandfather. Logically I knew that he wasn't to blame. I'd seen him change, and I knew that the beast was something separate from the boy I loved. But I still found myself staring at his hands—which had plunged a blade into his own flesh and blood. A man he'd loved . . . who had given him the gift of music, of composing. Tristen's hands had wielded the knife . . .

In my confused mind the images got tangled with imagined scenes of my dad being slaughtered, a knife dragged across his windpipe. "No, Tristen!" I cried, shaking my head. "I don't believe you did it!"

"*I* didn't do it, Jill," he said. But he didn't sound sure himself. "I mean, my body performed the act. But it wasn't me. You were there that night when I changed . . ."

I heard him, and I knew he was right, but my shock and horror overcame reason. I'd been lying next to a killer. Not a *potential* killer like Tristen had feared becoming but a *real* killer. Somebody who'd already shed blood. I kept shaking my head, backing away from him. Those fingers had just been touching me . . . "No, Tristen."

He stepped toward me, hand out, talking more quickly, the confession spilling out. "Please. Try to understand. My grandfather *begged* me to help him die. He knew the terrible things *he'd* done, and he couldn't live with himself anymore. He was bedridden, nearly paralyzed, and all day and all night, long-repressed memories flooded back, torturing him. He *implored* me to steal pills from my father, a lethal dose, but I couldn't do it. I loved him too much to lose him forever. I was selfish, too selfish to end his misery."

"Tristen . . ." I backed farther away, bumping against the wall in a room that was starting to get dark. Too dark. "Stop!"

He followed my retreat, confining me in the effort to reassure me. "You've got to understand, Jill. Grandfather *provoked* the beast inside of me, summoning it on purpose. He taunted me, calling me a coward, weak—too weak to face the truth about our family. And he spoke about the thrill of killing, talking directly to the monster, urging it to emerge, to have its way with a knife, to take its first satisfaction on *his* flesh. I begged him to stop . . ."

Although Tristen confessed without the slightest quiver in his voice, I saw a tear trace down his cheek, but my blood was so cold that I couldn't feel sympathy. I couldn't feel anything.

"I don't remember anything else," he said. "When I came to myself, I was at home, my hands spotless when the police arrived to say that grandfather had been found by his cleaning woman, dead in his bed, his wrists slit with a butcher knife. Suicide, they concluded." His eyes darted to the novel. "But I had the bloody book, and it had been inscribed. I tried to tell myself that, at worst, the beast had given him the knife. But I was kidding myself. Grandfather could barely use a pen, and his one arm had been cut to the *bone* . . ."

195

Tristen closed his eyes, grinding his palms against them, maybe shutting out the images or maybe punishing himself by crushing his broken wrist against his skull. "I've never said this aloud before. Oh, god, Jill . . ."

He was in agony. But I didn't reach out to him.

I used the opportunity when Tristen's eyes were closed to dart past him and run through the house, tearing out the door, jumping off the porch, and scrambling into my car. My fingers were so shaky that I seemed to take forever to lock myself in. Then I jammed the key in the ignition and pressed hard on the gas pedal, spinning out of the driveway and tearing across the grass in my desperation to get away, put space between us.

I looked back only once, checking the rearview mirror as Tristen's house got smaller in the distance.

I didn't see him standing on the porch.

I didn't think he even tried to follow me.

Chapter 59

Jill

IT HAD BEEN A LONG TIME since I'd needed Mom to hold me while I cried. Even when Dad had died, I'd understood that she was in no shape to be strong for me. But driving home from Tristen's, fighting back tears, all I could think was *I want my mom*.

As I parked the car in the garage, I saw a light on in her bedroom, and I hurried inside, running upstairs and knocking on her closed door. "Mom?"

"Come in!"

I opened the door, planning to fling myself into her arms. I knew that I couldn't tell her about Tristen, not what we'd almost done that evening or what he had done in England. But I thought I could at least say I'd had a terrible day at school and needed a hug.

But when I saw her, I stopped in my tracks. "Mom?"

Was she wearing a *dress?*

"How do I look, Jill?" She smoothed her skirt, seeming uncertain. "Is this okay?"

"You look great," I told her, not understanding. The dress was a black one she used to wear to nice restaurants when Dad would take her out. "Are you going somewhere?"

"Just out with friends," she said, turning her back on me and facing her mirror. "Some people from work."

"Oh." I fidgeted in the doorway, unsure, too. I still wanted to run to Mom. But she looked almost . . . happy. Who was I to intrude on that?

Mom must have misunderstood my mood, because she added over her shoulder, "I hope you don't mind. I know I should try to get some extra hours at the hospital now that I'm doing better. But Frederick thinks it's important for me to have fun, too."

Frederick. The beast who'd brought my mother back from the brink of oblivion. He'd healed my mother, but he was dangerous and *violent* . . . just like Tristen.

"Mom," I said, struggling not just with my sorrow but with sudden fear for my mom's safety, "do you think you still need to see Dr. Hyde? I mean, you seem like you're a *lot* better."

"Yes, Frederick agrees." She smoothed her hair, eyes fixed on her reflection. "I'm not seeing him professionally anymore."

I was so relieved by that news and so caught up in my own misery, my heartbreak, that I overlooked one key word.

"I'm going to my room," I said when Mom kept staring at her reflection, seeming to forget about me. A small smile played on her lips, and I *knew* I couldn't burden her with my sadness. "I'm kind of tired," I added. "I might go to bed early."

"Okay, Jill." Mom flipped open her jewelry box, chose an earring, and stuck the post into her ear. "I'll see you in the morning. Keep the doors locked!"

"Sure," I agreed, closing her door as tears started to well in my eyes again. Would my mother ever be there for me again? Tristen certainly wouldn't . . .

I wasn't sure how I held myself together as I walked down the hall to my room. Tristen had committed murder. His secret had become my burden, had destroyed us, left me completely alone again.

When I shut myself in my room, I let the tears come flooding out, but as quietly as possible, burying my face in my pillow until Mom rapped on my door and called goodbye. When I heard the back door slam closed I really sobbed. But it didn't help. Maybe I'd cried so often in the past year that tears didn't hold the power they used to. They certainly didn't wash away the anger and the hurt.

I *wouldn't* give my heart, my soul, my body to somebody who had ended a human life—especially in the bloody, violent way that my dad's life had been snuffed out.

Tristen should have been stronger, when his grandfather had begged for death.

He hadn't fought hard enough.

No. I would not love Tristen Hyde.

But the whole time I cried, a small voice inside of me kept protesting that I still *did* love Tristen.

That voice . . . that's what drove me to unzip the compartment in my backpack where I'd put the stolen formula. I'd planned to give it back to Tristen, telling him that I wasn't sure how it had wound up with me. But that nagging voice, the devil on my shoulder, the opposite of my conscience—which insisted that loving Tristen was *wrong*—it was that voice that made me pull out the stopper and take a sip.

I just wanted to silence that voice. Maybe for a few hours. Maybe for *forever.*

Or did I want something else, like the freedom to be bad and wrong that the voice represented? Because I was in such pain, I *wanted* to do something bad. Maybe even hurt somebody else, the way I hurt.

I guess my reasons didn't really matter as I fell to the floor, clutching my stomach, feeling the wicked pain course through my veins, shattering me and setting me free.

Chapter 60

Jill

THE DOUBLE ESPRESSO feels hot going down my throat. The new bra feels soft against my breasts. The stolen thong feels—

"What the hell are you doing here, Jekel?"

I smile up at Todd Flick, wondering what took him so long to approach me. What a gorgeous, detestable piece of shit he is. "What? Is this seat reserved for guys who lick Darcy Gray's shoes?"

Flick stops smirking, and his pretty eyes flash. "What's up with you lately?" he demands. "If you think having Hyde *as a* boyfriend *suddenly makes you cool, you are so wrong. That guy is* nothing. *"*

"He beat you up, didn't he?" I laugh, pointing to Flick's arm. "So what does that make you?"

"Hey—"

"And let's face it." I hold my hands about ten inches apart. "Tristen's twice the man you are in other ways, too."

"You bitch," Flick snaps. "That's bullshit!"

"Not according to the talk at school. I heard Darcy complain that you're small—and you don't know how to use it, anyway."

"Shut up!" he cries. "Darcy never said that!"

"Look, Todd. It doesn't matter to me. I'll never have to endure your groping and grunting. Thank God."

"You couldn't handle me!"

I laugh. "What? Would it slip right through my fingers?"

He stands mute, jaw flapping, so I down my espresso, plunk the cup on the table, and shove past him, making sure my tits graze his chest.

He watches me all the way to my car.

Chapter 61

Jill

I WOKE UP sprawled on top of my covers . . . and wearing new clothes. I felt them before I even saw them. A wire from the bra poked into my rib cage, and it felt like there was a string running between—

Oh no. I tugged at a tight skirt, trying to dislodge that string. What had I done? It was all hazy, like a dream I could barely recall.

Rolling out of bed, I ran to the mirror. My face looked the same, but my clothes . . . Where had I gotten them? I didn't have money for new clothes!

My eyes darted to my backpack. The formula. I remembered drinking some . . .

Sweat trickling down my back, I tore off the outfit and fumbled to check the labels, sucking in my breath when I saw the designer names. I glanced at my chest. And the bra . . . It was pushing my breasts together so my A-cups looked like they belonged in *Maxim*.

Had I *stolen* all this stuff? I couldn't remember . . .

My pulse raced and my head thumped. What else had I done? Where had I gone looking like that? Had anybody seen me?

I jammed the clothes into the back of my closet and hurried to the shower, where I scrubbed my skin until it was raw, like I could erase what I might have done. Then I put on my usual clothes and stole out of the house early, before I could see my mom.

Had I run into her last night? Talked to her? Was I in *trouble*?

And what would happen at school? Had I seen kids from school? Maybe . . .

I walked in the sunlight, gulping deep breaths of cold, fresh November air, trying to figure out what I would say if anybody mentioned seeing me. I also tried not to think about how I had felt wearing those clothes or wonder why I'd shoved them in my closet instead of the trash can at the back of our yard.

Chapter 62

Jill

I WAS IN ART CLASS clipping my junior year photo to the edge of my canvas so I could begin adjusting the eyes on my self-portrait for what seemed like the millionth time when a strange, uneasy hush fell over the room. In seconds all of the chatter that always went on while we set up our easels simply stopped.

Without even looking, I knew that Tristen had joined us, uninvited.

My hand fell to my side, and I turned to see that Tristen was indeed standing in the doorway staring straight at me while everybody else gawked at *him*.

I shook my head, trying to tell him to leave, but he came toward me, ignoring my teacher's disapproving look.

"Tristen," Miss Lampley said but without much authority. I think, like everybody else, she was leery of the gash on his face, the crude bandage, and his tired, hunted, but determined expression. "I don't think you should be here."

I shot her a dismayed look. Did she really think that half-hearted attempt would stop Tristen Hyde from doing anything?

"This will just take a minute." Tristen overrode her, continuing to cross the room, stepping around students who watched his progress with wary interest, moving aside if he came too close.

"Tristen, go, please," I hissed when he reached me.

He didn't listen to me, either, and tried to take my arm. "Jill—"

I pulled away, warning, "Don't touch me."

"Fine," he agreed, crossing his arms. "As you wish."

"Why are you here?" I asked, focusing on my canvas, where the innocent girl I'd been the previous year was smiling her not-quite-right smile. "What do you want?"

"The contest," he said.

I actually laughed a little. "There's no contest. That's *over*, Tristen."

Out of the corner of my eye I saw that Miss Lampley had stepped closer, monitoring him. I also saw Tristen turn slightly to face her for a second.

She took a step back, and Tristen turned back to me.

"No matter how you feel about me," he said, "you need the money, and we *know* our experiment works. We could still win."

"I don't care about the money," I lied, even though I was still paying the bills late.

"We could start working during the day," he added. "You wouldn't have to be alone with me."

I choked a little, and turned my face more squarely away from him. I wanted to be alone with him . . . But I didn't want that at all. "It doesn't matter, Tristen," I said. "We're not doing the contest."

"Jill." He spoke my name so firmly that, although I didn't want to look at him, I did.

"What?"

"I made a bargain with you," he reminded me. "You helped me; now I *will* hold up my end of the deal."

"Tristen, we haven't even thought about the presentation," I said, voice cracking, and not because I was sad about the pathetic state of our abandoned project. "How would we present what we learned in public?" And it wasn't exactly the contest entry I was talking about when I concluded, near tears, "We have *nothing*, Tristen."

Even though I'd told him not to touch me, he clasped my upper arm and leaned closer. "We can do this, Jill," he said. "You know we can." He squeezed my arm. "We can beat Darcy and everyone else. You and I are smart enough to use what we've learned and win."

I should have yanked my arm away again, but I didn't. Darcy . . . I wanted to beat her. And I did still want the money.

And I did want to *win*.

"All right," I agreed, pulling away from him then, decisively. "But we'll work during school hours, and this time I'll be in charge, because it's my money. You said so."

"I don't want or need the cash," he replied, crossing his arms again. "I will honor that part of the bargain, too."

I took a second to consider what Tristen was offering.

"Let me help you win," he said again so quietly that even I barely heard. "Let me make what's left of my existence worthwhile."

My heart, which I wanted to close off to him, nonetheless sank when he said that. His father . . . He knew his father would come back for him. I tried not to look at the gash across Tristen's cheek but couldn't stop myself. One of them might very well kill the other before long.

"Please," Tristen said. "Let me keep my bargain with you."

I couldn't imagine working closely with him. It hurt just to stand next to him for a few minutes. But if Tristen Hyde felt that helping me would somehow serve as redemption, somehow help pay for the human life he'd taken, then I would help him ease his conscience. Especially since I knew then what it was like to lose control under the influence of the formula my ancestor had created and that had corrupted him.

"We'll start this afternoon," I said, picking up my paintbrush, signaling that he should go. *Go, Tristen. Please, just go . . .*

He left without another word, and I didn't watch him walk out like the rest of the class. I just kept studying my self-portrait, darting glances back and forth between my photo and the face on the canvas until I was dizzy from comparing the two. It was almost like the girl in the photograph was blurry and vanishing and the girl I was trying to capture on the canvas was an unknown quantity, too.

How could I not know my own eyes?

Still clutching my brush empty of paint, I thought back to the night Tristen had played our old Steinway and I'd glimpsed that dark place in his eyes, heard it expressed in his music. I'd wondered then if that was what had been missing in my art.

But I'd been wrong. That *wasn't* me. I would never be like Tristen.

I wiped my free hand across my mouth, which suddenly tasted metallic, like the formula I'd drunk just the night before.

The rage I'd felt toward my father, the clothes I'd hidden, an arm sliced to the bone, and blood on white sheets and white paper . . .

No! That wasn't me.

Hand not quite steady, I jabbed my brush into a glob of pure white and painted over my eyes with broad, reckless strokes, thinking I had to start again from nothing. But no matter how I tried, I couldn't even figure out how to begin.

It was a relief when Miss Lampley finally told us to clean up, and when the bell rang, I walked into the hall, glad to be headed toward sociology, where all I had to do was listen and take notes.

As I slid into my seat, I felt somebody staring at me, and I turned around to see Todd Flick, who sat near the back of the class, glaring at me. And then he mouthed the word "bitch."

I slid back around, mortified and shaken, not sure what I'd done to earn such naked hatred, not to mention a name I'd *never* been called before.

Not . . . *me.*

Chapter 63

Jill

"I'M SO GLAD you two decided to enter, and with such a compelling project," Mr. Messerschmidt gushed, rubbing his hands together and beaming at me, Tristen, and the stack of old documents on the lab table before us. "To think, recreating such a famous experiment from the original notes! It's tremendous. Astonishing, even!"

Mr. Messerschmidt started to reach out like he was going to touch the notes, and I slid them closer to myself, out of his reach. Something about my teacher's enthusiasm for the partnership of Tristen and me still seemed strange to me, and I didn't like the way he was looking at the documents. It wasn't like I thought Mr. Messerschmidt would steal my family's stuff, but still . . . he was almost *drooling*. "These are kind of fragile," I said, resting my fingers lightly on the yellowed papers. "It's not good to handle them a lot."

"Of course," Mr. Messerschmidt agreed, withdrawing his hand. But he frowned at me. "Jill, why didn't you come forward with this before when I urged you to enter the contest? You need to present in less than two weeks!"

"I don't know," I lied, spreading my fingers wider, like I was hiding the notes from everybody. "I just didn't think about it, I guess."

"You didn't think about *this?*" Mr. Messerschmidt laughed, gesturing to the papers again. "That's hard to believe!"

"Not just hard to believe but total bull," Darcy interrupted from the front of the room, where she and Todd were working at their usual lab station: number one. She didn't bother to apologize for eavesdropping. "They've been collaborating for weeks."

"Is planning quietly against the rules?" Tristen asked rhetorically. As if he cared about rules. "Must we all make a big show of *everything* we do? Some of us are mainly concerned with results, Darcy."

Her blue eyes flashed. "Or else you're cheating—"

Tristen laughed. "You're the one who boasted that you're working alone. And yet I see you have a collaborator. Who, I ask, is bending the rules?"

"Todd is an *assistant*," she clarified, voice rising. "He's not a *collaborator*. He just does what I tell him. Grunt work."

"Jeez, Darce," Todd snapped as he rinsed some beakers in the sink. "Thanks a lot."

Tearing my eyes away from the curled, stained papers, I saw that Todd's ears were red. "You're so mean, Darcy," I said. "You even treat your *boyfriend* like a slave."

I'd barely even realized I'd said that out loud until everybody turned to look at me. My first instinct was to blush, but I controlled it and forced myself to look them all right in the eye, one by one. Darcy *was* mean, and I had a right to say it.

Mr. Messerschmidt seemed hesitant, as usual.

Darcy looked shocked and angry.

Tristen nodded, eyes twinkling with bemused approval.

And when I locked eyes with Todd, I saw that he was furious and sheepish at the same time, like my defense had hurt his pride. What had happened, or what *was* happening between us?

Mr. Messerschmidt cleared his throat in a weak attempt to restore order. "Now, kids—"

"We'll need lab rats as soon as possible," Tristen interrupted, addressing our teacher. "I'll need you to get about twenty from the school's supplier. The school will pay, right?"

"I suppose so," Mr. Messerschmidt mused.

"See that it does," Tristen directed.

Me, I started staring at the old documents again. The formula lurked in there. The dangerous, exhilarating formula. The papers should be hidden . . .

Tristen tapped my shoulder. "Jill, are you all right?"

I tore my eyes away from the notes and realized that Mr.

Messerschmidt had meandered off to Darcy's station. "Yes, sure. I'm fine."

"What do you want to do first?" Tristen asked.

"What?" Tristen Hyde had never asked for instruction before. Maybe not in his entire life. And certainly not from me.

"This is your experiment," he reminded me. "You're in charge."

Yes, we'd agreed on that, but I hadn't really expected him to give me control. "Um . . . do you think we should . . . ?"

"Jill." He gave me a level, encouraging stare. "I trust your judgment."

I took a deep breath. "Okay. We need to start at the beginning. We haven't even developed a solid hypothesis."

"I'll get a notebook," Tristen said. He glanced to the front of the room, where Mr. Messerschmidt was sitting at his desk watching us all work. "If you'll excuse me for a minute, though, I want to make sure Messerschmidt gets that order for rats underway. He's not being very proactive, given how soon we need them."

"Okay," I agreed, following him with my eyes as he walked to the front of the room, broken but with his usual confident gait. How could Tristen still make my heart race, and calm me, and make me want to laugh and cry and throw myself into his arms when I knew what he was? How was it that the more battered, the more *terrible* he became in my eyes, the more I seemed drawn to him? What did that say about me? What was wrong with *me*?

"Hey, Jekel."

I'd been so focused on Tristen that I hadn't noticed Todd sidling up next to me. I wheeled around, heart pounding with alarm. "What?"

"I didn't like that shit you said about me in the coffee shop," he hissed.

208

"What?" I repeated, struggling to maintain my composure. I'd been in a *coffee shop?* With *Todd?*

"If you ever want to find out what it's like to be with a *real* man just call me," he continued in a low snarl. But his eyes darted to Tristen, nervously, before he added, "I'll show you who has the bigger one, bitch."

"I don't . . ." What had I said to him?

"Oh, not so tough today, are you?" Flick sneered. "Or maybe now that I've called your bluff, you're afraid that you really *can't* handle what I can deliver."

"I . . ." Was he offering to *have sex* with me?

He gave me an evil grin and made a motion of raising a phone to his face as he walked away. "If you ever have the guts, Jekel, call me."

I waited until I could control my shaking legs before I walked, with as much composure as I could muster, to the door, avoiding Tristen, who was still talking with Mr. Messerschmidt. Then I hurried to the girls' bathroom, where I leaned against the cool tile wall, avoiding the mirror, afraid to see my own face.

What had I done?

I was still fighting to remember when the door burst open and in marched Tristen, without bothering to knock or announce himself.

Chapter 64

Jill

"WHAT HAPPENED BACK THERE?" Tristen demanded. "What did Flick say to you?"

"Nothing." I tried to edge past him toward the door. "It was nothing."

He moved, too, blocking my path. "If you don't tell me, I'll get it out of him, by force if necessary. He will *not* upset you, not for as long as I'm around."

"No, Tristen," I snapped, yelling suddenly. My voice echoed against the pink walls. "No more violence! I'm so sick of violence!"

"Jill . . ." Tristen seemed surprised, and chastised. "You're right," he said, bowing his head slightly. "I'm sorry. I just wanted to protect you. But you're right. My way isn't the right way, and you probably handled it much better on your own, anyhow."

I stared at Tristen, who looked so out of place surrounded by pink tile, and suddenly the whole world seemed as topsy-turvy as a boy in the girls' room. I saw everything from a distance, like I was a character in a movie filled with ambiguous heroes and unexpected villains.

The most gallant, self-sacrificing guy in school was a murderer. The hottest, most popular stud had just propositioned the plainest, least popular virgin. The virgin became some sort of crazy slut when night fell. Fathers stole from daughters and attacked their sons. Mothers were too damaged and preoccupied to hold their own children. Teachers heeded their students, and shy girls snapped at dominant bitches. Chemistry, where I'd once found order in the universe, wreaked havoc on souls.

"I don't know what's happening to me," I blurted, burying my face in my hands. "I'm confused, Tristen . . . Nothing seems clear anymore."

I think I expected Tristen, my guardian, to reach out and hold me like he'd done in the past. That was his role, wasn't it? But I stood there alone, and when I pulled my hands away from my face, I saw that he had his arms crossed over his chest.

"I'm sorry," he said with almost pained sympathy. "I'm sorry that you're confused. I wish I could help, beyond winning you a scholarship so you can have a better future. But I'm afraid I'm just not the right man to do more."

I knew then that when I'd pushed him away in art class, I'd severed something between us. He would still defend me against bullies. That was just his nature, and he probably would have risen to protect any weak creature. But he wouldn't fold me against himself again. He would respect the distance I'd put between us.

"Let's go," he said, moving toward the door. "We don't have time to waste standing around in here. I've an appointment in an hour."

I followed him, and of course Tristen, always a gentleman when not wielding a butcher knife, held the door for me with his bloodstained hand.

I really, really wanted to ask him who he was going to meet, but I had a feeling that I didn't have a right anymore.

Chapter 65

Tristen

"HOW MUCH WILL YOU give me for it?" I asked as one of our school's most dismal miscreants, Mick Soder, ran his dirty paw down the side of my Honda.

"It runs good?" he asked, continuing to caress the car.

"Yes, yes," I said. "It's fine. How much?"

Mick shrugged, squinting. "I don't know. Three hundred?"

"Are you insane?" I snapped. "It's worth more than a thousand."

"You gonna do a title transfer?" he noted, smirking. "You want to get the authorities involved?"

Dammit. He had me there. The title was in my father's name. I just needed to unload the car as quickly and quietly as possible. My ATM and credit cards had been canceled, leaving me with about thirty dollars that I'd scrounged from the pockets of unwashed pants. Apparently the beast was first attempting to starve me into compliance. "Four hundred," I offered.

"Three fifty."

I stuck out my hand. "Deal."

Mick had apparently come prepared to buy. He dug into jeans that were even dirtier than mine and pulled out a wad of cash, counting some out and handing it over.

I counted, too, before giving him the keys.

"That must have been a helluva fight," Mick noted, nodding at my bandaged wrist. "What happened?"

I jammed the cash into my pocket. "The other guy was better armed."

Mick nodded, as if armed combat was a regular part of his life. "Give me back twenty bucks, and I'll get you a blade that will mess up a guy so bad . . . well, he'll look worse than you, and that's saying something."

I kept my tone noncommittal. "I'm listening."

Mick held his hands about four inches apart. "It's only this big. The blade flips out and the guy'll never know you have it. Until it's too late."

I still kept my tone neutral. "When could I get it?"

"Tonight if you want."

I took a moment to weigh the deal. Then I handed over the requested sum, not even bothering to negotiate.

Chapter 66

Jill

WHEN I GOT HOME from school, I lugged my portfolio up the
stairs to my bedroom, got my easel, propped my canvas on it, and
clipped on the school portrait, determined to buckle down and finish my painting. The assignment was due in less than a week, and
my eyes were still a blank slash of white, which would guarantee me
a failing grade.

And yet, I didn't start working right away. I didn't even unpack
my oils from the box where I kept them neatly assembled like a
rainbow. Instead, feeling restless and out of sorts, I wandered
around my room, tidying up, telling myself that I wasn't stalling. I
was straightening. Keeping order.

And as I put my things in all their proper places, I kept an eye
out for one thing that was *definitely* out of place.

The missing vial of formula.

Had I hidden it somewhere? Lost it?

Why had Todd Flick made that comment about the size of
his . . . ?

I glanced at my closet. And those clothes. I had to get rid of them.

Opening the door warily, like the clothes might bite me, I knelt
to dig in the back for the short skirt and tight shirt, pulling them
out. But as I stood up, I rubbed the fabric of the shirt between my
fingers. It was silky and would feel good against my skin. I could try

the stuff on, just for a minute, and maybe find out that I hadn't looked *too* slutty . . .

Dropping my jeans and unbuttoning my blouse, I stepped into the skirt and pulled on the shirt, then moved in front of the mirror, dreading what I'd see.

But my reflection . . . wasn't so bad.

I turned to the side. Maybe I was showing a little too much bare leg, but the clothes weren't totally out of line. Relief flooded me, and I smoothed the shirt against my body, straightening my spine . . . and frowning. The silky fabric was lumpy across my chest. Would it look better with the bra I'd stole . . . The new bra?

I went to my dresser and pulled out the top drawer. The black bra was hidden near the back, and when I pulled it out, something rolled forward.

The vial.

I picked it up, noticing that it was still almost full. This . . . with this I could . . .

"Jill?"

"What?" I yelped, shoving the formula into the drawer and slamming it shut as I spun around to face my mother, who stood in the doorway watching me.

Chapter 67

Jill

"I—I DIDN'T KNOW you were home," I said, leaning hard against my dresser.

"I was taking a nap," Mom said, still watching me.

I tugged at the hem of the skirt, but was suddenly more worried about Mom than my clothes. She'd pushed too hard, was relapsing . . . "Are you okay?"

She smiled a little, maybe understanding my concern. "I'm fine, Jill," she said. "I'm just resting between shifts. I'm trying to work a little extra this week."

"Mom!" I forgot all about my exposed legs. "Are you sure?"

She nodded—and yawned. But she honestly didn't seem as *weary* as before. "Yes, I'm ready," she said. "I want to start taking more of the burden off your shoulders."

"Thanks, Mom."

She finally seemed to notice what I was wearing, and she frowned. "Are those new clothes?"

I tugged at the skirt again. "Um, I borrowed this stuff from Becca."

Mom stepped closer, looking me up and down. Then she met my eyes—and smiled again. "The skirt is a little short but probably in style for girls your age," she admitted. "You look cute, Jill."

"Really?"

Mom nodded, and to my surprise, wrapped her arm around my shoulders and squeezed. How long had it been since *she'd* embraced *me?*

"I just wish I could buy you more of your *own* new clothes," she said, pressing us together.

And I wish I hadn't just lied . . . wasn't hiding things from you . . . "It's okay," I reassured her, pulling away. "Don't worry about it."

Mom checked out my outfit again, and realization dawned in her eyes. "Jill? This new look isn't for *Tristen,* is it?"

"Tristen?" I jolted, wondering if she'd suddenly recalled meeting him the night he'd drugged her. "No . . ."

"I just thought maybe, since he did that favor for you—for *us*—"

"No, Mom," I promised, cutting her off. "We're not . . . together." We never would be. *That* was the truth.

"Oh." I'd thought she would be happy that I wasn't seeing a guy, but she actually seemed disappointed. "I get the impression he's a nice boy."

"Sometimes," I said with a shrug. *And sometimes not . . .* "Um, about clothes," I added to change the subject. "Could I borrow that blue blazer from you? For that scholarship presentation?"

"Yes, of course," Mom said, but her face got pale. "I'm afraid I forgot about that, though. I made some plans for that weekend . . ."

I cocked my head. "Plans?"

"Yes." She fidgeted and looked away. "Your aunt Christine invited me to visit her in Cape May. She thought it might be nice for me to get away."

I looked at her with surprise. "Aunt Christine? But you two hardly ever visit. I haven't seen her since Dad's . . ." I stopped myself, wishing I hadn't nearly mentioned my father's funeral.

"Yes, well . . ." Mom shoved her hand through her hair, our shared gesture. "I've told her about my . . . illness, and she thought it might be good for me to get some fresh sea air, even if the weather is cold."

"Well, yeah, I guess so," I agreed. Actually, I was relieved that my mom would miss the presentation. I was terrified of public speaking, and it only got worse if I knew people in the audience. "I really don't mind."

She hugged me again, and the mood lightened once more. "Thanks, Jill. I really think this will be good for me."

Then my mother left me to go put on her scrubs, and in spite of her approval, I took off the shirt and skirt, put them back in my closet, and went to bed early, trying not to think about the vial that was hidden in my drawer or about Tristen. But both of those wicked, wonderful things seemed determined to tempt me, while I, a *good girl,* did my best to resist.

Chapter 68

Tristen

THE SCHOOL'S EMPTY hallways seemed unusually dark and silent as I made my way to the second floor sometime after midnight.

Locating my locker, I spun the combination, opened it, and pushed aside a track jacket I never wore. Dipping my hand into a plastic bag, I retrieved a Gatorade bottle. Only the liquid inside wasn't neon yellow-green. It swirled against the plastic, murky and milky and toxic.

I held it up before my face—and realized that I'd licked my lip.

Just touching the formula, I got edgy and . . . something else. Deep in the recesses of my brain I could hear one of my favorite compositions, a thunderous variation on a traditional funeral march, begin to play, almost feel my hands on the keys. Keys I hadn't touched since curing myself. Keys I was afraid to touch . . .

"You'll drink again, Tristen, of your own free will . . ."

I could have sworn that I heard my father's—the *beast's*—voice not in memory but whispered directly into my ear, and a shudder ran down the length of my spine. I honestly wasn't sure if the cause was thrill or horror, but my hand trembled, too, and the formula sloshed loudly, breaking the spell. I spun on my heel, jamming the bottle into my messenger bag and heading for Mr. Messerschmidt's classroom, walking quickly.

Hurry, Tristen. Hurry; hide the bottle from yourself and get moving.

Breaking into the room, I went directly to where the newly arrived rats moved restlessly in their cages, busy with their nocturnal lives, and although I was eager to be done with the tasks I had planned, I took a few moments to observe the animals, keeping an eye on a pathetic white runt that was missing half an ear. A weakling. A loser bullied by others. It lay curled in a corner as if trying not to attract the stronger animals' notice.

Raising the lid, I sought him with my good hand, and he allowed himself to be lifted out. His little heart beat quickly against my palm, but he didn't squirm or nip. I cradled him against my chest, stroking him, gaining his trust, and no doubt used to being handled by humans, he was soon playing along my arm, sniffing at my shirt.

As my new friend crept to my shoulder, I went to my lab station and first unpacked a small video camera, setting it up so it would capture what happened next, and then switching it on. Then I located an eyedropper in the equipment drawer.

The rat's pink nose snuffled against my ear, and I would have laughed if I hadn't been so grimly preoccupied with uncapping the Gatorade bottle, dipping in the dropper, and retrieving about an ounce of the formula.

Oh, the smell of that stuff. The smell of evil. Of power—

Stop, Tristen.

"Come now," I told the rat, plucking it from my shoulder and cradling it again, offering it the dropper in view of the camera. "Have a drink, yes?"

The rat clearly didn't like the smell, but with a little prodding at its mouth, it opened up, and I squeezed nearly the full dose onto its tongue.

The reaction was almost immediate. The animal stiffened in my hand, and its pink eyes rolled wildly as it squealed in pain. I placed it on the lab table, where it wobbled and collapsed, sides heaving—just as mine must have done.

Had I convulsed so violently, too? I couldn't remember.

"Sorry," I soothed him, glad that I hadn't brought Jill with me. I'd known the creature would suffer when it swallowed the formula, and I'd wanted to spare her seeing that—again. "Poor thing," I muttered, wincing as the rat writhed. "Believe me, I understand your pain."

I swore those pink eyes were accusing me. And then they closed.

I rested my index finger against the rat's side. Still breathing but barely.

We stayed like that for what seemed like a long time, and I had just given up the animal as doomed to die at any moment when its eyelids fluttered and its paws twitched, then opened and closed, not convulsing but flexing. Gradually, with effort, the rat stood on uncertain legs.

"Welcome back," I said, lifting and resting it against my chest again, making sure I kept the animal in view of the camera. But the rat sat docilely in my hand, and after about five minutes, I thought that I'd been foolish to believe that I might actually see it change. It wasn't a human—wasn't a *Hyde*. "Sorry about putting you through all that," I apologized again to the animal, which seemed almost drowsy after its ordeal.

And sorry, Jill, that we'd have no proof of success for our presentation. I'd thought video of a wildly altered rat might just seal the deal, proving that the old formula really did create monsters. But it was apparently not to be.

I stroked the rodent's head for another minute until it seemed recovered, croughing on its haunches and washing its face, then sniffing at my fingers again. I allowed it to play in my palm for a while, and was about to reach over and turn off the camera when suddenly, without warming or provocation—it bit me. Hard. "Dammit!" Blood welled from the tender spot between my thumb and index finger.

The rat released my flesh—only to sink in again, and again, so rapidly that I didn't even have time to react. I barely had the presence of mind to steel myself for a short time, long enough to capture some images on tape.

And long enough to see the *look* in the animal's eyes.

When I couldn't stand being gnawed on one second more, I moved to the cage, and—just needing to be free of the little demon—dropped it in with the others.

As I stepped back, shaking out what had been my good hand, I saw the runt turn its new rage on its fellow rats, attacking randomly, viciously, until the cage was a seething mass of panicked, squealing rodents. Flecks of blood splashed on the glass.

"Shit!"

I swore not only at the carnage but at the realization that the experiment really seemed to have *worked*. "Dammit," I muttered again in disbelief as more blood hit the cage walls. "Son of a . . ."

I watched for just another second, stunned into inaction, then realized I needed to intervene and stop what threatened to become a massacre.

I hurried back to the lab table and switched off the camera—not wanting to record what I'd do next—and started to pull the switchblade from its hiding place in my bandage. But as my fingers touched the knife, I found that I couldn't do it that way. Couldn't bring myself to plunge in the blade, perhaps miss killing him, and need to stab the animal again, maybe more than twice. Instead I flipped open my messenger bag, searching for the vial of strychnine, glad, for once, that I never cleaned out things. Twisting off the cap, I dipped in my index finger and covered it with pure poison, then reached in among the frenzied, wounded rats, snatching up the runt. He wriggled and fought as I struggled to force the powder onto his tongue, biting me enough times that I feared I might be poisoned, too, if too much entered my bloodstream through the breaks in my skin.

But before the rat could do *me* in, the toxin paralyzed his much smaller nerve system and he lay still on the table again. This time his heart didn't beat at all.

"Sorry," I apologized yet again. "But I had to do all that. For Jill."

The rat's videotaped reaction—documented success with an animal—might just net her the thirty thousand dollars. It was worth the life of a rodent. Yet I still felt bad as I bagged the creature for disposal and cleaned the mess in the cage. A few of the rats looked to have serious injuries.

When the room seemed in order, I packed up the camera and resealed the bottle of formula, twisting the cap on tight. The motion left a smear of fresh blood, *my* blood, on the white plastic, and I shoved the bottle into my bag, ready to return it to my locker.

The funeral march I'd once composed still played faintly, now mockingly, in my head as I hid the bottle away and carried the corpse to the Dumpster outside the school. One of my most beautiful compositions wasted on a dead rat.

How could I have been tempted, even for a second, to become like that animal: convulsing, mad, and murderous? Who, what type of person, would want *that*?

I also wondered, as I often did, where the beast that took away my parents was hiding, what it was planning, and if I would have the courage to use the knife when it *really* counted.

Raising the Dumpster lid, I hurled the rat into its rancid coffin, gagging unexpectedly at the strong stench of rot.

Chapter 69

Jill

"YOU'VE ACCOMPLISHED a lot in a short time," Mr. Messerschmidt noted, nodding with approval. "Do you think you'll be ready to present in a few days?"

"Yes," I said. "But we're cutting it close."

"Jill's got it under control," Tristen said, dipping his hand into a cage and stroking one of the rats that we were systematically sickening, documenting their reactions to early versions of the formula that we knew weren't really effective. "She's going to win."

"*We're* going to win," I corrected him, thinking that Tristen seemed to be distancing himself more and more, not just from me but from any concept of the future. "Us."

Tristen didn't look at me. He was frowning, eyes trained on the rat, which shuddered under the influence of a weak acidic solution.

"It'll be okay," I promised him. I sort of meant the rat. I sort of meant . . . everything. I wasn't sure about either.

"You two don't have a chance, with your half-dead rats and stinking old papers," Darcy piped up from the front of the room. "It's not research. It's a publicity stunt!"

"It's a great experiment," I advised her. "So just worry about your own work, okay?"

"I guess *Jekel* told *you*, Darce." Todd snorted as he wiped down their station for the evening.

I stared at him, not sure if Darcy had been insulted or me.

"Do you two have a ride to Philly?" Mr. Messerschmidt asked me and Tristen, diverting us away from an argument.

"I just sold my car," Tristen noted, "so I'm no help."

I frowned at that news and not just because we needed a ride. Was Tristen low on money? Or did he expect not to need a car soon?

"I don't know if my car will make it," I added. "I never got it tuned up. And my mom can't take us. She'll be out of town."

"I'll drive you," Mr. Messerschmidt volunteered. "I'm going anyway."

I expected Tristen to flatly refuse, forcing us to hitchhike before he'd accept charity from Mr. Messerschmidt. Instead he simply said, "Thanks. That's great."

I was further surprised to see what looked like grudging but genuine gratitude Tristen's face, and I wished again that I knew what they'd talked about on that day he had shown up battered in class. Something had changed between them. Somehow Mr. Messerschmidt had gained a little of Tristen's trust.

Our teacher checked the clock. "Time to wrap up."

"We're done," Darcy said as Todd, finally free of his cast, tossed his backpack over his shoulder and hoisted her designer tote, too.

I looked with dismay at the chaos at our station. "Could we stay late? We have so much to do."

"You're not *supposed* to work alone," Mr. Messerschmidt noted, although he didn't seem very firm about it. "That *is* school policy."

Darcy, near the door, gave a wry laugh. "Oh, don't worry. They've already worked solo."

I glared at her until she rolled her eyes and marched out the door, followed by Todd, who gave me one last unreadable glance before departing. Then I turned back to Mr. Messerschmidt, pleading, "Please? We'll be careful."

"Jill, are you sure?" Tristen interrupted. "You want to stay with me?"

I knew what he was implying, and it tore at my heart suddenly, because I still trusted him. It wasn't what I feared he'd do that appalled me; it was what he'd *done* that I despised. "Yes, Tristen," I said. "I want to stay."

"Well . . ." Mr. Messerschmidt wavered—but only for a second. "If you promise to be careful."

"Really?" I blurted, surprised that we'd actually gotten permission. I'd thought Mr. Messerschmidt was a rule follower like me. "I mean, that's great," I amended before he could change his mind. "Thanks."

"I'll take responsibility," Tristen told Mr. Messerschmidt—but he was looking at me. "I'll keep Jill safe."

"Lock up when you leave," Mr. Messerschmidt said. "And don't tell *anyone* I let you do this." Then he got some stuff from his desk and headed for the door, too. But before he left, Mr. Messerschmidt paused, and for a second I thought he was going to change his mind. He looked nervous and sounded edgy as he offered us a weird farewell. "Good luck, kids."

Then he left me and Tristen alone— really alone— for the first time since we'd been in Tristen's bedroom kissing and confessing.

And the first thing Tristen did was lock the door from the inside, sealing us in the room.

Chapter 70

Jill

"TRISTEN?"

"Just being cautious, Jill," he said, rejoining me at our station.

My heart crept into my throat. "You think your dad . . . ?"

"I doubt he'd come here," Tristen reassured me. "He could easily kill me as I sleep in the house if he wanted. But I have a responsibility to look out for you."

I didn't know what to say to any of that, so I picked up Dr. Jekyll's notes to start working again. "We're on the experiment dated February eleventh. He starts with the base formula then adds two grams of magnesium." I lowered the papers and ventured cautiously, "But maybe, since we're alone, we should, um . . . jump ahead?"

Tristen measured out some magnesium and added it to the acidic mixture, then looked to me, eyebrows arched. "You mean . . . ?"

"Test the real formula, the final formula, on a rat. To see if it works."

I got nervous as I suggested that, because a terrible little part of me was thinking, *You could show me where you've been* hiding *your portion of the formula . . . Maybe I could steal just a little more if you turned your back . . .*

But Tristen silenced that traitorous small voice by advising me, "I've already done that, Jill. And documented the results."

I dropped the notes, and they fluttered to the desk. "What? When?" *Without me?*

"I came to school late last night and fed about an ounce to a rat," he said. "You'll be happy to know that the experiment was a complete success."

I realized then that he had stopped mixing the latest solution and was holding out his hand. Looking down, I noticed that his fingers were covered with small, but angry-looking, red marks. Some had scabbed over. I met his eyes again, seeking explanation. "Tristen?"

"The animal went from docile to berserk," he explained. "I have it all on video, so we can show it at the presentation."

I shook my head, not believing him. "You're kidding . . ."

But Tristen wasn't smiling. "No. I'm very serious."

"We should repeat the experiment," I said, getting excited. We were on the brink of winning thirty thousand dollars. And we'd be working with the real formula . . . "If we keep getting the same result, we could do it on stage at the presentation!"

"No." Tristen was firm, his jaw set. "I won't do it again. And you don't want to see what happens."

"But—"

"No!" he insisted. He rubbed the back of his neck with his scratched-up hand and averted his eyes. "I had to put the rat down, Jill. It was attacking the others. I hated doing it, but I had to."

Tristen was so obviously pained over killing the animal—or maybe admitting it to me—that I forgot my excitement.

"I—I understand," I said, forcing myself not to imagine how he'd ended the rat's life. I didn't want to picture Tristen killing again, maybe snapping an animal's neck with his bare hands, even to spare the other rats. Still, I glanced at his hands, his now *literally* blood-stained hands, and realized that the crude bandage on his wrist was getting really ragged. Without thinking, forgetting that we no longer touched each other, I reached for his arm. "I can fix that for you."

He pulled away. "No. It's fine."

I grabbed for him again. "Tristen, just let me . . ."

When my fingers wrapped around his wrist, I felt something narrow and hard under the torn shirt, and I looked up at him, confused. "Tristen?"

"Let go, Jill," he said, pulling back.

But I didn't. I held on to him. "What is that?"

He yanked free of me. "That, Jill, is my best hope against the *thing* that is coming for me."

I suspected then that Tristen was carrying a knife, and the thought made me sick. Only suddenly I wasn't disgusted just because he might use it to kill again. As I looked at his brave, determined face, I was mostly terrified because the weapon seemed way too small to do any good against an enemy—especially one that had already shown such ruthless power.

"Tristen," I said, all of the weak defenses I'd raised against him melting away, "did your father really say that he'll hurt you again? You never told me what happened that night."

He gave a short, rueful laugh. "No, you ran out, horrified by me, before I could tell you."

"I'm sorry."

"No need to apologize," Tristen said with a shrug. He resumed mixing the solution, avoiding looking at me. "But to answer your question: yes, the beast that controls my father, completely now, vowed to return, and if I haven't drunk the formula and restored *dis*order to the Hyde family, he will kill me."

I had sort of pieced all that together, but to hear him say it out loud . . . I got hot and nauseous. I was petrified for him. And how could I have played around with the formula? "Do you know where your father is?"

"No." Tristen finally met my eyes. "That phone call, when we were in bed . . ."

He said that casually, like that didn't matter, either. And maybe it didn't to him anymore. That made me sick, too.

"That was Dad's department head, asking why he'd stopped coming to the university." He tapped the stirring rod against the glass beaker, frowning even more deeply. "He doesn't still see your mother, does he?"

"No," I said. Not *professionally.* "The treatment's over."

"Good," he said.

"Tristen?"

"Yes?"

I found myself staring at the spot where Tristen's bandage bulged just slightly. "Will you be able to fight your dad to . . . ?" The end. That's what I meant.

As always, Tristen was able to finish my thoughts. "I'll do what I need to do, Jill," he said. He stared into my eyes, and I saw the same resolution I'd seen just before he'd drunk the formula, convinced that he was committing suicide. "When the time comes, I *will do* what I need to do."

"Tristen . . ." But what could I say?

"Let's keep working," he said, picking up an eyedropper.

"Although *we* know how this story ends, we'll want to show the judges that we followed Dr. Jekyll's notes from start to finish."

"Sure."

But I didn't move to help him. I just watched, sad and confused, as Tristen . . . doomed Tristen . . . bent and chose a rat from one of the cages, cradling it in the crook of his arm. "This won't taste good," he warned, raising the dropper to its mouth.

The rat squirmed, and Tristen spoke softly, "Come now. I don't like doing this, either, but it's in the interest of science and a scholarship—for the greater good."

He managed to squeeze a few drops into the rat's mouth before it writhed out of his hand, tumbling back into the cage. "Poor thing," Tristen said, watching it run in circles. "I hope it's not in pain."

Poor, poor thing . . .

I didn't know what came over me, but I started to cry then, and I moved close to Tristen and wrapped my arms around him, comforting myself and hoping that I comforted him a little, too. At first he stood rigidly, not accepting my embrace, but as I held him, I felt his muscles start to relax, and soon he wrapped his arms around me, cradling me against his chest, rubbing his cheek against the top of my head, soothing me, too. "It's okay, Jill," he promised. "Don't cry for me."

But I wasn't crying just for him. I was crying for me, too. I was crying for *us*.

"Oh, Jill," Tristen said, raising my face to his. "What am I going to do with you?"

I studied his warm, wonderful brown eyes, knowing what I *wanted* him to do. I wanted him to kiss me. I wanted him to tell me that he still loved me. Because I knew that he had. We'd both been close to saying it, that day in Tristen's bed . . .

He bent closer to me, resting his forehead against mine and closing his eyes, and I raised up on my tiptoes, thinking that I couldn't wait one more second for him to kiss me. *I* would kiss *him*.

But before my lips could meet his, we both heard a sound and jerked apart, staring at the door as the knob twisted from outside.

Chapter 71

Jill

TRISTEN AND I stood locked together, eyes fixed on the twisting, rattling knob. "Tristen," I whispered, fighting down fear, "who do you think—"

"Shhh, Jill," he hushed me. "Quiet."

My heart raced, but his remained steady. "It could be a custodian," he suggested. "Or Darcy, returning."

"A custodian would have keys, and Darcy would knock." My eyes were locked on the knob, which rattled harder.

"True." Tristen gently pried away from me—and removed the knife from its makeshift sheath. The blade, when he flicked it open, was thin, but looked reassuringly vicious.

The door began to shake—and then we heard a deep, growling, voice. "Tristen! Let me in!"

My entire body seemed to freeze at that terrible sound. It was Dr. Hyde's voice—and yet not his voice at all. I edged closer to Tristen, terrified. "Tristen . . ."

He clasped my wrist with his free hand and began tugging. "Come on."

I allowed myself to be dragged along, eyes darting around the room for a hiding place, although I knew hiding would be futile. "Where are we going?"

"*You* are leaving," Tristen whispered, dropping the knife and raising a window.

"Not without you," I objected, wriggling as he wrapped one arm around my waist, lifting me.

"Jill, stop fighting and go!"

I twisted against him. "Not without you!"

Across the room the door rattled on its hinges, and that terrible voice roared out Tristen's name, summoning him. "Open this door now, *son!*"

"Jill." Tristen spun me around to face himself. "This is inevitable for me. Allow it to happen."

"Not tonight." I shook my head. "I won't go *without you.*"

We stayed deadlocked for just one more second, and then, just as the door shuddered again, struck from outside by a beast whose rage was palpable, Tristen agreed. He didn't say anything, but somehow we both understood that we would go together.

"Run, Jill," he said, pushing me out the window. I watched from outside as he snatched up the old notes, crammed them in the box, grabbed the knife, and followed, dropping to the ground and clasping my hand in his. "Just run."

Tristen was one of the best runners in the state, and it seemed like I borrowed some of his power as we tore away from the school and into the darkness. I felt like we were both flying, like nothing could catch us, not even a monster as strong as the one I feared was on our heels.

But thinking back, I'm sure that Tristen slowed his pace to match mine.

That seemed like something Tristen Hyde would do, even if it put his own life at risk.

Chapter 72

Jill

"ARE YOU GOING TO BE OKAY?" Tristen asked, standing in the shadows behind my house.

"Yes," I said. "Mom's home tonight. I'll be safe."

"I'll stay until you get inside. Then lock the door behind you."

I started to step up onto the back porch. "Tristen . . . you're not going back, are you?"

"No, Jill," he promised. "He wouldn't be there, anyway."

"You could come inside."

Tristen shook his head and shifted the box under his arm. "No. I'll hide this and go home."

"Home? But—"

"It's too cold to sleep outside." Tristen attempted a joke. "And I think, now, that he doesn't plan to confront me in our house, anyhow."

"Why," I wondered aloud, "do you think he came to the school?"

"I'm sure he's watching me, knows what we're doing, and hoped to find me with the formula," he said. "For, more than killing me, he wants me to drink and continue our legacy."

A spark of hope flickered inside of me. "What if you did it?" I ventured. "You could always drink it and buy time, with the intention of changing back . . ."

But he was already shaking his head. "No. It's too risky. Who knows what I might do under its influence?" He paused, and I could hear the reluctance in his voice as he added, "You know that my father likely killed yours, over the formula?"

I stood in silence, letting Tristen's words sink in. And yet I knew that I wasn't as shocked as I should have been by the suggestion.

Had a part of me guessed that Dr. Hyde was involved in Dad's death? Had I pushed the clues and coincidences out of my mind as Mom had healed under his care—and as I'd come to love Tristen? Because to love the son of my father's killer would be so wrong . . .

"I'm sorry," Tristen said, hanging his head, like he really did share responsibility for Dr. Hyde's crime.

"I wonder," I mused with a bit of my old foolish hope for Dad's redemption, "if maybe my dad was trying to *help* yours."

"Yes, I believe so," he said, looking at me again. "I found an unfinished document on my father's computer in which he discussed working with an anonymous collaborator on a cure for the madness that he knew was overtaking him."

My heart started to race. "My dad?

"Yes," he confirmed. "Our fathers were also excited about broader possibilities for the formula if they perfected it. They saw implications for opening whole new avenues of study in personality manipulation and social control."

"You never told me that," I said, stunned. "Why not?"

His brown eyes clouded with remorse. "I couldn't bring myself to tell you. How could you look at me again, knowing what my father likely did to yours?" He gave a rueful laugh. "Not that my own sins weren't enough to drive you away."

A part of me still hadn't accepted, or absolved, Tristen for killing. A part of me also knew that it was terrible to love the son of my dad's murderer. But I loved him anyhow. "Forget that," I urged. "You aren't a monster—and we aren't our parents. I don't blame you for your father's actions."

"I think your dad really believed that he would restore your college fund and then some," he added. "They had very high hopes for professional—and by extension, financial—gain."

A huge lump grew in my throat. Tristen had largely just vindicated my father, like I'd hoped for. And yet Dad was still gone, Tristen's father was maybe worse than dead, and Tristen and I . . . the future didn't look good for us, either.

"Go inside, Jill," he finally said. "I'll be fine tonight."

Tonight. But not for long.

I hesitated, one foot still on the step. "Tristen?"

"Yes?" He stepped closer and raised his hand, brushing my stray lock of hair behind my ear. "What is it?"

I caught his hand in mine and laced our fingers, squeezing our palms together. Although it was very dark, I saw what I wanted to see in his eyes. "Come over tomorrow night," I offered. "You need something decent to eat, and you could rest." I felt myself blush as I added, "Mom will be at the hospital almost all night . . ."

He hesitated. "I don't know, Jill. It might not be safe for you."

No. It wouldn't be safe. Being with Tristen would be the riskiest thing I'd ever done, for my body and my soul and especially my heart, which would be shattered if anything really happened to him. But I was convinced that being with Tristen Hyde would be *right*. "Just come," I said, rising on tiptoes to kiss his lips lightly. "For me."

"Okay," he agreed.

He waited while I went inside and locked the door behind me. Then I watched from a window while he disappeared into the night, praying that he hadn't lied about going back to the school.

Chapter 73

Jill

"JILL, I'M GOING TO WORK," Mom said, poking her head into my room. "Don't stay up too late painting, okay?"

"I won't," I promised, checking the clock. Tristen would arrive in about a half hour. "I'm wrapping up soon."

She stepped into the room, joining me at my easel. She stared first at the painting and then at me, seeming confused. "I thought this portrait was due soon."

"I'll finish in time," I said, with more conviction than I felt.

"You'd better add some eyes!" Mom teased with a grin. She was subtly pressuring me to finish my assignment, but I didn't mind. I was just glad for the genuine smile.

"Do I ever let you down?" I asked—and pushed away a twinge of guilt. Mom would be very disappointed if she knew what I planned to do with Tristen that night. But we *had* to be together. It was like I didn't have a choice. I checked the time again. "You should probably get going, huh?"

"Yes," she agreed, giving me a kiss on the cheek. "Have a good night."

I would. I definitely would. "You, too."

I listened as she got her coat and keys, and when the back door shut behind her, I abandoned painting, too nervous and excited to work.

Was I ready?

I caught a glimpse of myself in the mirror. Did I look okay?

I straightened my back, checking myself in profile, then went to my dresser and reached into my drawer, feeling for the black bra, thinking that I would look better in that and that a guy would like it. But when my fingers touched the silky fabric I hesitated. *I* hadn't chosen it, *stolen* it . . .

I shoved the bra farther back, thinking it felt tainted somehow, and wrong for the night I wanted to have. As wrong as the formula, which was also hidden in there.

I didn't need that either, right?

But I could keep it in my nightstand, just in case I got nervous . . .

I was just about to wrap my fingers around the vial when I heard a knock on the front door and yanked my hand back, horrified by my own behavior. Tristen was here. He would be sickened if he knew I'd stolen—*tasted*—the formula.

Slamming the drawer shut, I raced down the stairs and threw open the door. "Tristen . . ."

But it wasn't Tristen who stood on the other side.

Chapter 74

Jill

"BECCA, WHAT ARE DOING HERE?" I asked as she stepped into the foyer, uninvited.

"I have to talk to you," she said. "Now."

236

"This isn't a good time."

But Becca barged past me into the living room. "It won't take long. I just need to tell you something. About Tristen."

I knew, before she went any further, what she wanted to talk about. I knew that I was about to learn the truth about what had happened between my friend and the guy I loved over the course of the previous summer. And from the look on Becca's face, that was a truth I didn't want to know.

"Not now, Becca," I said. "Please. Not now."

Not right before Tristen was about to walk into the house, go with me up to my room . . .

"I know you guys are together," she said. "But I also know a secret about him, Jill."

I shook my head. "Becca . . . you don't have to tell me—"

"I was with Tristen this summer," she blurted. "We had sex. By the river. And he *changed,* Jill. Tristen *changed,* and it was scary. It was like he got . . . *rough.*"

Becca probably thought all the blood rushed from my cheeks because she'd just told me that Tristen had a violent side. But I'd lived through that. It was the admission that they'd had sex, that's what sort of killed me. I'd suspected that they'd hung out. Kissed, maybe. But *sex?* "That's enough," I said. "You don't need to tell me more. Please."

"Jill." She rested her hand on my shoulder. "You *need* to know this."

"I don't . . ."

"We were on the riverbank," Becca continued, ignoring my protests, "and Tristen was kissing me, whispering this *amazing* stuff in my ear." Although she was telling a story that was supposedly terrible, a smile started to play on her lips. "I swear, I was thinking that Tristen Hyde was, like, the *best* guy I'd ever been with."

"Please, stop touching me," I begged, pushing her hand away. Her hand that had touched Tristen. "Stop telling me this!"

But she was lost in memory and still had that small smile on her red lips. "I mean, we couldn't tear each other's clothes off fast enough!"

"Becca." I couldn't bear picturing Tristen undoing buttons on Becca's shirt, her hands moving to his jeans . . . "Please!"

"Calm down, Jill." She interrupted her story, jerking back to reality and shooting me a look of frustration. "It didn't mean anything! We were just at a party and got carried away! You don't have to get all jealous!"

I stared at her, speechless. How could I not be jealous? Becca had Tristen first and it hadn't even really *mattered* to her. I knew that I was being irrational. They had been together before Tristen had even noticed me. And yet I couldn't think logically. I just kept picturing them down by the river, Tristen whispering in Becca's ear, removing her clothes . . .

"But suddenly," she continued, "and I mean, right at *the* big moment, Tristen got *different*, and I was *scared* of him." She paused, then added, like she was doing me a great favor, "I don't want that to happen to you, Jilly."

I glared at my "friend" through tears. "That" already *had* happened. I'd lived through the bad with Tristen. But Becca . . . she'd beaten me to the good part. *Stolen* it from me on a whim, without a second thought. And by doing so, and telling me too much, she'd stolen *Tristen* from me.

Of course, he was guilty, too. The searing, rending pain in my chest, the actual breaking of my heart . . . those were Tristen's fault, too. This time he couldn't blame his actions on an alter ego or a formula that *my family* had poisoned him with generations ago.

238

Tristen had chosen, of his own free will, to have sex just for the hell of it, with my friend.

And me . . . I'd been so stupid to think that he considered what we were about to do *special.*

What had Tristen whispered to Becca before he'd changed? Had he looked into her eyes the same way he looked into mine? I clenched my fists, struck by a terrible thought. If things hadn't gone wrong that night, would Tristen still be with beautiful Becca? Was Jill Jekel just a last resort yet again?

"Get out!" I cried, pointing to the door. "Just go!"

"Don't be mad at me!" Becca was clearly surprised by my reaction. "I'm doing you a favor. And I didn't think *you* would ever get together with him when we did it!"

"No?" I snapped. "Why not? Because Jill Jekel could *never* get a hot guy?"

"Jill . . ." she stammered. "I didn't mean that . . ."

"Yes, you did!"

"Look. You're *way* overreacting." She jammed her hands into her pockets. "Christy Hitchcock's parents are out of town. There's a big party at her house tonight. Why don't you come? It might help to be around people. Put things in perspective."

"A *party?*" I was incredulous. "You think a *party* will fix what you just did?"

"You're making a big deal out of nothing." Becca sighed. "I mean, everybody has sex! You didn't think Tristen Hyde was a *virgin,* did you?"

No, I hadn't thought that, and yet . . . "Get out," I ordered her again. "Just leave me alone!"

"Whatever." She headed for the door. I got the sense that she felt like she'd met her obligation to me and was wiping her hands clean of the whole mess. "I still think the party would do you good. You spend too much time in this gloomy old house."

The door slammed behind her, and I trudged upstairs and stood, once more, before my mirror.

Talk about a monster. The girl reflected there didn't just disappoint me. She *sickened* me. She was so stupid, and naive, and grotesquely innocent. She'd been pointlessly waiting, dreaming of romance, of *love*, when everybody else was busy screwing, randomly and meaninglessly, taking whatever satisfaction they wanted with no regard for emotions.

What a fool she was. What a pathetic *sucker*.

I wanted to tear off her carefully ironed blouse with the same violence that the beast had started to use back in the lab. I wanted to yank off her plastic eyeglasses and grind them under my feet. I wanted to rip out her childish ponytail and chop off her mousy brown hair, hacking at it painfully with the dull blade of a knife.

Turning my back on Jill Jekel, I went to my dresser and hauled open the top drawer, digging until my fingers touched smooth glass. Grabbing the vial, I yanked out the stopper and raised the beaker to my lips.

As the formula trickled down my throat, the pain seized me, and within seconds I was on the floor, and I did yank out my ponytail and tear at my blouse as I writhed against the hardwood in agony, my stomach seeming to dissolve inside me.

But not once did I regret what I'd done. And when I managed to rise to my knees, shaking, shirt torn from throat to navel, hair wild, I crawled back to the mirror and looked at my face, a smile— a *sneer*—creeping across my lips and a gleam forming in my eyes.

Jill Jekel as I knew her was vanishing.

Chapter 75

Jill

WHAT A NICE BIG NEEDLE. How it gleams on the dresser. How sharp it will feel inside of me.

Slowly, slowly, I press the point against the flesh of my earlobe. The metal pierces deep, penetrating virgin skin, a bead of blood oozing out and trickling down the instrument to dribble across my fingers, making them sticky and warm.

Yes, yes . . .

The point erupts through the other side with an audible pop, and the deed is done. I withdraw the slick instrument, twisting it in the hole, savoring the sting, and the blood, dripping on my shoulder, stains ivory fabric.

I raise the needle again, the process is repeated, and—both ears ravished—I go to Mrs. Jekel's jewelry box, digging until I find two big gold hoops.

Absolutely perfect for a party.

Chapter 76

Tristen

"JILL?" I OPENED the back door a crack. "Are you here?"

When she didn't answer, I entered the dark kitchen. "Jill? Sorry I'm late."

But I was speaking to no one. The house was obviously empty.

Assuming that she had run out for a moment, I paced around, waiting for her—purposely avoiding the very thing that drew me.

That old Steinway in the corner.

Did I dare? My stomach twisted just to think about it, yet I did risk a glance.

Find out, Tristen. Have the guts to play. You're alone, with no one to hear if you fail.

Taking a deep breath, I sat down, poised my fingers, and closing my eyes, I touched the keys, wincing as my broken wrist suffered the impact. But it wasn't just the physical pain that struck me as I struggled to bring forth something, anything, worth hearing.

Yes, I could still play. I had technical skills and could create a melody.

But the inspiration, the *darkness* that had driven my best work—it was gone.

Pounding the keyboard, but impotently, I gave up and buried my face in my hands, mourning not just the loss of my talent but finally the *thing* that I'd killed, too.

The beast. We had been bitter enemies—and yet collaborators, too. I'd suspected so, for longer than I cared to admit. And when I'd drunk the formula, slaying the monster within, I really had murdered my talent, too.

Pressing my palms against my eyes, refusing to give in to weakness and break down, I couldn't help but wonder. What would Grandfather have thought to see me stripped of my gift? Would he have said the bargain was a good one? Or that the price I'd paid for drinking the formula had been too high? Would Grandfather have perhaps ventured that the terrible beauty we'd both *known* I'd been destined to create might have been worth the price of even human life?

Long after the last notes died away, I sat in the silence, the absence of sound that would henceforth define my life, thinking that liberation from my demon wasn't as sweet as I'd anticipated.

"You will drink again, Tristen, of your own free will . . ."

Those words echoed again in my mind, and I forced myself to think not of music but of the way the beast had pressed Jill against the lab table, wanting to violate her, *kill* her.

I finally rose, aware that I would probably never sit at a piano again, but grateful that at least I had Jill. Her life, her happiness, were worth any sacrifice.

But where in the world was she on such an important night?

Impatient, needing her, I went up the staircase, headed for her room, looking for some clue as to where she might have gone. And when I opened the door and switched on a light . . .

Oh, hell.

Chapter 77

Tristen

THE PARTY at Christy Hitchcock's house was well underway when I arrived, pushing through the crowd of drunken Supplee Mill students, looking for Jill.

She had to be there somewhere. The party's existence was common knowledge, and the phone book on Jill's desk had been open to the correct page, as if she'd checked the address. Whoever "she" was . . .

"Jill's not here, Tris."

I felt the tap on my shoulder and spun around to find Becca Wright smiling. "Becca—what happened? Where is she?"

"Your girlfriend is totally out of control." Becca laughed. "Totally!"

I knew that. The first thing I'd noticed when I'd entered Jill's room was the distinctive smell of toxic chemicals. And the mess. Clothes were strewn everywhere. And then I'd seen the self-portrait on the easel. The wicked, wicked eyes that Jill had bestowed on herself.

Why had she drunk the formula?

"Is Jill *here*?" I repeated. "Is she all right?"

Becca rolled her eyes. "Oh, she'll be fine. Your precious girl-friend just went off the deep end because I told her we slept to-gether last summer."

"You did *what*?" I demanded, fighting an almost overpowering urge to shake her violently. "But that's a lie!"

"Whatever, Tris." She sighed. "We *practically* did—before you freaked out. It's splitting hairs."

"We did not even come close, Becca!"

"We had our shirts off—"

"And our pants *on*."

"Jill needed to know about you, Tristen," Becca said, trying to sound grimly serious. But she couldn't quite keep a smile from slip-ping across her lips. "I did her a favor."

I glared down at the perky, malicious little cheerleader, seething with anger. I could tell, just from the smug look on her face, that Becca had told Jill we'd had sex to hurt her. Or maybe to break Jill and me apart. Because Jill *would* split hairs. For me—not some uncon-trollable beast but *me*—to have slept with one of her few friends, that, of all the heinous things I'd done, might hurt her the most deeply. Might very well cause Jill to do something reckless and drastic.

I grabbed Becca's arm. "Where is she?"

Becca laughed, knowing that she was about to wound me, too. "She just left—with Todd. They said something about going back to her house."

God, no. Not Flick . . .

I released Becca and began to shove through the crowd. But she caught my wrist. "What?" I snapped, whirling on her. "What now?"

I expected her to deliver a cruel, final barb. However, she didn't sound mean, only hurt, as she asked, "Tristen, why Jill? Why not me?"

"You told me to get away from you," I said, confused.

"But you don't even *look*," she said, ego clearly bruised. "You only look at Jill."

Becca was wrong to come between me and Jill simply because I'd hurt her pride, but *I* ended up saying, "I'm sorry."

Then I plunged through the crowd and into the night, desperate to get to Jill before Todd got to her. Or vice versa. Honestly I didn't know who was in greater danger.

Chapter 78

Jill

TODD FLICK THUDS DOWN on to the couch, foolishly believing he's about to kick a field goal between my legs. I climb onto his lap, and he puts a clumsy hand on my waist. "I knew you wanted this," he says. "You uptight girls always get crazy for sex sooner or later."

"Oh, Todd," I sigh. Such a pretty, pretty corpse he will be. And not much stupider in death than in life! I swing my legs around to straddle him. "Pretty, pretty Todd!"

"You're weird, Jekel," he says, eyes glazing over with the lust that will make him vulnerable. "But I kinda like it."

"What about Darcy?" I pout. "Won't she be mad?"

"I'm sick of that bitch," Todd confides, clasping my hips with both hands and pressing me tighter against him. "She's too bossy."

"I won't boss you, Toddy," I promise. "You'll be the man *with me." The* dead *man.*

"No, you'll do what I say, right?" Todd says, closing his eyes and licking his lips as I rub against him. "Whatever I say, right?"

"Oh, yes . . ."

Just as I lean forward, prepared to kiss his disgusting lips and endure his fat tongue inside my mouth, the door erupts open and in bursts Tristen Hyde. The guy I really want.

Right on cue.

Chapter 79

Tristen

ALTHOUGH I KNEW that the girl writhing against Todd Flick wasn't really Jill, the scene in the Jekel's living room made me want to puke, or perhaps kill someone. And because I could never harm Jill—not any aspect of her—I chose Flick.

"Get the hell away from her," I snarled, stalking toward them, tearing Jill off his lap and hauling Flick to his feet.

"Get off me, Hyde," he snapped, pulling away. "This is none of your business." He jabbed a thick finger at Jill. "*She* hit on *me*, dude!"

I was all too conscious of the fact that I'd played a role in driving her to Flick, and I was fully aware that Jill was not really even in the room, yet his assertion nearly knocked the wind out of me. I'd never been jealous before, but this was *Jill.*

"I'm going to kill you," I growled, advancing toward him, grabbing his shirt, and shaking him hard. "Did you kiss her? Did you *touch* her?"

Flick laughed. Actually laughed up into my face. "You ruined my season," he spat. "And now I'm going to do your girlfriend. Tonight." He pried at my fingers. "So let me go and get the hell *out* of here."

I did let him go—just long enough to haul back my fist and smash it into the side of his jaw, sending him stumbling backwards. But he caught himself, regained his balance, and charged me, using his shorter stature to advantage by ramming me with his shoulder as if I were a tackling dummy on the practice field.

We both fell to the ground, Flick on top of me. I was so furious, though, that I easily rolled him off and pinned him to the floor. I was kneeling over his chest, not quite sure what I planned to do next—both of us regarding each other warily as we struggled for breath—when I felt a light tap on my shoulder.

"You dropped this," a throaty, seductive, feminine voice said. "And I thought you might want it."

I dared to look sideways and saw that my knife—blade open—was being offered to me by a delicate familiar hand.

And me . . . I accepted the weapon.

Chapter 80

Tristen

"DUDE!" FLICK'S EYES DARTED between the knife and my face. "What the . . . ?"

"The knife's not for you," I advised him, hurling the weapon across the floor so it spun under the couch. Then I rose off Flick, who scuttled backwards like a crab. "Get out of here," I ordered him. "And never mention this—unless you want me to tell Darcy what you were doing. And trust me, she really *would* kill you."

"You two are nuts," he said, dragging himself upright and starting for the door, keeping a good distance between me and the incarnation of Jill, whom I caught in my arms as she lunged toward the knife.

"Tristen, hurt him," she demanded, writhing against me. "Do it!"

Flick was almost at the door. "Something's wrong with both of you!"

"Remember that and consider yourself warned," I told him, fighting against Jill, who threatened to break free. The formula had made her strong. "Now *go!*"

Flick hauled open the door and darted into the night, and although Jill was powerful, I was still stronger, and I spun her to face me. Suddenly she went soft in my arms, accepting my hold. I looked into her eyes, desperate to see the girl I loved. But she was gone. In her place was a creature who looked like Jill Jekel if she were to wear tighter clothes, mess up her usually sleek hair, and— What had happened to her ears? The lobes were red and bloody.

"Jill, you hurt yourself," I said with dismay, forgetting for a moment that Jill was absent. "You're bleeding."

"Oh, god, Tristen." She scowled at me with eyes that were dead as a shark's. "You're such a coward. It's just a little blood. And there should be a lot more on the floor right now! If you loved me, you would have killed him!" She hit my chest, hard. "But you *don't* love me, do you?"

"I love Jill," I said. "I want her back."

"Jill is a coward, too," the creature snapped. "She lets people bully her! I had to take revenge!"

"Jill saved my life," I said. "She's strong, and sweet, and beautiful."

"She's pathetic."

"Where is the formula?" I demanded. "Where did you get it?"

"Jill stole it, that first night in the lab," she said, smiling at the shock on my face. "Jill—not me. Because she *wanted* to be me. She tasted it on *your* lips, Tristen. And after that she craved that side of herself."

Suddenly it all made sense. Jill's crazy behavior in the classroom: I had been responsible for that. I hadn't even thought about the formula that lingered on my tongue. "No," I said, choking on my guilt. "I didn't mean to . . ."

"Don't sound so guilty," she groaned. "It's good, what happened. The formula is *good* for all of us."

"That's not true."

In my shock and remorse I had loosened my grip, and she abruptly tore free of me and stalked to the piano, hips swinging. Standing next to the upright, she hit a note. "Why don't you play, Tristen? Compose something?"

I froze in place. "How did you know . . . ?"

"Because *I* understand that side of you," she said. "Jill didn't understand it, but I recognize the music you made. I know where that came from. And now it's gone, isn't it, Tristen?"

Seeing Jill's body on top of Flick had been like a punch to the gut. But to hear the pity in her voice as she spoke of the way I'd been diminished—that ripped out my soul. I couldn't even reply, and she walked away from the piano, drawing close to me, raising her hand to stroke my cheek. I closed my eyes, not wanting to look into hers.

"Tristen," she tempted me, "you could play again, tonight. Just kiss me. Taste the formula on *my* tongue, and you could play. Then *we* could play."

I shook my head, fighting rising desire. Dual *desires*, actually. "No, never."

She slipped her hands around my neck, and I felt her rise up, her chest brushing mine. "It would be so *good*, Tristen," she promised, digging her fingers into my hair. "We could be amazing together. You could have your nice girl sometimes. And you could have me, too. We have the formula, Tristen. We could have it all."

Oh, god, I *wanted* it all, right then. The creature in my arms was promising me everything that a man could possibly wish for. We could be saints all day and sinners all night. I could have my talent back, and play the world's greatest concert halls, have power and prestige. I would be able to control it. I wouldn't lose control . . .

"Do it, Tristen," she urged. Her breath was warm against my lips, and I could smell the potent mix of chemicals. "Just kiss me."

My talent . . . power . . . sex . . .

"Oh, Jill," I groaned, losing my fight with temptation, "don't do this to me."

I muttered that protest—yet I bent my head to meet her mouth.

Chapter 81

Tristen

AND THEN, JUST BEFORE I fell prey to all my darkest desires, I opened my eyes.

"No," I said, pulling back. There was nothing for me in her eyes. Nothing.

Of course I still grieved my old talent and yearned to hear, even one more time, the applause of a crowd. And there was a part of me, I was ashamed to admit, that missed some of the beast's most twisted, unfettered thoughts, the longings expressed and experienced freely without the slightest twinge of guilt. The way the beast was free to live without moral constraint—there was a seductive element to that, too.

But more than talent or accolades or freedom from the world's moral strictures and the pressures of my own conscience, I wanted Jill.

I didn't want the girl who was offering herself to me shamelessly right then. I wanted the girl I'd planned to *refuse* to make love to that same night, because I thought in the end Jill would regret sleeping with a doomed man mainly because she felt time was running out. Under different circumstances she would have waited.

I knew that most people would consider us too young to talk about lifelong commitments or marriage, but I couldn't imagine taking her to bed without that promise. Even if it meant never being with her, I didn't want to have one desperate, hurried, hidden night. I wanted to put a ring on her finger. I wanted a future—or nothing. I knew, in her heart, that she would want that, too.

"Where's the rest of the formula?" I demanded. "I want Jill back."

"Never," she insisted, shaking her head. "You're so weak, Tristen."

But the creature I held, she was the one growing weak. I could already see her eyes softening and growing weary. Her hands were loosening around my neck.

"Come on." I slipped my arms beneath her legs, lifting her and cradling her against my chest. "I'm taking you to bed."

"Finally," she said with a hint of a snarl. But her head rested heavily against my chest. "It's about time."

"We're just going to sleep," I told her. I wouldn't leave her alone that night, in case there was still some formula in the house. I doubted that she would get up and drink again, but I couldn't risk it. "We have a contest to win tomorrow, remember?"

"Oh, fuck that," she grumbled, yawning as I climbed the stairs. "We could have that money and so much more . . ."

"All I want is Jill back," I repeated. I was confused, though. The girl who uttered that curse had sounded like *Jill*. But she would *never* say that word . . .

I wanted to get her to talk again, but she was already sound asleep as I placed her on the bed. I removed her shoes, then gingerly pulled the earrings from her bloody ears. The wounds were small but obviously crude.

Oh, Jill . . . How could she have done that to her own body?

How could I have carelessly kissed her with the formula on my tongue?

After locating some rubbing alcohol and cotton in the Jekels' bathroom, I sat on the bed and, cradling Jill's jaw in my palm, wiped away the dried blood, making sure the disinfectant went deep into the holes. Jill grimaced in her sleep, and I flinched, too, knowing how the alcohol would sting. "Hush, love," I soothed when she whimpered. "This needs to be done."

When the wounds were clean, I took off my shoes, too, and lay by her side, wondering what she would say when she woke up to find me next to her. Would she be appalled to learn of her alter ego's behavior? Or had the incidents of the day—the lie of a friend and her own reckless, dangerous response—would those things change Jill so much that she would never be quite the same?

As she slept in my arms, I lay awake wondering, with more than a little apprehension, if I would *ever* recognize the girl I loved again.

Chapter 82

Jill

I WOKE UP in the middle of the night, felt an arm around my waist, and panicked. The last thing I remembered was Becca telling me she'd slept with Tristen, so it couldn't be him . . .

Bracing myself, I rolled over, and I didn't know if I was relieved or horrified to see that it really was Tristen in my bed. Had we . . . *done* anything after I'd changed? If so, I'd stolen from *myself*. Even though I didn't love him anymore. I didn't . . .

"Tristen." I shook his shoulder. "Wake up."

He opened his eyes, tensing. "Jill?"

I could tell that he wasn't sure if he was with me or a monster. "It's me," I said. "Just me."

His muscles relaxed, and he held me tighter, not saying anything.

I didn't try to pull away, and after a while he asked in a whisper, "Where's the formula, Jill? Do you have more?"

"No," I promised. "It's gone."

"If you do, tell me," he urged. "It's unpredictable. The novel says so. It's wearing off for you now—but what if it doesn't next time? And what if you don't have enough to drink and change back?"

"I don't have any," I insisted.

Then I started to cry and buried my face against his chest, and even though I was turning to him for comfort, and his concern for me was so clear, I spoke the thought that had driven me to drink the formula in the first place. "I hate you so much, Tristen."

He kept holding me, but I felt him suck in a sharp breath, and I knew that I could never take the words back. I kept crying against him, and he kept stroking my back, but his touch was different.

Downstairs the back porch creaked as somebody stepped on the boards, and although Tristen and I should have been terrified—whether it was his dad coming to kill him or my mom about to catch us together in bed—neither one of us seemed to have the energy even for fear. We just kept lying there together as the door opened and my mom's familiar, light steps stole into the kitchen and up the stairs, headed straight for her room.

"I never slept with Becca," Tristen whispered when my mother shut her door. "She lied to you."

I wished then that his dad *had* come to my house. I would have stepped between them and taken the violence that Tristen expected. It felt like I'd already been stabbed and was dying.

I shouldn't have trusted Becca, even though we'd been friends since kindergarten. I should have asked Tristen. I could have trusted *him* to tell the truth.

Me—ultimately it had been *me* who had ruined everything. And it was too late to fix what I'd said to him.

I hate you so much, Tristen.

He pulled away from me and swung his legs off the bed. "I'm going now."

I wanted to beg him to stay, but I knew he wouldn't. "Okay."

He sat on the edge of my bed, lacing on his shoes. "We have the presentation tonight," he reminded me. He didn't sound hurt. Just detached and practical. "We leave right after school."

"Tristen, you don't have to help me."

He stood. "We have a deal, and I'm an honorable person."

I didn't know if he meant to hurt me by rubbing my nose in my own shame or if he was just stating a fact about himself, but the words stung, and when he was gone, I curled up on my side and cried until dawn.

I never did learn what my alter ego had done that night, but later when I looked in my mirror, I saw two holes in my ears that hadn't been there before, and I hoped that they were the only way I'd let myself be violated.

Chapter 83

Tristen

AFTER I LEFT JILL'S HOUSE, I broke into the school one final time. I moved through the hallways without fear, because I had nothing left to lose. Jill had said she *hated* me, and her words had left me cold inside. To make matters worse, I knew that she was right to despise me. I had carelessly kissed her and cleaved and corrupted her soul.

Locating my locker, I spun the combination—one lock that I didn't have to pick—and tugged on the handle. Reaching behind my jacket, I dug into the plastic bag and retrieved the Gatorade bottle full of formula. Uncapping it, I went to the closest water fountain and dumped the contents down the drain, rinsing away every last drop.

I'd given up hope of curing my father, and I wouldn't leave any extra lying around for Jill or anyone else to find, in the event of my death.

Tossing the empty bottle in a trash can, I left the school and went home and waited for dawn, just wishing the contest was over. Because after we won the money, I would destroy the notes and the list of salts. And when they were gone, all that would be left of the formula on this earth would be the portion that Jill had just lied about not having.

Chapter 84

Jill

I RAPPED ON MOM'S OPEN bedroom door, and she smiled at me, shaking out a red dress. "Good morning!"

I leaned against the door frame, holding a bowl of cold cereal that I was trying to force down, although I wasn't hungry. "That's a pretty fancy outfit for visiting Aunt Christine," I noted, watching her fold the dress and tuck it in the open suitcase on her bed. "I guess you guys are going out, huh?"

She stayed bent over the suitcase, not looking at me. "It never hurts to be ready." She straightened and frowned at me. "I'm really sorry about missing your presentation. You're sure you don't mind if I'm away this weekend?"

I swallowed a soggy lump of Cheerios. "Just have a good trip, okay?"

She came over to me, arms outstretched. "Thanks, Jilly." Then she hugged me, nearly spilling my cereal. Her body finally felt substantial against mine. "And good luck. I'll call tonight for all the details."

"Sure." I pulled away. "I need to get ready for school. I have a chem test today, too."

Mom smiled again as she continued packing. "You'll do fine with both things, I'm sure."

"Thanks." As I turned to go to my room, I saw my mother folding her black dress, too, and I thought she was probably expecting too much excitement from a weekend in Cape May with her sister. But I was too preoccupied with a sadness that bordered on numbness, and a vengeful scheme I had planned, to dwell on Mom's life.

Chapter 85

Jill

"JILL, WHAT HAPPENED after the party?" Becca whispered.

"Nothing," I said, but the blood drained from my face. I'd gone to the party . . .

She gave me a knowing smile. "I told you the party would help. You definitely got over Tristen!"

"I guess so," I agreed. What had I—had that *thing* I'd unleashed—done to "get over Tristen"? Something with a boy? But it didn't matter, I reminded myself. The night was over, and Tristen and I were over. Nothing really mattered.

"You have forty minutes to complete the test," Mr. Messerschmidt said, beginning to hand out the exams, offering Darcy a stack.

She turned to pass copies to me, and Todd twisted around, too, giving me a weird, almost scared look. I didn't want to know why.

"Good luck tonight," Darcy said as I accepted the tests.

"Thanks." I kept one copy, handed the rest to Becca, and set right to work. When I got to the third question, I reached up to tuck my hair behind my ear—but not in a nervous way. I kept my hand there a long time, until Becca realized that my paper was exposed. I glanced to her, saw her questioning look, and gave a subtle nod.

She began to copy, eyes darting and hand flying, and we fell into a pattern: me racing ahead and Becca playing catch-up whenever I would adjust my hair.

Too bad all of the answers I gave her were wrong.

Too bad we'd have identical failing exams, which would probably land us both on academic probation in our crucial senior years. Maybe we'd both fail the whole class.

A part of me wanted to look back to see if Tristen saw me cheating. I wondered what he would think if he noticed. But I didn't check, because I had a feeling that he wasn't bothering to look at me at all, and that would have been even worse than his disapproval.

"Time's up," Mr. Messerschmidt eventually called.

We handed in our papers, and I smiled at Becca as we left the room, telling her, "I hope that repays the favor you did me. I hope we're even now."

Chapter 86

Jill

"READY?" MR. MESSERSCHMIDT asked, one hand on the top of his car's open trunk.

I double checked the contents, making sure everything we needed was inside. The display I'd designed, the box with all the papers, the chemicals we'd need for our demonstration, and some of the rats that had shown reactions to variations of the formula. "Do you think they'll be okay?" I asked Tristen.

"It's less than an hour's ride," he said, shrugging. "I'm sure they'll be fine."

"Maybe we should keep them up front."

"They're rats," he pointed out. "Who cares if they're comfortable?"

But I'd seen him stroke the animals and worry over them . . . Was he growing cold to *everything?*

"Just get in the car, Jill," Tristen said, preempting Mr. Messerschmidt by slamming the trunk shut. "Please."

I wondered then if *he* hated *me.* Or if he was beyond caring after what I'd said. Maybe I was like a rat in his eyes. A creature beneath concern or consideration.

I crawled into the back seat, Tristen and Mr. Messerschmidt got in the front, and we headed to the University of the Sciences in Philadelphia.

I stared out the window at the passing traffic, one hand in the pocket of my best wool coat, the one I'd worn to my dad's funeral, my fingers caressing the vial that contained what was left of the formula.

Chapter 87

Jill

THE ASTRAZENECA AUDITORIUM at the University of the Sciences was already crowded when we got there, and I got nervous just looking around at the students and teachers and parents who were lugging in plastic bins filled with their presentation materials.

Soon I would have to stand on stage in front of all those people, some of the top science students in the nation, and *Darcy Gray*, who'd laugh at how my voice would quiver like it always did when I spoke in public.

"Come on, Jill," Tristen said, nodding for me to follow him. He held the carrier full of rats. "Let's go."

"I . . . I . . ." I hung back.

"Jill, you're second on the program," Mr. Messerschmidt noted. "You should probably get backstage and set up."

I looked to Tristen, wanting to tell him that I was scared. I wanted to lean on him and borrow his strength. But his eyes were neutral, and he didn't encourage me.

"You go ahead," I said. "I need to use the restroom."

"Fine," Tristen agreed. "You're the boss."

I watched him lead Mr. Messerschmidt through the crowded aisle toward the stage. He was taller than most of the teachers, even, and I easily followed his progress. Even in a new setting where he didn't know anybody, and although his injuries didn't look as ominous anymore, people seemed to part and make way for Tristen Hyde. I didn't think they were picking up on some menace that lurked inside of him. I thought they just instinctively recognized that he was special somehow.

How could I have thrown him away?

I turned away, scanning the auditorium for a restroom. Seeing a sign, I began to thread my way through the increasing throngs— with increasing panic.

I was going to freak out. Darcy would laugh at me, mercilessly, as she accepted her check for thirty thousand dollars.

I touched the vial in my pocket with sweaty fingers.

The evening didn't have to end so badly, though. I knew somebody who was bold. Somebody not afraid to steal, or go to parties. Somebody who would probably *love* to be on stage with all eyes on her and who could win the money. And what, really, did I have to lose by summoning my alter ego one last time? I'd already lost Tristen, and maybe my virtue, at a party I couldn't recall, and I was about to be humiliated, anyway. Wouldn't it be better not even to remember?

But it wasn't just stage fright that made me reach again for the vial, as I stepped inside the ladies' room. If I had been honest, I would have admitted that it was my inability to live one more second with myself.

I'd destroyed my one chance at love. Becca had handed me the hatchet, but I was the one who'd hacked to pieces my relationship with Tristen.

Maybe I just *wanted* to drink the formula, too. Just plain wanted to do it, and everything else was just an excuse.

I hurried toward a stall and was just about to step inside when somebody spoke to me.

"Well, well, well, if it isn't half the losing team of Jekel and Hyde!"

Chapter 88

Jill

"WHAT ARE YOU doing here, Darcy?" I blurted, fingers curling around the vial in my pocket.

I realized the question was stupid as soon as it came out of my mouth, and of course Darcy laughed. "I'm here for the contest. Duh." She rolled her eyes and continued applying blush at the mirror. "I hope you're that sharp on stage," she added. "It'll be that much easier to beat you."

"Don't be so sure you're going to win," I warned her. "Tristen and I have a good presentation."

"I've seen you talk in public." Darcy smiled, dropping her makeup into her purse. "Remember seventh grade when you gave that book report? You ended up running out of the room!"

"This isn't seventh grade anymore," I reminded her.

"But you're the same person," Darcy said. "The same mousy girl you've always been—and always will be. You might be teamed up with a smooth-talking, arrogant thug, but at heart you're still a frightened little baby, Jill. It's just who you are."

I knew Darcy was deliberately undermining my confidence to boost her chances of winning. But I also knew that she was just being mean for the hell of it. And to make matters worse, she'd just insulted Tristen.

Pulling my hand out of my pocket, I walked up to Darcy and took the fingers that had just been clutching the formula, opened them wide, and slapped her across the face hard enough to make up for about a decade of abuse. My palm print stained her cheek, and she clapped her hand across her face, glaring at me in mute disbelief.

"I'll see you on stage," I said. "And don't ever insult me or Tristen again."

Then I marched out of the bathroom, forgetting all about taking the formula. I found Tristen backstage doing some last-minute rehearsal. He glanced up from his notes. "I suppose you'd prefer that I speak—"

"No," I interrupted, holding out my hand. "This is my experiment, right?"

Tristen seemed surprised but handed over the notes. "Of course."

"Jekel? Hyde?" A woman with a clipboard approached us. "It's time."

"Let's go," I said, shrugging out of my wool coat, dropping it with the rest of our stuff, and leading Tristen onto the stage.

Chapter 89

Jill

"YOU TWO SHOULD really be proud," Mr. Messerschmidt said as we drove down the turnpike. "You did a great job."

"We didn't win, though," I said, hunched in the back seat.

Tristen twisted around to face me. "But you were outstanding, Jill. Everyone loved you."

The compliment was bittersweet. *Everyone but you, Tristen.* I'd seen to that.

"Thanks," I said.

Tristen didn't turn back around. He kept facing me in the darkness. A car passed us in the next lane, and the headlights briefly lit his face, and I thought I saw a trace of admiration and maybe even affection in his eyes, and suddenly I didn't care so much about losing the money. At least Tristen had thawed a little.

"We did do okay, didn't we?" I sort of smiled at the memory of me, Jill Jekel, delivering a flawless speech in front of about two hundred people. "Third place isn't bad."

Tristen's white teeth flashed in the darkness. "Especially since Darcy got fifth."

It was mean to be happy about her failure, but I couldn't help grinning, too.

Tristen reached back then and gave my knee a shake. "I'm proud of you."

"Thanks," I repeated as he turned to face forward again.

Although the heater in Mr. Messerschmidt's car wasn't reaching the back seat, I felt warmer suddenly. Tristen had touched me. It didn't mean he still loved me, but it was better than the cold distance that had separated us. It was a start, maybe.

Hunkering down in my seat, I buried my hands in my pockets and stared out at the passing night. I was so distracted, thinking about Tristen, that we went about a full mile before I realized that the vial was gone.

Chapter 90

Tristen

MESSERSCHMIDT PULLED UP in front of Jill's house, and immediately something struck me as not quite right.

"Jill," I said, opening the door and flipping up my seat, "I thought you said your mother was out of town."

She clasped my hand and struggled to get out. "She is."

I continued holding her hand and directed her attention to the glowing windows—and the smoking chimney—of her house. "Well, someone's home. And they've lit a fire."

She started to pull her hand from mine, but I wouldn't let her go. I didn't want to release her. Not yet. For I had a very bad feeling about the scene before us. It was just an instinct born of my own knowledge of how the beast would behave.

I stroked Jill's hand with my thumb, hoping to convey that even if she hated me, I still loved her. I couldn't help loving her. I wanted to do so much more than just touch her hand. I wanted to take her in my arms and tell her that I was sorry for all that had gone wrong between us and for all of the awful things I had wrought upon her life, from forcing her to trespass in the school to carelessly altering her very soul with a kiss.

But of course I couldn't, with Messerschmidt watching.

"Maybe Mom came back," Jill said. She didn't sound convinced, though. In fact, I got the clear sense that alarm bells were going off for her, too.

The scene was so innocuous. And yet something was wrong.

Messerschmidt opened the trunk, offering, "I'll help you take everything inside."

I squeezed Jill's hand again. "You wait out here, eh?"

She looked up at me with those wide, wonderful eyes, which had just captivated an entire auditorium full of people as they'd always captivated me, and shook her head, her ponytail swinging. "No, Tristen. Let's go in together."

"Jill . . ."

"Come on," Messerschmidt prompted, lifting out the old box. "It's late and cold."

She pressed my palm, and I knew that she wouldn't let me go alone, no matter how I insisted. She truly had changed—and not only because she'd tasted the formula. The Jill Jekel who had emerged in the last few weeks was *completely* beyond my control.

"Let's get a move on," Messerschmidt urged, starting up the steps.

Releasing Jill's hand, I removed the box from Messerschmidt's grasp, stepped past him, and led the way inside the house.

Chapter 91

Jill

I WAS GLAD Mr. Messerschmidt came with us. Tristen knew something was wrong. *I* knew something was wrong. Mom wasn't supposed to be home. And she never lit fires. That had been Dad's thing.

"Jill, give me the keys." Tristen held out his hand. "Please."

I almost protested . . . then did as he asked.

Mr. Messerschmidt cleared his throat, almost like he was nervous, too, for some reason.

Tristen put the key in lock, opened the door, and we all stepped inside.

And what we saw there . . . it was even worse than what I'd imagined we might find.

Chapter 92

Jill

"MOM?" I CRIED. "What's happening?"

"I'm sorry, Jill," she said, voice trembling. She was sitting on the couch, a teacup perched on her knee, which was shaking, too. Violently. "I didn't tell you we were seeing each other. I thought it might upset you . . ." Her eyes darted to Dr. Hyde, who stood near the fireplace, smiling a crooked, evil smile. "And then he changed . . ."

"Yes, people do change," Dr. Hyde agreed, stepping away from the fire. "Don't they, Tristen?" His smile shifted to a scowl. "And sometimes they must change back."

"Run for help," Tristen directed Mr. Messerschmidt over his shoulder. "Hurry."

But for the first time our teacher didn't follow Tristen's direction. "I can't do that," he said.

"Then grab your cell—call the police," Tristen snapped, keeping a wary eye on his father. "You don't understand what's happening here. Listen to me!"

Mr. Messerschmidt turned as instructed—then slowly and deliberately spun the deadbolt, sealing us all in together.

Tristen whipped around. "What are you doing, you idiot?"

"I'm sorry, Tristen," Mr. Messerschmidt said, cringing. "I have to do what your father says."

What? I stared at my teacher, not understanding.

"What the hell is going on here?" Tristen demanded, turning

267

back to his father. "How do you know Messerschmidt? And what are you doing to Jill's mother? This is about you and me!"

Dr. Hyde walked behind the couch and rested his hands on my mom's shoulders, and I wanted to scream. Mom's hands shook so hard that the contents of the teacup spilled out onto her pants. I followed the spreading stain and realized that her ankles were bound. My throat tightened like the duct tape was around my neck, too.

"Don't spill that, dear," he said, squeezing Mom's shoulder. His hands appeared gnarled and he stood slightly hunched, the monster finally casting off the mask it had worn. Dr. Hyde had changed, physically, like Tristen had done in the lab. Only this time the transformation was complete. The handsome, if imposing, psychiatrist was gone, replaced by a grotesque—and completely terrifying—creature with eyes that seemed barely human.

There were hints of Dr. Hyde: the beard, the suit, the shape of his face. And yet the beard wasn't neatly trimmed, the suit hung wrong on uneven shoulders, and the features on his face were warped and irregular. The bent nose, the lopsided mouth—they were awful, physical manifestations of the twisted soul that had emerged.

This thing . . . It was someone—something—else. And it was terrible to behold.

"Steady, now," he urged again when Mom's hand kept trembling. "You might be thirsty later."

"What are you doing?" Tristen repeated, his own tone ominous.

"Blackmailing you," Dr. Hyde said. "Tonight you will drink the formula or watch your girlfriend's mother drink what is in *her* cup. And then we will all sit and watch Mrs. Jekel die, slowly and in agony. And if *that* doesn't convince you, I will break your little girlfriend's neck with my bare hands."

I stifled the urge to cry out as tears began to stream down Mom's face.

"Over my dead body," Tristen said, putting a protective hand on my arm.

"As you wish," Dr. Hyde agreed.

"What's in the cup?" I spoke for the first time since coming in the door.

Dr. Hyde released Mom's shoulders and stepped around from behind the couch. "Household bleach. A common but effective corrosive—as I'm sure you, a chemist, know perfectly well."

"No . . ." I shook my head, looking to Tristen. "No . . ."

"We don't have any formula," Tristen pointed out. "If you thought we made some at the contest, you're wrong. It was just a demonstration. I didn't add the final ingredient. I won't ever again."

"You know how to make it, and you have everything you need in the car," Dr. Hyde growled, stepping closer. His eyes were so metallic, and the smell of him . . . He smelled like a corpse already rotting in the grave.

Is that what Tristen would have become? What I would have become if I'd kept drinking the formula?

Where *was* the formula?

I shot Mr. Messerschmidt a confused glance. And how—why—had our teacher betrayed us?

"I don't have *all* the ingredients," Tristen insisted. "I don't have the altered salt!"

This revelation seemed to anger Dr. Hyde further—but didn't sway him from his plan. "You will tell Messerschmidt what is needed, he will get it, and you *will* drink the solution!" he snapped. "Tonight, as I planned!"

"Tristen, don't!" I cried. I couldn't let him become like the monster that stood before us. It would only delay the inevitable for my mother and me. I didn't believe Dr. Hyde would let either of us leave the house alive. There was no reason for Tristen to destroy his soul again. "Don't make more."

"I *can't* do it," Tristen said. "And neither can you."

And with that, he drew back his arm and hurled the old metal box into the fireplace, where the unlocked clasp opened on impact, the papers flying into the flames.

"YOU FOOL!" the beast roared, staring into the flames, curling and uncurling its fingers as the documents were consumed. "YOU IDIOT!" He spun to face Tristen. "You were the best of our lineage. Young, smart, ambitious—and talented! With your gift and our legacy you could have commanded incredible power. Been worshiped—and feared—around the world. Now you've ended everything!"

"On the contrary," Tristen said. "You and I—we are just beginning." He stepped closer to the beast. "Now let the women go, and let us conduct our business in private. Because I am *very* eager to see this through to the end."

I had seen Tristen Hyde's imperious side many times, but I'd never seen him be that commanding, and I thought he probably *could* have inspired both adoration and outright terror if his evil side really had been unleashed. Maybe he could do it, just on his own. But even the powerful guy who stood, feet planted wide on our old wooden floors, wasn't strong enough to slay the monster that seemed to be growing more hunched, and more vile, with every passing second. Not without unleashing his own terrible side . . .

"You have made a grave mistake, Tristen," the beast growled, stalking even closer. Tristen stepped in front of me, guarding me. "And now all of you will pay! You have cost your lover and her mother their lives, too."

I had no doubt then that we were all going to die as the beast reached out for Tristen, to take him first.

But suddenly, into the surreal silence that had descended upon all of us, Mr. Messerschmidt cried out, "Wait!"

Chapter 93

Jill

"I HAVE THE FORMULA," Mr. Messerschmidt announced, stepping out from where he lurked near the door.

We all spun to face him, and I saw the vial from my pocket. "How did you get that?" I demanded.

"From your coat," my teacher said. "I knew you'd made some. I listen to you kids, Jill, when you think I don't. I heard rumors about you changing. I thought, maybe, given how shy you are, you might take some to the contest. *I* would have done it if I had been you." His face reddened. "The formula is so . . . liberating."

"You—you've taken it?" Tristen asked, sounding confused.

"Oh yes," the beast chimed in with a deep, gloating laugh. "Tell them, Messerschmidt. Tell them how you were a paid guinea pig for Jill's father, testing the formula to 'cure' Dr. Hyde."

My mind struggled to keep up. "I don't understand . . ."

"I wasn't a guinea pig," Mr. Messerschmidt protested, sounding hurt. He looked to me. "Your father and I were *partners*. We were all going to share the accolades when we found the proper formula. I was going to be a respected scientist, in league with your dad!"

"You were never going to earn respect." The beast laughed. "You were a very well-compensated lab rat."

The final piece of the puzzle fell into place. My dad had paid Messerschmidt to help him in the lab. That was where my college savings had gone.

"You're wrong," Mr. Messerschmidt objected. "Dr. Jekel treated me fairly. We were *collaborators!*"

"Then why did you bite your master?" The beast laughed again, turning to me. "Your father was so determined to 'save' Frederick. What a miserable martyr Jekel was—killed by his own assistant!"

I spun to face my teacher.

"I didn't mean to, Jill," he said. "But when I took the last formula, I changed. I followed him to the parking lot, needing to know how to make more, but he wouldn't tell me the secret . . ."

The room started to whirl around me. Mr. Messerschmidt— my *teacher*—had killed my father?

Across the room my mother was sobbing loudly. I looked over and saw that the fire had spilled out onto the floor, and the rug was smoldering at her feet.

"Jill." Tristen grabbed my arms. Maybe I was swaying. "It's okay," he soothed. "It's okay . . ."

"You came to his *funeral*," I accused Mr. Messerschmidt, hearing the disbelief in my voice. "And you faced me, every day in class. How could you? How could you not *turn yourself in?*"

He didn't answer, and I saw not just guilt but shame on his face. A shame I recognized.

"You *still* wanted more!" I screamed. "That's why you forced me and Tristen together to do the contest. You wanted us to make more so you could change again. Even after what you did to my father!"

"Yes," Mr. Messerschmidt confessed, breaking down before our eyes. "Your father . . . he never did tell me the final ingredient . . ." He buried his face in his hands, starting to cry. "I knew you and Tristen were smart enough to figure it out. I pushed you two together . . ." He raised his face to me. "God help me, I craved it . . ."

"I don't understand," Tristen said, turning to face the beast. "When did Messerschmidt start working for *you?*"

The monster in my living room was grinning again. "When you destroyed yourself, Tristen, I went to Messerschmidt, thinking he'd somehow figured out the formula and 'cured' you. But that idiot didn't even know you were already working, let alone had *solved* the mystery. I figured that out. After that I made sure he pressured you to make more. Your teacher became *my* pawn." The beast snorted a laugh. "While I was enjoying myself, relaxing in a quiet hotel room and courting Mrs. Jekel—"

My stomach lurched again. I'd kind of known Mom was up to something, with the fancy dresses and new social life, but I had conveniently ignored the signs, having grown tired of taking care of her. I looked to my mother quaking on the couch and saw that the rug was starting to burn more brightly, the flames spreading. *Oh, Mom . . .* We were all going to die . . .

"While I was amusing myself," the beast continued, "that *mess* of a man was keeping tabs on you, reporting to me, so I could confront Tristen at the proper time."

I wheeled to face Mr. Messerschmidt again. "You told him that night Tristen and I worked alone in the lab. You set us up! You delivered us to Dr. Hyde *twice!*"

He didn't say anything, and Tristen squeezed my arm again, either holding me up—or holding me back.

"Here," Messerschmidt said, avoiding my eyes and stepping past me and Tristen—giving us a wide berth in a room that was getting warmer, filling with acrid smoke—to hand the vial to the beast. I saw my teacher's hand shake as he offered up the solution. "Just give this to Tristen, and let me be done with all of this."

NO.

Tristen would not drink the formula. And I was not done with my father's murderer.

Lunging forward, I tore free of Tristen's grasp and snatched the vial from Messerschmidt's hand just before the beast could take it, and I tore off the stopper and poured every last drop down my throat, ignoring Tristen's cry.

"Stop, Jill! Don't do it!"

He was too late.

I turned on Mr. Messerschmidt and saw raw fear in his eyes.

Chapter 94

Jill

I DRANK THE last few drops . . . and nothing happened.

Maybe nothing had ever happened. Maybe all along the beast I'd unleashed had just been . . . me. Or maybe I was so full of rage that there was no room for a worse self to emerge. I *was* my worst self that night. "I hate you!" I screamed at Messerschmidt.

"Jill . . ." I heard Tristen calling my name, but his voice seemed to come from far away.

"I'm going to kill you," I advised my teacher, who backed away from me. I wheeled to face the beast, who stood too close to Tristen. Behind them both the fire began to spread in earnest. "And then I'm going to kill you, too, you fucking monster."

I think Tristen was too stunned to move. Either that or he wanted to let me have revenge. Regardless, he didn't move as I bent and smashed the vial against the floor so the glass broke raggedly. Swinging my arm wide, I swiped at Mr. Messerschmidt's face, wanting to maim him first.

I saw my teacher raise his hand, but I was too quick, and the glass caught him right beneath his eye. He howled in pain, and as he covered the spurting wound, I pulled my arm back again, aiming for his throat.

"Jill, no!" Tristen caught me, swinging me to face him. "Don't become like him. Stop—for me!"

I breathed hard and raggedly, staring into his eyes. I wanted revenge. I wanted nothing less than full retribution. But more than that I wanted Tristen to love me again. I didn't want to see the fear and dismay that I saw in his eyes then.

I dropped the broken glass.

"Jill . . ." Tristen was searching my face, and I knew he saw that I was still *me*. "Don't kill him."

Mr. Messerschmidt cowered on the floor, whimpering, and behind us the fire was still spreading, starting to consume the curtains. My mom struggled to free herself, crying, "Jill! Get out of the house!"

Yet the world seemed to stand still, revolving around me and Tristen.

"Kiss me, Jill," he said, holding my arms. "Kiss me and share the formula."

I shook my head. "No, Tristen. I don't even know if it's working . . ."

"It will work for me. You know it will. I am a *Hyde*."

The beast was coming closer to us, taking its time before killing us all—and giving Tristen one last chance to drink from my lips. Out of the corner of my eye I could see the twisted smile of anticipation on its face.

"Kiss me, Jill," Tristen repeated. "Kiss me goodbye. Then go save your mother."

"We don't have any more formula," I said. "You won't be able to come back . . ."

"It's okay, Jill."

I shook my head harder. "No."

"I love you," Tristen said. "I love you so much."

They were the words I'd longed to hear. And although we were probably both going to die, I suddenly felt curiously at peace. "I love you, too," I told him. "I'll always love you."

"Then do this," he said.

I thought I'd gone beyond taking orders from Tristen Hyde, but how could I disobey as he bent his head to mine and pressed our lips together? And although I knew I was corrupting him again, ruining him, I kissed him so tenderly and so hungrily that, for the brief moment that we had, we really did feel like one soul. I felt like I lived and breathed as part of him, and shared that glorious strength that he always possessed, whether he was a man or a monster. For a moment I *was* Tristen and he was part of me.

Then he released me, and as I darted to save my mom, I saw Tristen Hyde turn to face his waiting father as the house burned down around them.

Epilogue

Jill

"I'M GLAD YOU came with me," I told my mom, taking her hand in mine.

"I worry about you in this city." She shook her head. "It's not safe. Are you *sure* you want to live here? You could wait a year, reapply to Smith."

"I'll be fine," I promised. "The NYU campus is very safe, and Tristen will be close by. I don't want to go to Smith anymore."

Mom looked at me with sad, worried eyes—the expression she always seemed to have since that night our house burned down. We never talked about it anymore, but I always saw a shadow of the experience in my mom's face. "I don't know that you being with Tristen reassures me," she said. "It's a big city."

"It's a miracle that I got into NYU's art program—and a scholarship," I told her. "I'm *going* to school here."

"Your paintings are so different now." Mom's brow furrowed more deeply. "They're so dark. I worry about you . . ."

"Mom." I squeezed her hand. "It's *okay.*"

A smattering of applause interrupted us, and I looked to the stage with the same anticipation and excitement that I always felt when Tristen entered a room.

He smiled at the small crowd, and without a word, sat down at the baby grand piano, closed his eyes, and began to play.

I watched him, mesmerized, like everybody else who heard him. His reputation was already growing in New York, where he'd gone after his father's death, quitting high school and never looking back.

High school had never seemed right for Tristen, anyway.

The stage where he sat, that was right for him. And soon he would play on bigger stages, for larger audiences. Although he was barely eighteen, some of the city's best musicians were already taking notice of the young man who played the haunting, beautiful, powerful music.

Mom leaned over to whisper, "He *is* very good, Jill."

It was an understatement. On the stage Tristen bent over the piano, his fingers swift and sure, his blond hair gleaming under the spotlight. I glanced around at the audience, watching their faces, gratified that they were as captivated as I was by the dark, thunderous song that Tristen conjured.

Returning my attention to him, I pressed my fingers against my chest, feeling the engagement ring that I wore hidden under my shirt on a chain around my neck. My mom liked Tristen in a way, but she was wary of him, too, and she had strongly objected to us getting engaged so young. But I had nearly lost Tristen, more than once. I wanted to be joined to him, as tightly as law and sacrament could bind two people.

He wanted that, too. He insisted on it.

I smiled in the dark room. And when Tristen Hyde insisted on something . . . Well, it was still hard to refuse him.

Bowed over the piano, Tristen brought his composition closer to a crescendo, and I could feel the audience tensing, and I wondered what they would think if they knew the price that he had paid to get his talent back.

For that night in my house . . . the formula hadn't worked for Tristen, either.

We couldn't quite figure out what had gone wrong. Whether there just hadn't been enough solution on my tongue or if the ingredients had simply expired, having sat a little too long.

Regardless, whatever had happened between Tristen and his father back in the that burning house, it had been Tristen's handiwork alone.

He never talked about what took place after I'd dragged my mom onto the porch, and the fire had all but destroyed Dr. Hyde's body, so there was no investigation.

Sometimes I would look at Tristen and wonder if he'd used a weapon or if they'd fought hand-to-hand to the death. All that really mattered to me was that it had been *Tristen* who had emerged from the engulfed building, stumbling, choking on smoke as he collapsed in the yard, his face and hands and clothes black with soot. So black that if there was blood on him, it didn't show.

No, I would never know exactly what Tristen had done that night. But whatever had happened, it had reopened the dark side of his soul, or created a new dark place, and he could compose again.

Did he think the price he'd paid was too high? Even though we loved each other, I didn't ask. I had a feeling he couldn't answer if he wanted to.

Around me I could feel the collective excitement in the crowd as Tristen drew them into his mind, his soul, bringing his composition to a deeply satisfying, beautifully corrupted end.

There was a moment of almost stunned silence, during which Tristen sat, head bent, recovering, like he'd done that evening so long ago in my former house. Then the applause began, some people rising from their seats.

Tristen stood then, too, and smiled warmly. "Thank you." He

went backstage but emerged a moment later and dropped down into the audience. People tried to grab him, wanting his attention like he was already a star, but he politely excused himself, eyes fixed on me as he made his way toward my seat.

"I'm glad you made it," he said, kissing my lips.

I couldn't wait until we were alone, so I could kiss him more. Would his touch ever seem ordinary to me? Not thrilling?

No.

"It was wonderful," I told him.

"You're biased," he teased, eyes twinkling. Then he turned to my mother. "It's good to see you, Mrs. Jekel. I'm glad you came."

"Tristen." Mom gave a polite nod. "It's good to see you, too."

"We need to get to the train station," I said, checking my watch. "We're cutting it close."

"Sure." Tristen clasped my hand and led us toward the exit. "Let's go."

When we reached the street, he hailed a cab and we rode in silence to Penn Station. As we moved through the city, I watched, as I often did, for a rotund little man who might bear a scar under his eye where I'd slashed him with a broken vial. Mr. Messerschmidt had disappeared that night, taking advantage of the chaos of flames and fire trucks, and we always wondered where he'd gone. The Manhattan sidewalks were crowded, and I scanned the faces, thinking a city with eight million people would be a good place to hide. And if I found him . . . ?

I honestly wasn't sure what I'd do.

"We're here," Tristen announced, sliding out and holding open the door for Mom and me. Then he paid the driver, refusing Mom's attempt to shove money into his hand, although it probably meant he'd skip a meal later that week. He'd inherited his father's money and possessions, but seemed unwilling to touch either, preferring to make his own way. A fresh start for a new generation of Hydes.

I led the way to the train, where I hugged my mom. "I'll be home on Sunday," I promised. "In time for school."

Mom frowned. "You're not coming with me? I thought—"

"No, I'm going to stay with those girls I met during my weekend at NYU," I lied.

Of course I would stay with Tristen, as if *that* would be very romantic, in the cheap, dirty efficiency he shared with five other struggling musicians. But Mom wouldn't like to think of me even curling up on the couch with him for the night, so I fibbed.

I didn't lie because I was afraid Mom would be mad and drag me home on the train. No, I was so far beyond her control, so much an adult, that I made all my own rules. I lied only out of respect for her feelings.

"All right, Jill." Mom hugged me. "Just be careful, okay?"

"I'll watch over her," Tristen promised, placing an arm across my chest, pulling me to him. "Don't worry."

Mom boarded the train, and Tristen and I waited, waving until it was out of sight.

"Have I mentioned that I love you?" Tristen asked, turning me toward himself and pushing my stray lock of hair behind my ear, a gesture that he had largely assumed responsibility for.

"You can say it again," I said, slipping my hands under his coat and around his waist, just like I'd done at the cemetery on that cold January day. I rested my head against his chest, feeling his heart beat.

"I love you," he whispered, lips brushing my hair.

As always, when he said that, my eyes welled with happy tears. Would I ever get used to those words, either?

Never.

"I love you, too," I promised, voice cracking.

Alone . . . I would never be alone again. No matter what happened, even when death did eventually separate us, I would never really feel alone again.

After a few more moments just holding each other, I pulled away, and Tristen and I clasped hands and left the station, walking into the night together.

ACKNOWLEDGMENTS

Like no doubt every book that features only one or two names on the cover, *Jekel Loves Hyde* was actually a collaborative project, and so I want to try to give credit to all the amazing, talented, supportive people who helped bring it to bookshelves.

I was fortunate to have two wonderful editors—first Kathy Dawson, who saw potential in the initial draft, and then my new and gifted guide, Margaret Raymo, who tirelessly helped me polish, and polish, and polish . . .

Thanks, in fact, to everyone at Houghton Mifflin Harcourt, especially Betsy Groban, Adah Nuchi, Jenny Groves, Laura Sinton, Linda Magram, Karen Walsh, Christine Krones, Lisa DiSarro . . . and the list could go on and on.

A special nod also to Cliff Nielson, who created the beautiful jacket for this book and the one for *Jessica's Guide to Dating on the Dark Side.*

Speaking of which—many, many thanks to all the e-mailers, bloggers, booksellers, and YA librarians who supported my first novel and helped to ensure a second, from Adele Walsh in Australia to Donna Rosenblum in New York, as well as Betsy Rider, Michelle of Michelle's Minions, and the fun people at YA Reads, who seem to be scattered around the globe. I wish there was room to acknowledge you all!

I also want to again credit my agent, Helen Breitweiser, for always making me feel as if I'm the one and only author she has to handle, and for doing such a great job on my behalf. Finally, I have to acknowledge my friends and family—including my Pilates pals, and Patti and the Lewisburg, Pennsylvania, McDonald's crew, as well as everybody in our little town who cheers me on.

And the biggest thanks to my husband, Dave, my parents, and my in-laws, who not only support my projects but help to watch my wonderful girls, Paige and Julia—both of whom encourage me with their boundless enthusiasm.

Without all of your help and guidance and good wishes, this book wouldn't exist.